Deception Has A Name

Y. Deonna

Y. Deonna
authorydeonna@gmail.com

Printed in the United States of America

Second Printing: Sept 2019
Crown Ruby Publishing

I'm dedicating this to my big little brother. D, as long as there are pen and paper, you will live in every book that I write. I'll miss you forever & I love you always.

CHAPTER 1

Death

Silence encompassed Olivia as she watched her best friend...her only family...fall to the asphalt pavement below with a thud so loud it crushed her eardrums. The world stopped, time paused, and her heart palpitated. It was like she was in slow motion...in a movie...but it was reality; she saw it with her own eyes. She screamed, as her mind battled between believing it to be real or fantasy, and then she ran to Deek and held his head in her lap and begged for him to hold on, trying unsuccessfully to make him hold her back. Blood seemed to escape from every part of his toned body and stained her clothing; she tried without victory to stop the waterfall of blood that dressed his beautiful brown skin. Her hands covering his wounds and his eyes rolling uncontrollably, he was gasping for air and trying so hard to hold on. Seconds later, Angelo ran attempting to help. Her brother whispered his last words; what they were, she did not know. She could not hear because of her own screaming. She assumed it was Deek asking Angelo to take care of her, because he said to her brother he would; and then Deek's eyes closed. Sirens could be heard in the distance, but Olivia knew he had taken his last breath. Her pink shirt and blue jeans were now entirely soaked with his blood; she was dressed in red. Still, she tried with all her might to breathe life back into him. She tried to revive him and refused to let him go as the paramedics arrived. They tried unsuccessfully to resuscitate him; even if they had been right there when it happened, he would have died. This was a kill shot; an entire clip had been emptied on her brother. She had no idea why, or who would want to kill Deek. He was about to give up the gang life so they could have a real life; it was an attempt to get back the childhood stolen so long ago. He was all that she had in this world. She collapsed; there was no energy left in her body, and she begged for death. She wanted to die too; the loss was too great. The tears came, and she sat back in his blood shaking violently and rocking back and forth. She felt strong arms encompass her weakened body and walk her away from the horrible scene, but it was too late; her mind was already replaying it repeatedly. She was having nightmares without sleeping. "Why; why God why," she mumbled repeatedly to herself, chanting it like a lullaby to calm her anxious nerves. She watched as police and detectives came to investigate and ask questions. She watched as the yellow tape was pulled out, and she watched as they searched for bullets. This was Hollow Hill, nicknamed Hood Town; there was nothing but death and destruction, and no one told if they knew because of fear. The smell of it was so thick that she found it hard to take a breath; the odor of fear was bitter...so very bitter. She looked around at the eyes looking at her, knowing if they knew who caused this catastrophe...this calamity...they would not tell. Fear had already attached itself to all of them. It was the fear of revenge or even murder; this was Blanco Wild Deuces' territory, and her brother should have been safe. Around here a loose tongue was like walking into a battlefield of spraying bullets with no protection, and Angelo was here. No one was going to talk when the leader of one of the most violent street gangs was an onlooker. He ran Hollow Hill. Besides, this part of Georgia was so rough and violent that even rodents stayed away. She would have shouted if only she had known who the coward wearing the doo rag was, but he was unknown to her.

Olivia jerked from the hands that held her and went back to her brother, but she was not allowed; it was officially a crime scene, and he was gone on into the next world...no longer in this one. She was angry, full of rage, and mixed with vex as she saw people drive by—some looked mockingly, some in shock, some just looking to have something to gossip about later—but he belonged to her. She needed the world to stop. She wanted God to turn time backward in order to allow her to save him or take the bullets for him. Deek could not be dead; he would not leave her alone. He would not. Her brother had made her promises, and he never broke a promise.

Coldness attacked her body with a precise vengeance, and she started to tremble uncontrollably as she heard others shouting and screaming. "Shut-up," she wanted to scream, but her mouth would not open; her lips felt like magnets locked tightly together as she looked angrily at the spectators. Why were they screaming and sobbing? It was she that had lost her only connection in this world. It was her brother lying on the ground in a puddle of his own blood; dead. Then, she heard voices and saw a detective approaching her, but it sounded like gibberish and she could not understand. Her heart was beating so loud that all she heard was thump, thump. It was like a time bomb ticking; she wished it would explode. All she wanted was for the night to be over. She was just so cold, so confused; her heart was still longing for her brother. She wanted to beat her brain so it could stop playing the scene continuously. She felt like she was the only person in the world—the only one suffering, the only one caring, and the only one who had lost. He was all she had; he was her one protector and the only person who loved her. The combination of emotions were almost too overwhelming for her. She could not think clearly or focus. She just wanted Deek to get up and hold her. She longed to hear his baritone voice speak soothingly to her, telling her it's going to be all right, that she was safe, and he will take care of it.

"Olivia, come on with me," a voice said, and like a lost puppy she obeyed the command and followed. She said nothing but walked in silence, wishing she would wake from the nightmare that seemed only to get worse. Her eyes hurt from the constant flow of tears, and her jaw was sore from clenching her teeth. None of that mattered because the worse pain was the pain unseen. Her heart had physically been detached from her body. It was an unknown pain; it was a violent, relentless, intense agony that reached the depths of her soul...wounding her, ripping through her body, and destroying her from the inside out. Each step was becoming more difficult. It was like she was in quicksand, sinking deeper and deeper. "Save me Deek, save me, please; I need you," she whispered.

Warm hands gently touched her sunken shoulders. Her head was unable to rise; she tried but to no avail. Everything took more effort than she had strength for.

"Listen to me. I am going to take you home so you can change clothes, and then I am going to take you with me," he said to her.

She could not focus. She only knew it was a male voice, and for a moment she thought it was Deek; at least she wished it to be him. She looked and then stared, trying to bring in focus the image in front of her. It was Angelo. He held her hand and walked her back to the apartment—their tiny little home. It seemed like a mansion when Deek was alive, but now, it felt like a prison. It was holding all her memories, her childhood secrets and regrets, and the last memories she would ever have of her brother. These walls that once brought her comfort now only echoed pain—bland and white, colorless, lifeless; it was a reflection now of her bleeding heart. She was still numb...just going through the motions. If Angelo had not held her hand, she would have probably been still sitting on the ground waiting...just waiting for her brother to wake up and tell her it would all be okay.

While inside the apartment, her mind was lost. She had no idea what to do next. She just stood there in a daze waiting for an order...waiting to be told what to do and how to do it. There was a silence, and then Angelo again was by her side directing her to remove her clothes and take a shower. She gazed at him, her lip and chin quivering, but she did not move. She could not, though she wanted to lift her arms to remove her clothing. Although the blood was cold on her skin, it was her brother's blood and all she had left of him; she longed for any remembrance of him. Angelo pulled her near and undressed her and walked her into the bathroom. He turned on the shower, and she stepped in. He retreated, following the bloody trail she left behind. Hours, minutes, or seconds later, a loud knocking on the front door startled her, but she did not move. She stayed in the shower, trying to wipe off all that she had witnessed...trying to erase the pain that seemed to instantly imprison her as she watched her brother fall to his untimely death. It happened so quickly. Olivia did not even see it coming until it was too late. She felt such emptiness watching him fall. It should have been her. They were going to move away from here; he said that there were too many ghosts, and they needed a fresh start. They were going to South Carolina to start anew. He thought some of their paternal relatives might be living there. She did not know if that were true. Fifteen years of living, and she had never seen any other family. She never received cards on birthdays or any holiday, and there were no pictures to her knowledge; they were just forgotten. They were the children that no one wanted. Their mother had no family that she knew of, and Livvy never knew her father. So, she was not sure who Deek was looking for, but she would have followed him anywhere...even to death, but the bullets ignored her. He was the only man she trusted, the only man that ever loved her without seeking to take anything from her, and the only man that she loved with all her heart and soul. Deek was her life. The thought of that truth renewed her tears. She was an orphan. How horrible it was to be one...to be alone...to live in solitude.

She heard voices speaking low. She could tell that the police had found their way to their humble apartment; she guessed they were looking for clues, seeking some kind of information. It did not matter; it would not bring her brother back. If only she didn't want him to walk her to the store. If only she had waited, maybe they'd be watching television. She turned off the shower, dried off her tired body, and put on a clean shirt and a black skirt. Her long dark hair was still dripping...wetting the clean shirt she was wearing, but for some reason she did not care. She did not even feel the water soaking her back. She felt nothing.

She entered into the den; several strangers all looked at her, pretending to feel sorrow and mouthing how sorry they were. They were not sorry. To them, Derrick was just an uneducated Black gang banging criminal; to her, he was everything. He was her hero, protector, and provider...and her heart. She said nothing but stared blankly at them; words had yet to formulate, and she distrusted her voice. These men were an unwelcome inconvenience to her. Angelo was sitting in the chair looking lost, but no tears kissed his cheek and no emotions showed in his eyes; she wondered why. Deek and Angelo were best friends; maybe he was in shock or pretending to be strong for Olivia. Angelo was not one to show weakness. The only time he ever showed emotion was when his mother died; he did not even cry when his brother or father were killed. She knew he loved Deek and Carlos, especially after losing his own family. They were the three amigos; all of them were orphaned at a young age. Now she, too, shared their fate. Each looked after the other; they all had lost their parents and longed for family. They found it in each other; she found it in Derrick. Now that he was gone, she had nothing and no one. She was lost.

"Ma'am, we are sorry for your loss, but we need to know what you saw," the detective said, his pale blue eyes looking sorrowfully into hers. He wore a well-designed button shirt; tailored crisp, creased, khaki pants; and shiny shoes. He was probably from that side of town where the upper middle class lived, not far from the rich folk; the white side of town was where people like her were not permitted, because they were not seen as civilized, productive members of society. Olivia wondered what their judgmental minds were thinking as they stared at her. It was not like she cared. She had her opinions of them as well. She no more cared for them than they cared for her. She wanted this interaction to be over with quickly.

She eyed him cautiously, stayed alert, and took a long deep breath before she spoke. She knew better than to trust police because in her brother's line of work, they were just as much the enemy as a rival gang. "I want to see Deek. They won't let me touch my brother, and I want to see him. It's cold outside, and I don't want him out there for others to see. He needs me," Olivia said as calmly as her frightened voice could manage. She walked to the window to see if they still had him lying in the streets. The idea of that infuriated her. He was not roadkill but a human being, and he deserved to be treated with the utmost respect. She placed her small hands on the cold window, wishing for things impossible...yearning for things that couldn't be undone.

"Sweetheart," he said, and before he could finish Olivia spoke.

Hearing this stranger call her sweetheart hit a nerve. "Sir, my name is Olivia. Please do not refer to me as sweetheart," she said, still not turning to look at him or the two other men with him. Why were there three men all here to talk to her? Shouldn't at least two be canvassing the street to talk to others? This was not how they did it on television. She did not like how this was going already. There could be no law in a lawless society. They took care of things in house; the street handled the street. She heard her brother say that. White men in tailored clothing would not get the respect from poverty-stricken folks living in the Hallow. She didn't trust any of them. They were the others.

Angelo almost snickered at Olivia's defiance toward the officer. If it was not such a horrible situation, he would have given Olivia her props for checking the cop. But now was not the time. He shifted in his seat uncomfortably as he eyed the other detectives. Then he glanced back to Olivia but kept silent. His mind was replaying the sight of his best friend dying.

"Olivia, the coroner is coming to remove the body. A sheet has been placed over him. Once the coroner takes him, we can take you to see him. I need to know what you saw," he said again as gentle as he could be. Her distress was evident, and he did not want to cause her any more pain. His eyes darted around the apartment and he noticed no picture of a mother or father. He wondered if her brother had been her only parent. If so, it was even more disheartening. This was what he hated. No child

5

should have to witness what she had, and sadly it was becoming a daily routine; with no jobs, no community centers, and nothing positive to occupy their young impressionable minds, they turned to breaking laws and joining gangs. It was a sad reality.

Again, she placed her small hands on the window. She longed to be where he was; she wanted death to take her. She could not live without her brother. She had no idea how to be without his guidance. Life was hard, but with Deek everything was easy. He provided for her and kept her safe; now she had no support and no one to love her. She needed to be loved. Growing up with a crack addicted mother and absentee father gave her great insecurities; suffering like she had all of her childhood angered her, but her brother was the antidote for all that pain. With him gone, she was a target. There was no one to keep the pain away or the predators at bay. Where would she go? How would she live?

"Livvy, talk to the detective," Angelo said trying to coax her to turn around and speak so the police could leave. As the leader of BWD, he did not like this kind of heat; the quicker they left, the more comfortable he would feel. He had his own investigation to do.

She turned to face the detective with the pale blue eyes. The other two were looking around as if they would find something, but they would not. Deek never kept anything associated with Blanco Wild Deuces in the apartment for his sister's protection. There was no gun or drug stash; nothing was here. "There is nothing here," she said looking boldly at the two gentlemen who she felt were violating her home. She looked back toward the primary detective who had spoken. "I saw a guy wearing a doo rag pull out a gun. He said nothing or, if he did, I can't recall...and then bop, bop, bop," she said shaking. Each time she said it with her mouth, she could hear it in her ears and see it in her mind. "I don't know why. Deek did not have enemies, to my knowledge," she said trying to remain composed and fearing if she said too much Angelo would check her. She walked back to the couch and sat down. The tears rushed her at once, and her body began to violently shake; she could no longer control her emotions. She was still in shock...still not believing that she saw what she saw. It could not be; this was just a nightmare, and she needed to wake up. She pinched herself, but it did not work; this was real. The growing wet spot on her t-shirt reinforced that.

"Detectives, can she do this later? She just saw her brother get killed right in front of her. She's just a kid; she has lost everything in less than an hour," Angelo said as he reached over to console Livvy. She rested her weary head on his chest, and he embraced her...holding her tightly.

"We understand but is her mother or father around?" he asked, as he observed Angelo. He was not sure, but he thought he had gang tattoos. He wondered—being that the area was known for violence—if the homicide had been gang related. He looked at the young girl before his eyes; she could be no more than fourteen or fifteen, and she had just seen a horrible sight. He wanted to comfort her, as he had a daughter around her age at home. She would be inconsolable if anything had happened to him or her brother. The young girl standing in front of him was pretending to be strong, but her eyes said so much. He wanted to tell her it would be all right but, in all honesty, he could not. This would be a difficult case to solve because the perpetrator could be anyone.

Through the tears she managed to answer him, "No, my momma died of an overdose about five years ago. I never knew my daddy. Now I don't even have Deek; I am alone." She choked, and the tears ran down her face again; she was comfortless. No words could ease her, and no touch could calm her because no one was Deek. She wanted her brother back so badly. She thought she could wish life back into him. If she could just touch him and let him hear her. He would come back.

Silence dressed the room, as the others heard her confession. The lead detective looked at her as she held her head down, and he quickly wiped away tears from his own eyes. There was sadness in her eyes and body language...a sadness that seemed to hold a lifetime of heartbreak. He wanted to hold her tightly; no child should be alone and attacked by death at such a young age. He wanted to take her home with him, for the battle scars she had seemed incurable. He mourned for her, but he had a job to do. He could not lose sight of that, no matter how heartbreaking her situation was. Something was not right here. He was missing an important piece of the puzzle, and he knew it had to be gang related. This was not an accident.

Angelo sensing that the detective might ask more questions quickly began to talk. "She has me. I told her brother I would take care of her if anything ever happened. She got family. Like I said, I can bring her later if need be. She needs to go to bed; she has school tomorrow," he said watching all three detectives methodically as they watched him.

The detective looked skeptical but said nothing. He and the other two left; as they exited, they whispered among themselves. Olivia wondered what they were saying, but through her weeping, she could hear nothing but her heart breaking.

"Angelo, what am I going to do?" she asked, afraid to live one second without Deek. She leaned on him for everything. She was lost without him; she was only fifteen with no guidance, no protector, and no one. Life was not worth living if it had to be lived alone. Whoever killed Deek...would they kill her too? Would she be the next to be assassinated? She did not know. She could not understand why her brother was gunned down on his own street, just minutes from home. There was no reason for it to happen; none at all.

Angelo inhaled and exhaled his breath. He hated this for Livvy. She suffered so much, and she loved Deuce deeply. He would take care of her now. He would always take care of Livvy, as that was what Deuce wanted. "Don't worry Livvy; I will take care of you. Get some clothes, and I'll take you back to my place," he said kindly.

She got up and did as she was told. He watched as she left and turned back to the scene outside the window. It was not supposed to go down like that. He wanted Deek hurt...not killed. He thought if he roughed him up a little, then he would not want to leave the gang. Deek was his right-hand man, and he did not want to lose him. He did not want it done in front of Livvy; he adored her. This was going to change his entire plan; he had to rethink. He had to keep Livvy's trust. She was the prettiest girl in the hood—sweet, innocent, like a little lost puppy. She was loyal to Deek and him to her. It was that loyalty to her that caused this matter to even occur. He had to make sure no one could connect anything to him. He had to be the hero and not the villain. Who had violated his order? Why would Avery kill him when he knew that was not the plan? Things had gotten crazy and out of hand; he had to find out why. "Livvy, you ready to go?" he asked; she looked as though she had lived an eternity. He reached out for her, and they walked out of the apartment complex with her body shielded by his.

**

As they walked to Angelo's SUV, she heard people saying, "I'm so sorry, Olivia; Deek was good people." She said nothing, and the ride to Angelo's was a blur. When they arrived, Angelo's girlfriend was waiting on the porch with a few of the other BWD's. Olivia sat there inside the SUV and looked at them; she would not have moved if Carlos had not come forward and opened the door. He picked her up, and she collapsed in his arms, resting her aching head on his shoulder as he carried her inside placing her on the bed. She found no comfort as she rested her aching body. He pulled up the covers and kissed her cheek. "It'll be okay Livvy. You are with family," he whispered. He then turned off the light and returned to his friends.

"Angelo, what is she doing here?" Leah asked with an attitude. She had made it clear that she was the only chick in the house, and she did not want another...especially Olivia. It was well known that Angelo had feelings for her. The only reason he had not acted upon them was because Deek would not allow it. That might all change, and Leah was not ready to be downgraded.

"Shut-up, Leah. Her brother just got murdered. You know she ain't got nobody but us, and we take care of our own," he said and walked past her. She knew better than to test him. No one would treat her that way; how was she going to do that to Livvy? She was just fifteen.

Leah was not one to be overlooked or hushed easily. His attitude did not halt her anger. "Dinah ain't a BWD. What you mean?" she pressed. She walked behind him as she rolled her neck and finger. The others looked on wondering, when Angelo was going to pop her to shut her up. She had been drinking and talking foolishness since

Angelo had called and told them what had occurred. It was no secret that she was jealous, especially of Livvy.

He despised being questioned; no one had the authority to demand any explanation from him. "You ain't either, but you here. I mean if I want her here, she stays. I'm the boss. I run this; I pay for this and you ain't got anything to do with this. Don't call her Dinah, she hates that name; remember you are replaceable, Leah. You don't like it then leave, but don't you mess with Livvy," he said, tired of her annoying voice. It was getting near time to upgrade and let her go. She was becoming a liability. He eliminated liabilities. Besides she was just a pass around, and she had served her purpose. He had grown tired of her.

"I'm your girl, and I don't like being disrespected," she shouted.

He stopped in mid stride, turned around, and violently slapped her. "Shut-up. I got real issues to deal with. You disrespect me again, and I will put you in ICU. Get out of my face; you are getting on my nerves," he yelled, wondering why he even let her stay around. She was a stupid, embarrassing mess.

She retreated in haste and said nothing more. Her anger still lingered. Either she or Dinah had to go, and it was not going to be her. She had grown accustomed to a certain lifestyle, and some fifteen-year-old kid was not about to take her throne.

The fellas watched and laughed. This occurred at least once a week. It was a break from dealing with what they had lost. Carlos walked over to Angelo, seeking information about the murder. "Ace, what happened?"

"A lot, man. Some dude shot Deek, like right in the street; just straight ran up on him. It happened so quickly I didn't even have time to react, and poor Livvy saw the whole thing. If she had been a second sooner, she probably would have caught a bullet too. I don't know who did it, but we'll get him," he vowed looking at Carlos who agreed. No one knew Angelo's secret. But what really pissed him off was that Avery could have shot Livvy too, and she had nothing to do with it. Everyone knew to not touch Livvy, never. That was an immediate death sentence.

"I hate that for Livvy. She's a good kid; you know, Deek was really proud of her. He said she was going to college and do big things," Carlos said, shaking his head.

"We gonna retaliate tonight? We ready," he said, cocking his gun and ready to revenge his friend's death.

"Not tonight; the cops are hot. But we will get him. All in due time, he will get got," Angelo said, knowing exactly who it was. In order to keep himself safe, he was going to personally handle him.

"You right," Carlos said, putting the gun back up and pouring his beer on the ground in remembrance of Deek. His heart was hurting too, because they were the three amigos; life without Deek was going to be an adjustment. He dropped out of school, but he was bright. He cared about his neighborhood, his friends, and his sister. He was the last one who deserved a bullet. He was a good manager of money

9

and ran the drug operation like it was a Fortune 500. He didn't have to use a gun to get the job done. He had a reputation around town because he never lost a fight...never. Deek walked on the right side and stayed out of the spotlight because he had to take care of Livvy. Now he was gone. He recalled that long conversation they had. Deek anticipated that he might die; he left behind a box for her in case he ever got killed. He did it on her fifteenth birthday, which was just a few weeks ago. He must have had a sense that death was near. It was too much to comprehend, but it was real...too real.

***

It was a tortuous first night lying in a foreign bed, in a home that was not her own. She knew them; she knew all of them, but they were not her blood. She was not a member of the gang, Deek was. She had no one now; her only companions were her thoughts. She had no idea where she would be tomorrow, what would happen to her, who would take care of her, or who would love her. Deek, she just wanted her brother back. He was all she had. She needed him to come back. She closed her eyes, but all she could hear were the gun shots and then the eyes of those detectives assuming they knew who her brother was because he was in a gang. He deserved justice, too; he deserved for someone to care enough to find his murderer. He was not bad; yes, he was in a gang, but only to provide for them. He was a young man forced to grow up too soon because of the bad decisions their parents made. He was a good guy and had a good heart. He never allowed Olivia to do anything wrong or break the rules. He was good to her. He taught her how to live, how to love, and how to grow. She angrily began to beat the pillow beneath her. She was raging on the inside. She wished she could hunt down the person who did it. Who was he? Where was he? She had no idea. She was not street wise, like Deek. He tried hard to separate her from that world and protect her from the evil his eyes had seen. She had long ago been touched by evil; her innocence was lost, and her faith was betrayed by unworthy men and an unkind mother. What kind of life could a poor, parentless, girl live when no one was there to teach? She had nothing, now. There was no clarity through the fog that had overtaken her mind; there was no way for her to navigate through a path in which she had no map. Death had found her again and left her a victim. This time, death had not done her a favor. It only caused more suffering. What did she do so horrible to death for it to violate her with such eagerness and precise aggression? What sins had she committed in her young life to be punished so harshly? Why did God find her so disgusting, so unimportant, and so worthless? She could not understand; she would apologize if only He would reveal her faults. She just wanted Deek back. It made no sense to her; no matter how she calculated it in her head, it just did not add up. Deek should not be dead. He was her only reason for living, her only helping hand, all that she was, and all that she had. It was all stored in him. They were their only family, depending heavily on each other for survival.

Who was this adversary that came out in the night, hiding behind a hoodie and doo rag, and shooting her brother like he was an animal? What was the coward's name? This was why she hated gang life; they said the gang is family that they protected their own. Who protected Deek? It sure was not Angelo, and he is the leader. Why did he allow it to happen? Why did he betray her brother and let him die in the street? Oh, the pain...this unexplainable pain. She felt her heart mourning and then splitting in two. She felt so sick, so sad, and so disconnected with the rest of the world. Her mind was paralyzed by the pain, and sleep was denied to her as she looked out the window; wishing, wanting, even attempting to pray for Deek to come back and take her home. She twisted and turned as silently as possible. She feared her future, wondering if she even had a future. She would become name unknown—another negative statistic—because she had no family. Her brother had worked so hard to allow her the best life that he could provide. In one night, it was all destroyed by some unknown coward. Did he understand what he had stolen from her? Did he even care? Who would walk her to school each day and back home again? Who would take her to the skating rink on the weekend? Who would listen to her silly stories and comfort her when she had horrible nightmares? Who would call her Belle—from Beauty and the Beast—because she loved to read books? She was afraid for tomorrow to come...afraid of what tomorrow meant and the dangers that it held. The fears associated with it were too much for her fragile mind to conceive. Tomorrow would be a harsh hellish reality that she was unprepared for. She had to find a way to live in the world alone. The thought of it made her physically sick, and she shuddered with fear, crying herself into a fitful slumber.

CHAPTER 2

The Aftermath

There is no manual on how to deal with grief. Deek had never prepared Olivia for his leaving this world; he assumed he was somehow immortal and would be with his sister always. She believed that he was a superhero—an immortal too—but he was just human like everyone else and susceptible to the challenges of life. As she stood there at the cemetery, her heart ached worse than it ever had. She wished she knew who had done it. She would have hunted him down and beat him until he felt the misery she had; then she'd shoot him the same number of times he had shot Deek. She would make him pay. Olivia didn't care that she was poor. She didn't care she had no parents. She didn't care about fitting in at school, because as long as she had Deek, life was good and nothing else mattered. All she cared about was her brother, and now he was gone. His presence kept all the bad away. She never went without, and she never needed. When he needed her the most, she let him die. She hated herself for that. She whispered to him how sorry she was. She was not nearly as brave as him, but she would have taken all those bullets to save his life; she wished it had been her who died and not him. She had nothing to offer to anyone. She was just a reject, and now she was an orphan. The word sounded so ugly...orphan. She belonged to no one. No one would miss her, care for her, or provide for her. She was just in the world. How sad—how very sad—to have to be the one left behind. The tears met under her chin, and she let them remain untouched. It was like she heard her brother crying from the soil, like the story of Cain and Abel. How she longed to breathe her life into Deek so he could come back. But she was not a suitable replacement, because evil hands had scarred her body and made her an unworthy sacrifice.

"Come on, Livvy...come on with me," Angelo said, reaching for her and holding her close to him.

She needed his embrace; she needed to know she was still present. She felt like she was in a bad movie. So much of her wished the arms that held her belonged to Deek and not Angelo, but he was all she had now.

"Liv, you stay close to me and I will protect you until my last breath. That is a promise," he said, seeing how sad she had become. Each day she awoke another spark left her lonely eyes. He longed to see her spirit back. Even in sadness she was still the most beautiful girl he had ever seen. She had this spirit—something truly special inside of her—that made her glow. She had those diamond, clear beautiful rare gray eyes. She was unaware of how wonderfully beautiful she truly was, and maybe that was because of how much she lost. The things that Deek told him that happened to her made him want to kill every man that ever touched her. She was too special to be misused in such a way.

Olivia wondered how long this would last, as Angelo embraced her. In the days she had been living in Angelo's house, Leah was growing impatient and agitated with Olivia being around because Angelo was giving her more attention than Leah. She wanted Olivia gone, but there was no place for her to go. She could not return home; it was contaminated. However, she did not like Leah either, or her current living arrangement. She never liked Leah. She was not to be trusted. Deek told Olivia to always be wary of Leah. Leah liked bad boys, but she had no loyalty. She'd lay and love whoever would let her. She was the worst kind of woman. She only sought self and cared less about others. She wanted to fight Olivia. It was obvious in the tone of voice she used when she talked to or about Livvy, and she saw it in Leah's actions. They had a quarrel from way back, and Leah was not the type to live and let live. Olivia was thirteen when it happened. She went after Deek, he didn't want her, and Olivia made her feelings known; Leah still held on to that, even though she was dating Angelo. Leah also knew he wanted Olivia, and it pissed her off. Olivia was not looking to be competition; she just wanted a place to sleep until she could find a better situation. She did not like living with gang bangers either, but she believed it better to live with beasts than to be hunted by them. Still, she was not prepared for this; their lifestyle was not the one she was accustomed to living. Livvy came from a world of academics, not one of violence; true, she had been a victim of violence, but she was not an aggressor. She wished Deek had not died. The thought of her brother brought new pains and worries. He was beyond her reach now. As she stood there watching them pay their last respects, she grew angry. She hated cemeteries; they were sad, and the mark of the end...at least the end in this world. Sadly, her brother hated the dark and the cold; now he was surrounded by both. She wanted so badly to take his place. She'd rather die and stop feeling than to be left behind dealing with the aftermath. She sat quietly as they drove back to Angelo's house and was surprised to see a barbecue in full swing. BWD members had left long before Angelo and Olivia had. She assumed that had been preparing the barbecue, but she wanted no part of it. This was not a time of celebration; it was a time of mourning. She retreated to the back bedroom and took off her black dress. She just sat on the edge of the bed, wearing only her underwear and bra. She thought that exposing her bare skin would help her feel something again. She was just a walking zombie, a numb mess, a misfit of agony; depressed. She was so tired; was this the life God had planned for her when she was born to her mother? He could have it back. She would gladly give it to him, for it had done nothing but bring sadness and agony to her. She was defeated, weary, and broke...far beyond repair; nothing could feel worse than what she was feeling now. In a moment, she lost her brother and parent. Warm tears fell from her eyes again, but no matter; they had become part of her everyday life. They spoke the words her mouth could not form. She did not even wipe them away anymore. They reminded her that she was still human, still alive, and still caught up in this pathetic life. She lay back on the bed, recalling all the good times she had with her brother; he taught her how to ride a bike, how to play spades, how to tie a cherry stem with her tongue, and how to dream. Dreams kept the reality of the hood at bay. Dreams offered hope, opportunity, and possibilities. Dreams let her communicate with her dead brother. She closed her eyes—trying to dream, trying to find him—but a knock at the door ripped the dream away. She popped up, and there was Angelo standing at the opened door. Instantly, she used her hands to cover herself and looked for clothing; something about his eyes reminded her of the men who had abused her before. He walked in and shut the door. "You alright? I mean besides not having on clothes?" he said, looking at her lustfully. Deek had told him she was hands off but, now that he was gone, he felt he had every right to do as he liked. He did not want to hurt or harm her, but he longed to love her and to feel her untouched skin near his. It was a thought he had replayed over and over in his head since she had moved in. She reminded him of a time of innocence...a time stolen from him so many years ago.

She nodded her head and turned her attention to the chest of drawers adjacent to the bed to find some clothes. He walked closer to her, making her nervous.

"You look cold; let me hold you so I can warm you up," he said.

His touch made her body shiver. "That's okay Angelo; I am not cold. I just need to get dressed," she said, looking feverishly for anything to put on. His presence made her so nervous. She did not want his hands to violate her. She had been violated enough. She only wanted to be loved.

He slid her hair back and gently kissed her neck. She could smell the beer on his breath. "You are beautiful, girl. I love your eyes. I could get lost in them forever," he said.

She felt fear as her pulse quickened. She knew at some point it would come to this. All men reacted this way, at least all the ones she knew. Every man her mama had brought home had done the same. Angelo had always looked at her like she was dessert. Deek had kept him away, but now no one was around to protect her. She was as defenseless as a sea turtle trying to make it to the ocean through the sand, with predators everywhere. "Can I put my clothes on?" she asked in a quiet voice.

"Yeah, and then come outside with me. Everybody is asking about you," he said, admiring her toned body.

She nodded in agreement and started to put on her clothes, but he did not leave; instead he watched her. The door again opened, and Leah came in. She was angry. She began to swear and call Olivia names. Leah accused her of having sex with Angelo, saying she knew that Livvy wanted him. She called Livvy a slut, among other derogatory insults and slurs. Leah was incorrect. Olivia's mind was not on that man but on another man: her brother. She had long ago become disgusted with men. Her brother was the only person she trusted and, with him gone; she was a sheep among wolves once more. She would be devoured.

Angelo removed Leah so that Livvy could finish getting dressed; Leah's voice could not be hushed. She refused to be silent, and her agitation with Olivia grew. When she walked outside, Leah was still heckling Livvy and taunting her. Then she threw the drink she had in her cup on Olivia. Her outfit was now soaked by beer, a smell she loathed; something switched in her. Olivia—angry, miserable, and needing to release her rage—was happy to oblige Leah. She never was one to do a lot of talking, but Olivia could fight. She was undefeated, and Leah—being older at twenty-one—did not scare her at all. She would show these wolves that this sheep was no coward. She walked right up to Leah. It was like the world went silent. In that moment, all Livvy saw was Leah, and she punched her with everything she had. Leah, she went down. Livvy waited; she wanted her to get up so she could do it again. Blood trickled down from Leah's nose, and Olivia felt a surge of power course through her body. The first thing one learns about fighting is never to underestimate the opponent. Deek taught her how to fight after he found out what happened to her. She knew the power she used had dazed Leah; she did not get up. Olivia eyed her hatefully, still ready to attack again if necessary.

"Now finally we have some peace and quiet; Angelo, your girlfriend talks too much," Olivia said. Then she went back to the porch and sat down. She had no idea where it came from or why, but she did it; she dared anyone to touch her. She just wanted to grieve her brother in peace without the ignorance of others. She just wanted Deek. Her reaction even caught her by surprise, but she just wanted to be alone with her thoughts. Now that Leah was quiet, she could be. Creeper handed her a towel to dry off with, and Livvy thanked him. Then the music stopped, the talking stopped, and everyone looked at Olivia as if they could not believe she had just knocked Leah out. Olivia should have done it sooner because it showed them all she was not one to be messed with. She had lost too much, and she didn't care anymore. All she wanted was quiet so she could mourn. She had just buried her brother; why did Leah have to taunt her. Why? Any other day of the week she would have overlooked Leah's aggressions and ignorance. This was her brother's funeral, and she had no patience and no compassion for idiots like her.

"It is official. Livvy is now known as Knockout," Angelo said impressed. He had no idea she had that kind of power, and that made him want her all the more. Everyone was looking at her; Olivia wondered if Angelo was going to punish her for beating up his girlfriend, who was still unconscious. Some of the guys were trying to bring her around.

Angelo walked over to Olivia, and she dropped her head wondering what the consequence for this action would be. There was always a consequence. "Am I in trouble for knocking her out?" she asked, still not looking at him. She was mad at Leah but afraid of him. Angelo was unpredictable. All that energy she had felt when she hit Leah instantly disappeared, as he approached; he hovered over her like a storm cloud. Her bravery erased instantly by his approach.

He laughed. "No, not all; I didn't know you had that in you. Deek would have been proud," he said, placing his arms around her shoulders. "Go on over to the grill and get something to eat," He said, pulling Olivia up and smacking her butt.

The affection caused her to momentarily hesitate; this would be the repercussion of her action: unwanted attention and advancements from Angelo. She did not want that kind of attention from him, but she was afraid that now it would start.

Like a good girl, she obeyed and went over and fixed herself a plate although she was not hungry. The guys started to tease her. She wished she had let Leah beat her up instead or just ignored her, because Livvy knew now, there was nothing stopping Angelo from making her the replacement. If Deek had been alive, he would have told her to walk away and not react. Unlike Deek, she always led with her emotions; it was a weakness she had yet to learn how to control. She knew Angelo had eyes for her; although, she had many men assault her throughout her adolescence, this was different. There was no one to save her r. She sat down at the table and started eating. Leah finally got back to her feet. She silently went into the house, got her belongings, and left. Olivia turned her attention back to what the day really was about: Deek. It was real now; he was gone to a place where human and spirit could not meet; she needed him, and she was convinced that he needed her too. How can a goldfish reign among sharks? If she ever needed him, it was now. She thought to herself. Her stomach began to cramp, and she pushed the unwanted food aside. All Olivia wanted was to go home, but there was no home. She began to regret every decision she had made after Deek was killed. She should not have left with Angelo. It was an emotional decision. This was why she needed Deek. She knew nothing; she had no idea how to make this work. This was a dangerous world, and she was not strong enough to live in it without her protector.

"Don't look so blue, baby girl. You can smile; you are with family," Carlos said. He had watched her for some time now. He felt so sorry for her; she literally had no living blood family now. She had suffered so much at such a young age. He recalled how she had been beaten so badly it hurt her to even lay in bed. That was the worst he had ever seen anybody be beaten. They all had a rough upbringing, but she got the worst of it. Life in the hood was more difficult for a female. His heart was breaking for her. Looking at her made him regret so many things. He wished things had worked out differently.

"Nah, I lost that when Deek died. No one else is going to look out for me like that," she said sadly.

"Angelo will, and so will I. Deuce was my boy. I'll find who did that to him, and I'll take care of him," Carlos said as he looked into her eyes. She had the most beautiful gray eyes that could shine like diamonds; now they were dull and sad.

She said nothing. She knew full well what Angelo wanted to do and what it would cost. Carlos meant what he said; he was one of her brother's most trusted friends. She wished he had been there that night instead of Angelo. Carlos was like Deek—a victim of his environment, but a good-hearted person.

"Yo, Tres, send Knockout this way. I want to dance," Angelo said, as he sipped the last of his Corona. He did not like anyone else talking to her, not even Carlos. He wanted her all for himself. He had waited long enough.

She looked at Carlos with pleading eyes, but there was nothing he could do. No one disobeyed Angelo; to do so would be a deadly mistake. Olivia gave Carlos dap and then went to dance with Angelo.

***

When night came, so did fear. It was only a matter of time when she would have to share a bed with Angelo. She hoped it was later than sooner. She closed her eyes and tried to dream. She was searching to find Deek so he would come to her in her dreams and tell her what to do and where to go. However, sleep would not come to her no matter how hard she tried; it too refused her, as it had done every night. Her mind worried about Deek. They had never been separated—never lived a moment without the other—and now she had to walk alone; she was not prepared. This house was not peaceful; people came and went at will. Gunshots, screeching wheels, and loud music broke the quiet that she longed for. Tonight, was no different, so she got up and walked around the room; sadly, this would be her life, at least for the next three years. She hoped she had the strength to survive. She wanted to walk out the room and look at a television show that Deek and she loved—to somehow connect with him—but fear kept her in her bedroom. She believed if Angelo saw her, he might make her sleep in his bed. She did not want that. She heard footsteps come toward her bedroom; she quickly jumped into bed and pretended to be asleep. She knew it was Angelo, because he had a heavy footstep. You could hear him long before you saw him. He did not knock; he just walked right in and came up to her bed whispering Olivia's name. It reminded her of her deceased mother's past boyfriends. They used to do that to her. She did not move and continued to pretend she was sleeping, although she was terrified. Her stillness did not seem to deter him. He started to shake her awake. She relented and gently opened her eyes.

Even in darkness her eyes shone. "Hey sleepy head, I want you to come sleep with me. I just want to hold you," he said, taking his hand and playing with her unbraided hair.

Olivia looked at him and wanted to say no, but no one told him that. He was the boss. It was not that he was unattractive; he was very handsome. He had a lovely face; deep ebony eyes, curly shoulder length black hair he kept pulled in a ponytail, flawless Colombian tanned skin. He had an athletic build; he worked out daily, and it showed. But Olivia was just fifteen, and she had been a victim of men almost her entire life. She just wanted rest. He was at least seven years older than she was. The things his mind thought, her mind did not. As much as she wanted and needed the connection of another…to know love…she knew Angelo could not provide that. "What about Leah? She will be angry and hurt," she said, hoping there was some sense of respect for her in him. She did not want to lie in his bed. She wanted to be alone with her own thoughts and dream of Deek. She wanted her brother to come and save her. Wanting something does not make it happen; if it did, she would have a different life. Her eyes pleaded with Angelo's to let her be in her own pool of depression, but he was not to be denied. He took his hand and gently caressed her cold cheek. His eyes said so many things—things that she wished she could have hushed—but her feelings, thoughts, and needs did not matter.

"It's okay; I am done with her anyway. You don't have to do anything except let me hold you. I don't like sleeping alone," he said very softly. He took his hands and helped Olivia get out of bed. They walked to the master bedroom—his bedroom. The walk seemed like the green mile; only destruction awaited her. She got tense for a moment as she thought of what he might do, and she would have run if he had not held her so closely. Sadly, no one was there…just those two. She guessed the rest of the gang had gone to their homes or were hanging out. She wanted to know what he expected of her, and she wanted to find a way to ask that would not offend or anger him. "Angelo, you are just going to hold me, right?" she asked sweetly. "I mean, I just miss Deek so much, and I just want to sleep," she said looking down at her feet, praying that her fear would not show. She was so frightened and traumatized. Her mind was filled with vivid images of all the unkind things men could do to orphan girls—girls who had already suffered at the hands of evil. The idea nauseated her.

He placed his rough hand upon her small chin so that his eyes looked directly into hers. "Yeah, I miss him too. We need to console each other. I know what you are thinking. I would not do that unless you wanted too. I don't rape, I don't force, and I don't beg. I know you need somebody, and I told you I am here for you. I like you, Knockout. You are a knockout; you beautiful, you lovely, you tough. You are the kind of woman I need around here. You are going to be my Thug Princess," he said, kissing her forehead and pulling back his covers for her to lie down. She felt relief, knowing that he would not make her do anything. She could not handle that and losing Deek too. It was all too much. She positioned herself under his cold sheets, and a second later she felt his warm body conform to hers and his strong arms connected under her navel; she did not move. She slowly and quietly drifted off into a deep sleep; hours later, she awoke screaming. Angelo jumped up and reached for his gun. "What is the matter?" He turned to her with his eyes wide, as he tried to focus in the darkness.

She did not know; she must have had a nightmare. She was sweating and shaking...looking for her brother but he was not there. "I'm sorry Angelo; I had a nightmare," she said, still shaking as she noticed the gun in his hand. "Are you going to shoot me?" she asked naïvely.

He looked at her, his dark eyes gazing into hers; she could see him clearly because of the moonlight shining through the window. The man on the moon did not exist; if he did, she would have implored him to come and save her.

"No, never. Come on and lay down. It is okay; I am here. I will always be right here," he said, placing his arms protectively around her. His words brought her no comfort. With the knowledge that he had a gun ready to shoot and kill at will, a new fear emerged inside of her. She would not defy or deny him. Angelo had many sides; she would do what she must to stay on his good side. He fell asleep before her, and she watched him. She didn't know what she expected to see or learn from observing him, but she watched him. Several times he flinched, as if he were dodging a bullet; only he and God knew what terrible sins he had committed. She wondered about many things. Who was the man she was sleeping beside? Who was the man who promised her brother he would take care of her? She turned back around and waited on sleep to find her.

When Livvy awoke the next morning, Angelo was still fast asleep. She showered, put on her clothes, and started breakfast. She left him a note, got her book bag, and walked to school. She didn't like riding the bus; it was always some kind of drama. Deek used to walk her to school and come back to get her. Now, she had to walk alone, which was scary. Even this early in the morning, bad things could happen to a girl walking alone. Criminals and crime never rest; they just waited for the perfect opportunity...kind of like a lioness stalking prey. Deek had taught her well; she was always cautious. She knew three different ways to get to and from school; she never took shortcuts or walked in alleys, and she always watched. The school had metal detectors; knives, blades, and guns were forbidden and nearly impossible to sneak in. School was never her worry; getting to school was. The school was actually nice because of the way the district was set up. Most parents opted for private education or just moved. They feared the effects of what a hood presence upon their children would do. Olivia passed the ABC store, and the local drunks were already waiting; she never understood that. It seemed to her that if you could get up early to get drunk then you ought to be able to get up and go to work. She continued to walk swiftly, as she was nearing the pimp and prostitute area. This area was more dangerous at nighttime, but it was always a very violent section. It scared her the most. Pimps were dangerous because they saw women as fish, hooking them into a life of sex slavery and eventually killing them. It was a horrible life for women on these streets. If not for Angelo, sooner or later, one of those opportunists would have found her and made her live that life. Angelo was the best of the worst, she thought as she powered through. She was not unnoticed, but she guessed it was too early for them to prowl and attack. Or, they may have feared the wrath of Angelo if they touched her. She had one more block to go. Drug city was not bad for her, because BWD ran the drug scene. It was true that a new gang had entered, but they were no match for BWD. If Angelo felt like it, he would eliminate the entire sect. She eased her stride. There was no fear here; she knew the dealers, and they knew her. She waved and continued to walk until she made it to school. Crazy it may seem to be waving at the local dealers, but they were under her brother's management until he was murdered. They never bothered her; if anything, they looked out for her. They were her street sitters; most people had babysitters, but not Livvy. Those guys were a safety net. Finally, she could get a reward for all her hard work. This was her place...her escape for eight hours. She loved school and did well, considering the circumstances; she worked hard because she promised her brother she would go to college. Even though he was gone, and she was heartbroken; she never broke a promise to Deek. Her brother said, "Your word is you; if you don't keep it, people will label you a liar and no one will trust you." Deek was like her mother, father, and brother all in one. His wisdom was all she had left.

She walked inside, went through the metal detectors, and walked right into math class. School had not started yet, but she loved math. Mr. Douglas always had some equation waiting for her. She started on it. She spent her free time here and ate lunch here. She had no friends; she never needed any because she had Deek, but now he was gone. The kids in school never made fun of her or bullied her; that was mainly because, last year, she beat a girl so badly she had to be hospitalized. Deek got mad at her for that—even threatened to give her a whooping—but the girl had been messing with Livvy for four weeks, so she had to let her have it. The crazy thing was that she got suspended and not Livvy; it pays to be an A student; people incorrectly think nerds don't battle. Well, they know now different.

Mr. D always had a juice and muffin for her when she came in the mornings. After all that walking, she was hungry again. She started her day and said nothing about burying Deek. She felt it best never to open yourself up too much to people; it was a liability, and it made you vulnerable. You should never give anyone ammunition to use against you later; Deek taught her that too. She solved the equation. When she showed Mr. D, he was impressed. The rest of the day went by too quickly; she was in no rush to return to the party house. She walked out the building with the purpose of going to the library. There were some books she wanted to read. Her English teacher had given the students a reading list, and she wanted to read all the books. As she was about to start her journey, a horn blew, and her name followed. She turned to see Angelo waiting for her. He motioned for her to come on, and she walked quickly. "Thanks for breakfast this morning; that was sweet. I am taking you shopping today for some new clothes. You get whatever you want," he said smiling.

"Well, can I go to the library too? I need to check out some books," she said.

"I'll buy you the books at the bookstore. How do you like that?" he asked with animation.

"Okay, thank you," she said, but wondering to herself what price she would have to pay later for the generosity he was showing her now. Nothing—not one thing—was ever free. Even salvation and enteral life had a cost; eternity came at the expense of Jesus, who died to save savages who still chose sin over salvation.

She sat back in the car and said no more. She would have preferred to go to the library, but she guessed owning the books was better than borrowing them. It could be he avoided the library because it was near the police station. Angelo did not like police. He despised them with a passion. She looked out the window as he drove to the outlet store. He grabbed her hand, and they walked from store to store. He picked out what he liked, but she had to remind him that her school had a dress code. There were certain things deemed inappropriate that could cause her to get suspended. In all honesty, it was the one rule that was rarely enforced, but she did not like dressing sexy. Besides, she wanted to blend in, not stand out; she didn't like drawing attention to herself, especially from men. It made her feel uncomfortable to be noticed, so he allowed her to choose her own clothes. She assumed he was in a great mood. He was laughing, smiling, and talking; and he openly displayed affection, no matter who was around. It bothered her, as she was still depressed about losing Deek; he was enjoying himself, like Deek had not died. That both angered and hurt her. She didn't like his attention, but she did not complain. She just let him do as he pleased. She kept reminding herself it would just be for a little while...at most three years. Once she graduated high school, she was going to college and she would never see Angelo again...she hoped.

CHAPTER 3

Two Sides of Angelo

As weeks turned into months, Olivia felt like she had incorrectly judged Angelo. He was gentle, patient, and kind to her. Maybe she was thinking of him too harshly because of his past; he had returned to the old apartment and gotten all her belongings and Deek's. She had not been back since her brother had been gunned down in the streets. The police still had not made any progress in the case, and no one had called to interview her again. They did not care anyway; she could tell that from their attitudes. To them it was just one less gangster on the street. But he had told Olivia he was leaving the gang and would have if he had not been murdered that night; no one seemed to understand that. BWD was not his life or legacy; he had much more to offer society than that. Angelo assured her, like Carlos, that they would find out who did it; but they had made no progress either. The room that she once had slept in at Angelo's house had now been turned into a study for her. He made everyone leave by 10:00 every night, except the weekends and school breaks. He said he wanted her to keep up her good grades. He had bought her a new wardrobe and new tennis shoes that cost one hundred dollars; plus, he gave her an allowance. In the back of her mind, she thought that, in some way, he would be looking for repayment; nothing was ever free.

After a month, she was his; all his kindness was being repaid. It was not what she wanted, but it was what he wanted, and she submitted. It made life easier for her. Leah, of course, did not take this well; she vowed to get payback. She attempted to make life hard for Olivia; Livvy wasn't really worried about Leah. She knew Leah was a coward. Her concern was finding out who killed Deek and why.

Angelo, though temperamental with most, was very easy with Livvy...at least most of the time. That might have been because she said very little and did as she was told. He had his expectations. He wanted breakfast on the weekend; she was exempt from making it during the school week. He wanted dinner every night, even if he was not at home at dinnertime. She could not have outside friends; he was very jealous when it came to her. But she did not have friends anyway, so she did not care. She was not old enough to legally attend clubs, nor did she want too; but if he wanted her to go, no one refused to let her in. She had to dress up for him when he asked, keep the house clean, and count his money. He only trusted her with it; it used to be Deek's job. She was good at math and loved numbers; he knew that from Deek. From the age of eight, she could balance a check book; and by eleven, she had written out a budget for herself and Deek. At twelve, she had taught herself how to do taxes; that was her side hustle. It was legal; she never defrauded the government, but a lot of people from the hood could not afford to pay the price to have them done; so, they came to her. She still had savings from doing it. Deek taught her to never steal or commit any other crimes. However, she did not like being Angelo's personal accountant because sometimes the money did not add up, and that meant he was going to hurt or even kill someone. If she could, she would add money just to save one of the dealers; most of them were just kids like her. He caught her doing that once, but only warned her never to do it again. She didn't. Angelo only gave warnings to people he liked; other than that, you were gone. She was learning her place in his chaotic, violent world. She tried to separate herself from it as much as possible. He trusted her and kept her close to him. She knew things that only his inner circle knew. The way they spoke—like people were disposable—made her nauseated and afraid. They were soulless and thought nothing was wrong with being that way. She was stuck with them; how could Deek ever have been part of this?

**

It was a quiet Saturday, as they sat on the couch. She felt his eyes staring at her, and she waited for him to speak. "Baby, go get me a beer," he requested.

She closed the book she was reading and got up to get his drink. When she returned, he took the beer from her and pulled Livvy onto his lap. "You know why I love you," he said, planting kisses all over her body.

She shook her head no. She hated when he kissed her like that. It felt so unnatural, but it was what she had to do. He liked to be affectionate, and he liked her to be affectionate back. She never pulled away or complained openly. She had seen him strike Leah for that plenty of times previously. He thought the world was his, and he lived as though he was the master of all.

"Cause you do as you are told and don't ever talk back. I love that," he said.

"Okay," she said, turning to get up and return to her book "Agnes Grey." She enjoyed reading literary classics and Christian fiction; it helped. She had just finished two Virginia Woolf novels, mostly for her English class; she liked doing extra credit. She had a 100 average in her AP English class, and she planned to maintain it. It was the only part of her life she felt she had control over. At school, she had some freedom.

"You little bookworm; leave that book over there and tend to me. Now I see why Deek use to call you Belle," he said, tugging on her hair.

She turned toward him, wondering what he wanted her to tend to. She hated having her hair tugged at; it triggered terrible memories that she longed to forget. She had gotten his beer, and the boys would be over in about an hour. So, what he wanted her to do, she did not know.

"What do you want me to do?" she asked politely, placing her finger on the page so she would not lose her place. She looked at him, waiting for a response.

"I just want to kiss on you and hold you. You feel good in my arms," he said. "You want to sip this beer?" he asked, as his hands ran unchecked across her body.

"No, thank you," she said shyly, looking down at her feet.

"You are so polite. 'No, thank you,' my sweet little princess. Look I might not be back tonight because I got some business to take care of. You going to be alright without me?" he asked.

She nodded yes, trying to conceal some of her excitement. It was not that she was not enjoying his company; he went out of his way to be good to her. But she liked reading her books in silence. She didn't mind being alone in the daytime, but at night her fears, thoughts, the sight of Deek being killed, and her past swarmed her all at once paralyzing her defenses. It had gotten worse. She guessed it was because she was so stressed. It was nerve racking dealing with Angelo at times. Though he was kind to her, he was also demanding. She tried her best not to slip up or do anything to anger him.

"Why do you do that all the time? You just shake your head and hardly ever talk. Why? I like to hear you talk. You my girl, right?" he asked, looking into her youthful face. She was so enduringly sweet and so spellbindingly beautiful. He understood why Deek would not let him have her before. Now that he did, he would not let anyone touch her. There was still innocence in her eyes that years of abuse by her mother's boyfriends and pimps could not erase. Something in her was magnetic, hopeful, and untouched. He would find out all her secrets.

She looked at him, not sure why her silence was an issue. "Yes; I just don't talk a lot because I don't have much to say, I guess," she said. He did not allow her to talk to anyone but him. She had no extracurricular activities, no friends, and no life outside of him; there was nothing for her to talk about.

"Okay, well talk to me. You can ignore the rest of the world, but not me; it makes me feel like you're hiding something from me. I don't want to get paranoid," he said, sipping his beer and looking at her.

She almost nodded her head again but caught herself. She did not want him to get paranoid either. "Okay, I will talk more. It's not that I am thinking anything; I'm

24

just used to not having to talk. You don't have to get paranoid or anything. I'm sorry," she said, not sure why she apologized but hoping that would ease any uneasiness that may have been lurking in his head.

"Don't apologize baby; I am not mad at you. I just like to know what you thinking. Go ahead and read your book."

She kissed his cheek and went back to her book. She snuggled up to him and began to read. He placed his arms around her and held her tightly. They stayed that way until some of the guys came over and he left. She immediately fixed dinner and then went back to her book. She found that living in fiction was much better than reality. She missed Deek in moments like this. He sometimes read to her; he had such a pleasant voice and sweet laugh. A part of her loved the silence and the solitude, but part of her hated it because the silence mocked her broken heart and reminded her of what she had lost so unjustly. That feeling she felt as she watched her brother die came back to her, along with that fear of the unknown and the pain of being alone. Warm tears formed at the bridge of her eyes, but she would not allow them to fall. She had to be stronger than that. However, four hours of hearing nothing but cars and not being able to talk to another person left her lonely. She was hoping that Angelo would be home soon. She longed for companionship. She thought about calling Carlos' girlfriend, but she was older than her, like most of them, and she had nothing really in common with the other girlfriends.

Darkness seemed to scare her even more now. Her mind began to wonder; what kind of business was he doing? Had he found the person who murdered Deek? If so, she wanted to be there. She needed to look into the eyes of the one who had ripped her heart out. She thought about calling Angelo but decided against it. He did not like to be nagged, and she did not like receiving violent blows to her body. It was not that he had attacked her, but he could; and that was enough to keep her from doing it. She finally went to bed; at least she was alone. She preferred to sleep alone. However, Angelo did not like that; he liked having someone to hold. He never touched her sexually unless he asked first. The first time she said no, wondering if he would keep his word and not force her; and he did keep his word. But what he did do was daily remind her of how much money she cost him, what kindness he was bestowing on her, and that if she loved him, she would show him. But at fifteen, what did she know of love? Only Deek loved her—not her deceased mother; or her absentee father, whoever he was; and, in honesty, not Angelo. She knew the biblical definition of love; this was not it. She accepted him because he was all she had, and a little of something was better than nothing. She took what she had to in order to find out who killed Deek and keep a roof over her head. She had endured ten years of abuse. What was a few more? She just hoped she could keep her sanity and not slip up or anger Angelo. She was a witness so many times to how his anger could escalate and how badly he beat people when disobeyed; it was frightening.

Midnight came with the rattling of keys. She held her breath, trying to make out the footsteps. It did not take long for her to know it was Angelo and some of his friends: Carlos, Biggs, Jose, and Creeper. She heard them in the kitchen; she was glad she made a lot of food because, if not, Angelo would have come and got her and told her to fix more. She never understood why grown men could not fend for themselves in the kitchen...especially thugs like them.

They were eating and talking, as if they were the only ones in the house. She dared not get up and look out. If he had been alone, it was possible. But because of his jealousness, she couldn't roam the house in her nightclothes when there was male company. It was almost like having a daddy; except they shared a bed and daddies didn't do that...well...not good daddies. He treated her very differently than Leah; he said it was because he loved her and only used Leah. Livvy just lay in the bed gazing out the window, as she did every night, wishing for Deek to come back. When she thought about the good times she and her brother shared, it made the hard times better. The door to the bedroom opened gently and he tried to walk softly, but to no avail. She turned around and looked at him but said nothing.

"Did you miss me?" he asked, as he took off his shoes and lay beside her; she felt like velvet in his hands.

Only an idiot would say no, but of course she missed him; he was her link to the outside world. If she was not going to school, she could not leave the house without him; he said it was for her protection. "Yeah, I missed you. I started to call, but I decided against it because I know how you are when you are doing business," she said.

His face softened. "You could have called; you can call me anytime," he said kissing her forehead. "I know it can get lonely, but I can't take you with me; it would not be safe," he said, caressing her arm.

"Okay," she said.

"I'm going to take a shower; that food you cooked was good. I might get a second helping. You wait up for me," he said.

She looked at him; her eyes were already so very heavy. "I'll try," she said.

He smiled and left. Two hours later, he returned and gently woke her with tender kisses. The lights were on, and he pulled off her nightgown with ease and said, "I want to love you tonight."

She was not the mood for that; she never was. She was too young for sex to be on her brain. She had other things to think about. She wanted to sleep, but she did not deny him. His hands dressed her entire body, tickling her back and below; she jumped and tried to reposition, because she did not want him to see or touch the scars. Even after half a decade, her scars still lingered, telling the tale of her miserable childhood. It shamed her.

"What is wrong?" he whispered, looking concerned.

26

"I just don't like you to touch me there, and I don't like the lights to be on," she said, not looking in his eyes.

"Why?" he asked, flipping her over and discovering what caused her so much shame and embarrassment. That explained her hesitation all the times before; she was hiding her scars. "What happened to you?" he asked, his fingers touching the scarred skin. It looked like the shape of a belt buckle. He had not noticed it before, but she had scars all around the area.

"One of my mama's boyfriends did it. Please don't look at it and don't touch it; I beg you, it embarrasses me," she confessed, trying not to cry. As much as she tried not to connect with him or let him into her past, she wanted to be wanted and needed to be comforted. She hated herself for her vulnerable hungry heart. He softly kissed each part of it and said she was still beautiful. Something in his tone eased her dismay and penetrated the wall she worked so hard to create. That was the Angelo she liked; easy, kind, soft spoken, and tender...but there was another side to him...one she hoped never to see. He was so kind in his touch that it was like a father rocking his newborn baby, and she fell asleep in his arms.

**

A new school week started, and Olivia was happy to go. When she arrived, Coach Lydia Geter approached her. She told Livvy that one of the varsity cheerleaders had gotten hurt and could not finish the rest of the school year. She wanted to know if Olivia would replace her since she was an alternate. She also said that she thought it would enhance her college application. Livvy was an underclassman and found it odd that she had asked her out of all the others, but she told Coach Geter she would...anything to enhance her college application and up her chances of leaving Hollow Hill. Coach Geter nodded and told her to be at practice tomorrow. Although it sounded silly, Olivia always wanted to be a cheerleader. They seemed to be everything she was not: popular, pretty, and peppy; she was nerdish, quiet, and frightened. The idea of becoming a cheerleader made her heart dance because she always wanted to belong to something. She went through the rest of the day with glee. She could not wait to start; well, she had one obstacle—Angelo. She walked outside, and he was waiting on her. She told him what Coach Geter had said and asked if she could do it. He said it was all right as long as it did not interfere with what he required of her to do. She hoped it didn't; she wanted to be a normal teenager just once.

"I have a surprise for you," he said, after she finished talking.

She looked at him in wonder and waited for him to tell her what the surprise was.

"I'm going to teach you how to drive, and take you to get your permit," he said.

"Really? I can drive the Escalade?" she asked. He had a nice sedan too, but she liked the SUV best.

"Not at the moment, but I will let you drive the sedan," he said, pulling her face to his lips.

She smiled and looked out the window, wondering if Deek could see her wherever he was and what he thought. She wanted to go to his grave and talk to him. "Angelo, can I go see Deek?" she asked eagerly.

He looked at her somewhat taken back by the request. "This weekend I can take you, but right now let us concentrate on you learning to drive," he said, placing his hand on top of hers.

She nodded and drove back to the house. She didn't have a lot of homework, so she went into the kitchen to cook. The house already had some guys hanging out, and she kicked them all out of the kitchen. But Creeper requested she make him tacos instead of burritos. She nodded and began to slice and dice, placing the burritos in the oven. Then she started to make Spanish rice, refried beans, and avocado dip for the tortilla chips. She set aside Creeper's tacos and started to set out plates, utensils, napkins, and glasses. She did so with extra pep in her step because she was so excited about being a cheerleader. To her dismay, she noticed that the guys had drunk most of the lemonade, so she just made some Kool-Aid. Sometimes around these grown men, she felt like she was their babysitter and personal chef. As she was placing the Kool-Aid in the refrigerator to chill, Angelo entered the kitchen. "Babe, is that all the lemonade that is left?" he asked, resting his hand on the table.

"Yeah, but I'll make some more tonight. I just made some Kool-Aid. Your friends drink it as soon as I make it," she giggled; they acted like the lemonade was elixir the way they drink it.

He nodded and drank the rest of the lemonade. He looked around the kitchen, seeking something to nibble while the food was cooking, and noticed a plate set aside. "Why you make me tacos? I don't like them," he said, looking strangely at them and making a gross face.

Olivia laughed at the face he made. "I know, but those are for Creeper. I am taking the burritos out now," she said and turned to the oven to pull them out so they could cool. "Everything is ready now so you all can eat. I can get the guys," she said, untying her apron. She looked at him, but he was glaring at her. "Does the lemonade taste too sour?" she asked, figuring since there was only a swig left it must have tasted really tart.

His lips curled and his eyes narrowed at her like she was a target. She could not figure out why. His glare began to make her nervous. "What is wrong?" she asked nervously. Her eyes widened in wonder as she waited to see what he was about to do.

"Why are you fixing Creeper a plate? You didn't make me one?" he said in an annoyed tone. Did she have feelings for Creeper? He would eliminate him too. Olivia was his and his alone. Unlike Leah, she was not to be shared.

"Huh? Um, he asked me to set aside some tacos. I will make your plate; the burritos just got done," she said, somewhat confused. She thought she was doing right.

He walked toward her, and her heartbeat began to quicken. His hand grabbed her arm, and he pulled her near him. "You messing around with Creeper? Did he give you a place to stay? Why are you being so disrespectful?" he demanded.

She looked at him, not understanding the anger and jealousy. "What did I do wrong? I'm sorry," she said. She wanted to retreat. But he was taller and stronger, and he would not be moved. He slapped her so hard that it penetrated through her entire body. She grabbed her cheek to ease the pain. His reaction startled her. She had done nothing for him to react so violently towards her. She looked at him completely shocked by his reaction. Her eyes asked why, but he gave no reply.

"Go to your room and don't come out until I tell you," he yelled. His voice dressed the entire house. As she retreated, the guys looked at her with pity. She walked to her study crying. That night, she went to sleep hungry, angry, and frightened. He never came to get her; she didn't want him to. She slept on the cold floor, warmed by her tears.

***

Friday night lights shone brightly as the girls stood ready to hold the sign, they had made for the football players to run through. The football team was undefeated, and this was Olivia's first game cheering. Angelo and all the other BWD were there. She easily found them because they all sat together with bandanas, hats, and flashy jewelry. The school colors were white, baby blue, and gray; they were the mighty sharks. Olivia never really thought about school pride but now, being a cheerleader, she felt...well...excited, like she had a life again. She kept a picture of Deek pinned inside her uniform close to my heart. She wanted him to share every new experience with her. The guys crashed through the banner, and she did a few back flips. She was really good at gymnastics, jumping, and flexibility, which probably was the reason why she was recruited. Practice kept Angelo at bay sometimes. He came to her practice or had one of his goons come and watch her. They were making sure she was 'safe,' but that was code for not talking to anyone, especially boys.

"Carlos, you see her out there tumbling and flipping; she looks good don't she," Angelo said, his mind polluted by impure thoughts.

"Yeah, Ace, she do. She almost looks like a kid again. Deek would be really happy with that. It's good she got you to look out for her," Carlos said, admiring how well Livvy had adapted to her new surroundings.

"Yeah, that's my baby out there," he said. "So how much we making tonight with two undefeated teams? I put a stack on the home team."

"We got this, Ace. We making some big bucks. You know I got a new contact I want you to meet. He's big timing...beyond drugs and petty theft. He is into human sex trafficking; if we can get into that, we are set for life. Uncle Luis will be very happy," Carlos said to him.

Angelo saw dollar signs. "Do this, find out some things, do a background and underground check, and make sure he is legit. We don't need FBI or police tapping us. Let them continue thinking we are uneducated, illiterate, bastards. I like when they underestimate us; it makes it so easy. I'm going to contact my Uncle Luis, too," He said laughing.

Carlos laughed too and then turned his attention back to the game.

Olivia was so excited to be cheering with the rest of the girls; and she was even more excited as they ran the last touchdown and won the game. The people in the stand erupted with cheers.

"Livvy, you want to come to the party at my house tonight?" Bianca asked.

It was kind of her to ask, but Olivia knew that was not even a possibility. "No, I have to get home. I have a project I need to complete for history, but thanks for the invite," she said, wanting to go but knowing that Angelo would not allow it. She told the ladies goodbye and began to walk up the stairs to where Angelo was. A guy from school stopped her in mid stride. "Olivia, hey; where you headed?" he asked.

She knew who he was, but he had never spoken to her before. His name was Jacoby; he was the basketball 6'0 feet star phenomenon who played varsity. "I am headed home," she replied, not sure why he was talking to her and fearing that if Angelo saw it the repercussions that would ensue would be horrible. She had not forgotten the slap he had given her a few days' prior for fixing Creeper tacos. Thank God Creeper explained to him, and he apologized; but she was still wary.

"Bianca is having a party tonight; why don't we go together," he said.

She was lost; he never talked to her...never even acted like she existed...and now he wants to go out. "No, I can't," She said, preparing to leave. He reached for her arm and, on instinct, she jerked away. "Look, for your own safety just turn around and walk away and pretend I don't exist." she said. All she needed was for Angelo or one of the others to see, and they would both be beaten.

He looked perplexed and started to speak, but Angelo had already spotted them and was on his way down the bleachers while the other looked on. "Knockout, is this punk bothering you?" he asked.

"No, he was just confused; he thought I was somebody else. We all look alike in our uniforms. He is leaving right now," she said, looking at him with pleading eyes. He understood and turned to leave. But before he could, Angelo jacked him up and whispered something in his ear. Olivia could not hear what it was, but she knew it was bad because he turned bright red and, when he released him, he dashed off.

"You cool?" he asked her.

She nodded yes, and he walked her back to his car. He was a little aggressive with her. His hands were gripping her tightly. She guessed it was because he thought she was flirting, but she was not. She was trying to save her butt and Jacoby's also. There was no need for his aggression. The home team won; they should be celebrating.

"Don't let that happen again. I told you; do you need me to smack you around to remember rules? Any more of that, and I will...and I will make you quit the cheerleading squad. Do you understand? You act about as stupid as Leah," he barked at her.

His harshness hurt her feelings. "Sorry, and I do understand but, Angelo it wasn't my fault. I was walking, and he approached me. I promise, I was not flirting with him. I was telling him I was not going to Bianca's party and to leave me alone," she said in defense of herself. She should have said nothing. His fist connected with her lips and blood poured like sweat from her face. It was the second time he had hit her. The pain was unimaginable...far worse than before. It was a painful connection she did not deserve. She looked at him, her eyes asking why. How did Leah stay so long with him? He was a brute and a bully. That was unnecessary. She wanted to run away, but there was no place to go. She was stuck with him.

"Don't get blood on my seats," he ordered, looking angrily at her.

The Angelo she feared—the other side of him—had just been revealed. She quickly retrieved a towel she had in her bag and placed it to her pulsating bloody lips. She did not cry; she did not flinch. Olivia just sat there motionless and quiet until they reached his house. She quickly retreated from his view and cleaned herself up. The bleeding still had not stopped; it hurt so badly. She wanted to leave but she knew she had to stay. This was her new world. There was no safe place. She had few choices: the state, a pimp, or Angelo. She just had to work harder at not making him angry. There was no need for her to be upset with him or ask him why he hit her. She just had to pretend like it never happened but remember that it did...because simple mistakes had deadly consequences. She had an entire weekend with him; it could be pleasant or painful. She would have never left the safety of the bathroom, but his knock at the door told her it was time to come out.

She was thankful at least that no blood had escaped onto her cheerleader uniform and none on his leather seats. He probably would have beaten her again for getting his seats messed up. She opened the door, and he stood before her. He was apologetic and embraced her. She did not want his touch, his phony apology, or his pretend love; she wanted to leave. She wanted Deek. Her brother would have beaten him...even killed him...for placing his hands so violently on her. She did nothing wrong and was attacked. She felt something new in her heart. She felt hate.

CHAPTER 4

Balancing Act

Olivia locked herself in the study room, leaned her aching body against the wall, closed her eyes, and tried to be invisible. This was a foreign lifestyle, and Angelo was the dictator who could be kind or harsh depending on his whim. She was held captive by him. She wanted him to be what Deek was—her protector—but his demands on her were becoming too harsh. Her silence had originally kept her out of trouble but, upon his insistence, she stopped being silent because it made him paranoid. Now it seemed like the sound of her voice unleashed an uncontrollable anger—a rage that was only calmed by him beating her. She just wished to disappear forever. There was no safety in this place; no one cared about her. The loneliness was the worst feeling she ever felt. There was a sermon that she heard before she stopped attending church. Jeremiah was lonely during his time as a prophet, as he attempted to help Israel and they condemned him. In the New Testament, Jesus said he was not alone because he had the Father. But unlike Jeremiah, she was no prophet; she was not God in human form; she was a mistake, a burden, a wasted creation. Every day that she woke up and saw Angelo beside her reminded her how sorry and sad her life was, making her wish she was never born. No one claimed her, and all had left her. Her eyes opened to the sad reality that she was still confined to the walls of Angelo's house. No amount of time spent reading books would help her escape him. She tried; she tried to recall something good and beautiful so that Angelo could not steal the little ray of hope she had left. She felt it dimming. Fear surged through the marrow of her bones when she heard his voice call her name. Her lips were still swollen by his angry reaction; her body was still sore from his selfish apology; he was so rough and brutal. She wished her entire body was paralyzed so that she never had to feel his hands cascading down her body or his lips connecting with hers. That was a kindness not extended to her. She had to feel his rage, his hatred, and his paranoia. Maybe it was her; she had this ability to upset him without trying, and everything she did to help only made things worse. She just felt that, if he did not see her, he would not feel it necessary to hurt her. "Yo, Knockout, babe. Where you at?" she heard his voice yell. It was not angry but gentle. She did not want to leave the study for fear of what he would demand of her. She took a deep breath and opened the door and walked into the den. "I'm right here," she whispered. Watching him as he turned around, his eyes met hers and, for a moment, she saw regret in them. Her body was physically shaking as he looked at her. She wondered if he would again assault her battered body.

He inwardly winced at how she looked at him. Her diamond gray eyes were pale with fear; her lovely, soft skin glistened with sweat and tears. He almost felt sorry; almost, but it was her fault and she had to learn. "Babe, you need to put some ice on that or something. It looks kind of ugly. I was going to take you out for lunch but...um...you need to stay here looking like that," he said as he walked toward her. He reached out his hand to touch her, and she flinched. "What is wrong?" he asked softly.

She started to tell him he was what was wrong but knew better. "I just thought you were going to touch my lip, and it still hurts," she said without making eye contact. He scared her.

He knew it was fear that made her recoil from his touch. That frustrated him. "I told you I was sorry. You are overreacting. Don't be like that; just get some ice. I have some business. Carlos is coming over. So, fix him something, and tell him to hang here till I get back," he said and turned to leave.

She watched him go, and her body relaxed. She went into the kitchen and made an icepack for her throbbing lips. She closed her eyes to rest and retrieved the sleep that was denied her the night before. She was not Angelo's girlfriend but his slave, and he was not a good master. Something was eating at him, and it made him meaner to her—harsher and impatient. She would never escape him until he found another. She hoped he found his new interest soon. The slamming of a car door revived her, and she quickly walked to the window to see who it was. Carlos was walking toward the door; she opened it before he knocked, and he gasped at her hideous sight.

"Livvy, what happened to you? How did your face get like that?" he asked walking in and examining her face.

She shook her head, but he persisted. "I made Angelo mad. He said he was sorry. I should not have said anything," she confessed.

"Angelo did this to you. Why? What did you do for him to do that?" he asked.

She looked bewildered. She had done nothing. Why did he hit her? What made him think he had the right to put his hands on her? The question should be why does he hit? People always blame the victim and not the villain. "I don't know. A guy was talking to me, and I told the guy to leave; Angelo saw it and got mad. You were there. I was trying to explain, and he punched me in the face. Will you just ask him not to hit me anymore? He listens to you. I don't know what I have done wrong, but he gets so angry. Deek would never do this to me," she said.

Tres shook his head in disappointment. Angelo should not have put his hands on Livvy that way; it was wrong. It wasn't like she was entertaining the guy. "I am sorry," he said and embraced her. "This is not what Deuce would want at all. Have you had lunch?" he asked.

She shook her head no.

"Let's go out to get something to eat. You can get whatever you want," he said.

"I can't. Angelo said for me to fix you something to eat. I thought that was weird because the last time I fixed a meal for one of his friends, he slapped me for it. Besides, I am not supposed to leave the house without him. He said for you to wait till he gets back," she said recalling what he had told her. She knew he meant it.

"Well, you can go with me. I will tell him. Come on, you need to have some fun," he said as he reached for her hand and walked her to the car. His girlfriend worked at Soul on the weekends. She was happy to get out but worried about what Angelo would do to her when he found out. It was a brief ride; it only took fifteen minutes to arrive. They sat outside and waited for their orders to arrive. She ordered a milk shake, chili cheese fries, and a bacon cheeseburger. It was nice to not have to look over her shoulder because she was worrying about Angelo. Carlos kept the conversation light. He asked about school. Olivia wanted to know what if anything he had found out about Deek and how to live with Angelo without getting hurt. "Carlos, have you found out who killed Deek?" she asked as she took a small bite out of the burger so her mouth wouldn't hurt.

Her questioned almost made him choke, but he quickly regained himself. "No, I am trying, but it's hard. Angelo thinks he was trying to get a new deal started, and it was just a drug deal gone wrong. I can't confirm that. I told Ace it is not like Deek to do anything like that. Don't worry about it; I mean, don't let it consume you," he said.

Too late; she was consumed by it daily. It was the only reason she had not given into her darkest thoughts. "Well, can you tell me why Angelo hates me? I have to get out of his place. I keep pissing him off," she said.

"Livvy, he doesn't hate you. He really cares about you. He's overwhelmed because he can't find who killed Deek; Leah is an angry ex-lover and is causing mad heat around us; and he trying to be good for you. Relationships are hard on anybody," Carlos said to her.

Olivia nodded. She thought about saying more but held her tongue. Carlos was loyal to Angelo, not her; and if she said too much, he would repeat it. She had said nothing condemning; at least she did not think so. She would remain silent. "We should get back. I don't want to get into trouble," she said.

"You won't. I will take you home. Let me go see my old lady really quick, and then we can go," he said and dashed back inside.

Olivia gazed out, watching cars going back and forth, and saw Angelo's SUV. Her pulse quickened, and her breathing became labored. All she needed was to see him. If he saw her, he'd beat her like she had snitched. Sweat started popping out on her skin, and she reached for the milkshake to cool herself off. She hoped he would just pass by, but she was disappointed. He parked across the street and walked into the music store. She was silently praying for Carlos to return so she could beat him home. Five minutes later, Carlos returned. She told him they had to go and explained why but instead of running home, he walked over to the store to see Angelo. She slumped in defeat and sat in the car. Her lip was again hurting; she used a wet napkin to ease the pain. She kept a constant eye out by looking in the review mirror. She watched the two of them retreat and walk toward her. She could almost feel Angelo's fists bruising her flesh. She wanted to bolt out of the car and run for her life, but they were swifter then she. Angelo opened the passenger side door and reached for her. She closed her eyes and braced herself for the infliction of pain she knew she would receive, but nothing. She opened her eyes and he stared at her, confused by her reaction. "Babe, what is the matter with you?" he asked perplexed.

That was a dumb question if she ever heard one. How can you inflict pain on a person and then not understand the impact that has on a person? "Nothing, I am just in pain," she replied.

"Come on and ride back home with me. We need to talk," he said kindly. It was obvious that she was afraid of him. Carlos had told him so. He had been unnecessarily harsh to her, because of his own stress.

She got out but walked slowly. There would be no talking; it would be more like his fist walking all across her body. He reached for her hand to speed her up and opened the door so she could get in.

"What is wrong with you? I know it is something. Is it about what you said to Carlos?" he asked her.

She was glad she said little. "Am I in trouble?" she asked.

"What? Why would you ask that?" he said, as he placed the car in reverse and started the short drive back to his house.

"I make you mad all the time. You looked like I disgust you," she said not looking at him, but fiddling with her fingers.

He let out a sigh. "No, it has nothing to do with you. I am frustrated and I took it out on you and that was wrong. You my baby; you are going to have my babies. Don't sweat that stuff that happened; it's in the past," he said.

Olivia found little comfort in his words. She did not want either to be his baby or to have his babies. That was a frightening prospect. When they arrived back at his home, she wanted to retreat. But Angelo wanted to talk some more. She was scared now.

"Sit down and talk to me. I want you to feel like you can talk to me about anything, the same way you would with Deuce. You and I are family now, so you don't need to be scared with me. All I ask is that you respect my rules and live by them, like you did for Deek. You do that, and we won't have any problems," he said.

She nodded in agreement. He gazed at her, and she remembered how he felt paranoid when she did that. "Okay," she said. She was not sure what to talk about.

"Okay, well talk to me. How is school going? How is cheerleading going?" he asked.

"Good," she said. She had no life, and he knew that.

"Great, well you can go back to your studies. The guys are coming over, and we have some things to take care of," he said.

"Can I go to the library?" she asked.

"I told you, I have some business to attend too," he said.

"Don't you trust me to go alone? I won't do anything wrong. I just want to read some books," she said.

Her eyes lit like stars when she talked about reading books and doing mathematical equations. "You have one hour," he said. "I'll drop you off now and then come back."

"Thank you," she said. Joy overcame her as she rested in the comfort of pages written by authors long ago. She found power and hope in the pages. She found peace in the absence of Angelo; although it was a brief peace, it was one she found great pleasure in. She spent forty minutes inside the library and the latter twenty minutes outside. The sun warmed her skin, and she closed her eyes to bathe in its rays. She had been denied that since she lived with Angelo. He did not even like her to go outside to check the mail unless he was home.

"Hey, Livvy what's going on?" the voice asked.

She opened her eyes and turned slowly. She tried to cover her mouth so it could not be seen. "Hey, Bianca. I'm good. You?" she asked standing up and using her books to shield my lips.

"I'm great. The party was awesome; I wished you could have come. You would have loved it," she said.

Bianca looked as though she didn't have a care in the world. Olivia wished she could be like her. "I bet I would have," she said recalling the pain that was caused. "Bianca, I have to go. My ride just pulled up, and he doesn't like waiting," she said.

"Oh, okay. I'll see you at practice Monday," she said with a kind smile.

Olivia nodded and walked toward the car.

"Who is she?" Creeper asked as Olivia got into the car. She did not notice he was inside until he spoke.

"Bianca. She's a cheerleader...the one that invited me to her party. She's a junior this year. She is really nice," she said.

"Yeah she looks nice," he said and winked at Angelo.

Angelo smiled at Creeper.

Olivia ignored the comment and focused on the books she checked out. Bianca was way beyond his league. She was not impressed by money because her family had it. Creeper couldn't creep with her. She would blow him off, and Livvy would make sure of it.

**

Practice was enjoyable. Her lips no longer looked super horrible. A casual observer would assume she had bumped them into something. She was surprised that Angelo had not come to watch or sent any of his goons; she was glad though. Once practice was over, she walked outside and saw no Angelo. So, she sat down on the step and waited. She figured if he did not show in thirty minutes, then she was walking back to his place. She pulled out her bottled water and a honey bun. She plugged in her headphones and started bopping to the music. She felt comfortable, since most of the girls were gone. She never chit chatted with them anyway. When she looked up again to see if Angelo had arrived, she saw a familiar man walking toward her. She removed her headphones and watched him. A smile crossed his face, but not hers.

"Hey, Olivia. How are you doing today?" Det. Hoover asked.

"I'm fine, sir," she said somewhat suspicious of why he was standing in front of her; he was still wearing his signature rich boy outfit. He stood out like a sore thumb.

"Good; I wanted to talk to you again about what happened that night to your brother. I know he was part of Blanco Wild Deuces. I assure you that does not matter. We will use all the resources we have. We have a reliable lead. I thought I'd come by and tell you personally. Is there anything you'd like to tell me?" he asked. He had worried about her from the first night he met her. He hoped that she would trust him enough to tell him all that she knew.

She was elated that he had some news. "Can you tell me more?" she asked thirsting for knowledge.

He watched her closely and looked around seeing that no one else was nearby. "No, not without jeopardizing the investigation. But when we make an arrest, we will be able to answer your questions," he said.

"Okay," she said disappointed. That was not really worth coming to her school. "What do you really want? I am fifteen, but I am no fool. You came sniffing around for something. I mean no disrespect, but I have no information," she said. Angelo had already given her precise instructions on this subject.

"I just thought you might need to talk to someone. You're in danger, and I just want to help you," he said as he looked at her injured face.

She gave him a sarcastic smirk. "I've lived in danger my entire life. No one can help me since my brother is gone. I'm good. If you would kindly leave, I would be better," she said. If Angelo drove up and saw her talking to the detective, he would rip her a new one for sure. She was still healing from the last one. They didn't seem to understand their presence was not helpful but harmful for her. Anyone who talked to her was in danger and a danger for her. She was never sure what would set Angelo off.

"What happened to your lip and face?" he asked attempting to read her baby face. It was apparent she hit something, or someone hit her.

"She had an accident," the male voice said causing her to become startled. She glanced up and, as she feared, Angelo stood before her. She leaped up and walked toward him like an obedient dog. Where had he come from? She did not even see him pull up. He always did that...just showed up. It was scary.

Det. Hoover turned around slowly and eyed Angelo. "I was asking Olivia, not you," he said staring at him. He knew Angelo's kind and remembered that his brother had been killed in a police chase. His father founded BWD twenty-five years ago. Angelo was used to dealing with cowards and running the show, but this was his case and he was running things, not Angelo.

"Livvy, answer the man so we can go," Angelo said.

"I had an accident," she said looking down at her feet.

She had an accident, all right Det. Hoover thought to himself. "You be really careful, Angelo. She is fifteen. If you are having a sexual relationship with her, whether consensual or not, I will make sure special victims arrests you for statutory rape, endangerment, and anything else we can think of. You understand me?" he asked.

"I am her guardian. She never misses school, she is not a danger to society, and she has been more than willing to help you in the investigation of her brother's murder. There is nothing illegal going on in my home. I don't appreciate being harassed or threatened. I will make a formal complaint. You won't be talking to her again without me present. Do you understand?" he asked. Angelo grabbed her and they walked to the car. He was irritated by the police. He disliked and distrusted them. They didn't help; they only harassed.

Fear made Olivia start speaking and, though she wanted to stop, she could not. "I didn't say anything. He said he found a lead in Deek's murder, but he did not tell me what. He asked if I had anything to tell him. I told him no. I did just like you told me," she said hoping that would help her not get a physical beat down.

"I know you are a good girl. You got my back. It was my fault; I should have been here. It won't happen again. I love you," he said. He could tell she was nervous because she talked a mile a minute, but he had spoken with Carlos and he was not going to beat her for his mistake. It would not occur again if he could help it.

"Me too," she lied. She wondered what lead they had in her brother's case. She bet none; it was probably a ploy to get her to talk and turn on Angelo. She was more afraid of him than them. She knew that Angelo was capable of anything. If he felt that she was speaking against him or putting his gang into harm's way, he'd teach her a lesson. She had learned enough. She didn't need a review.

CHAPTER 5

Joyride

"**B**reathe baby, you got this," Angelo coached.

She had gotten her permit, and now he was teaching her how to drive. It was exciting, but also scary. It was a freedom she looked forward to, but knew it was limited to when he said she could drive or where she could go. It was only another way for him to extend his power over her. Her lip had healed completely, but the emotional damage his aggression caused had not. He ruled by fear, and he had shown her just what he truly thought of her. Now when Jacoby saw her at school, he would scatter. She tried to warn him way before it happened. He chose not to listen, and that got them both hurt. She tried to concentrate on the task at hand. Angelo still had not taken her to the cemetery; he said she should not have done what she did at the game and needed to be punished. It was cruel of him to deny her a visit to her brother, but that was how he worked. She asked Carlos to put flowers down for her, and he promised he would.

"Now you got it. Just relax. You are good at this," he said smiling at her.

His smile was genuine. When he looked at her his dark eyes shimmered, and Olivia wished he was that way all the time. For a brief moment she felt normal, but that feeling never lasted long; nothing about her circumstances was normal. She pushed the thought aside. "Can I drive to school?" she asked as she pulled into the driveway.

"Yes of course, but only with me on the passenger side," he said with a side grin.

She knew that. "Okay," she said and exited out the car. She could not walk to the end of the road without him, so she knew he would not allow her to drive alone. According to the law, she was not supposed to drive alone with a permit. But she was going to get her license soon enough. It was not like that mattered with Angelo around.

"You just gone walk away like that?" he asked.

She looked at him, not sure what she was supposed to do. Her body stiffened, and her words stammered out. "I... I don't know wh...what you mean," she said as her voice trembled, but she managed to walk back toward him.

A smiled emerged from his face. "I thought I'd take you to see Deek today," he said.

Olivia let out a sigh of relief. She thought she had angered him and was about to taste his fist again. "Oh, thank you so much," she said. "Do you want me to drive?"

"Nah, I will. We can take the Escalade," he said knowing that would make her happy.

She followed her heart and was happy to be able to see her brother again, even if it was just a simple tombstone. The ride was quiet, but she walked with felicity at the notion that she would be able to talk to him. There was so much she needed to tell him and ask of him. She was glad that Carlos had done as he promised and placed flowers on his grave site. She began to talk to him, mostly about general things. She wanted to tell him how controlling and mean Angelo could be. But she heard his footsteps behind her and said no more. She just sat back on her legs and stared at her brother's grave. She was glad that he was at least resting in a place nicer than the one he had left behind, and she hoped he was at peace. She wanted her brother to have peace. Peace seemed to elude him, but she hoped that he had peaceful moments before he was killed. She hoped she gave him a fraction of the joy he had given her.

Angelo watched Olivia. Before he had arrived, it seemed she was talking to him, but once she noticed him coming, she went silent. He wondered what she was talking about. "Well you wanted to come here, and all you are going to do is stare at him?" Angelo asked looking at her leaning over her brother's grave.

"I just like to be in his presence. It is calming to me," she said.

He knew better than that. "You want me to leave you alone? I will give you ten minutes, and then I'll blow the horn so you can come," he said placing his large hands playfully on her head and kissing her. "I know you love him; I do too. You belong to me now. It's the way Deek wanted it. I'm going to take care of you," he continued and turned to leave.

She suppressed her tears until she was sure he was gone, and then she poured out her heart to Deek. "Brother, this could not be what you wanted for me. I would never wish this to be bestowed on you. I miss you so much now; and the things I have seen and the words I have heard have been horrible. Angelo is meaner at times than any of those men Mama used to bring home. He was even meaner than our mother was to me. I don't know what to do or how to live without you. I am a puppet on Angelo's string. I want so badly to find out who did this to you, and why. The streets won't talk. I know someone knows. I wish I did. I am dying a slow miserable death without you. I would sell my soul to have you again. I am so broken, so worthless, so used up. I'm tired; I'm tired of being misled and used and tired of feeling the way I do. I can't escape anymore. I don't dream at all. My mind is never at rest. I live in constant fear. Angelo watches me like a hawk. He is kind, then harsh...loving, then hating...gentle, then rough. He gives me just a little to make me hunger, and then he takes it back. You never prepared me for how to live without you," she sobbed cleaning off his tombstone and kissing the ground that held him now. She wanted to say more, but Angelo had started blowing his horn; she dusted off her clothing and walked back to the car. She wanted to run, but where could she go? Maybe this was how her mother felt and why she had allowed so many men to use and abuse her; she wanted to feel. Her daddy leaving her alone after her birth must have made her mother feel empty. To fill that void, she offered her body to any man who asked so she could feel good, wanted, and special. In some ways, as much as she hated to believe it; she was like her. She knew Angelo was not good for her, but she needed someone, and he was all she had.

He was on the phone talking in code about business. Olivia pretended not to hear. He drove to a little diner and told her to go ahead and order while he finished the phone call. This was a nicer side of town that was an hour from home and had yet to be invaded by the decay that had defeated Hollow Hill. She walked in noticing no one, quickly sat down, and told the waiting waitress what she and Angelo wanted. As she rested, she began recalling the good times she had with Deek. But then a gentleman approached her. He was tall and stout, with fatherly eyes and a gentle smile. He reminded her of the detectives that had been in her apartment when Deek was murdered. "Olivia, I am Det. Alan Greene. I don't know if you remember me, but I am assigned to your brother's case. We have had a hard time locating you, so I thought we could talk a little now," he said.

How could that be? Det. Hoover had found her just fine at school two weeks ago. She was not hard to find. He could have come to the school, which she would have preferred since Angelo was right outside in his car.

"Please, Olivia. You are the only one that knows what happened," he pleaded.

She did not know who the murderer was; she only saw a guy and a gun. "I don't know who killed my brother. I honestly don't. No one will tell me. Besides Det. Hoover said you had a lead," she said feeling fresh tears forming and getting ready to fall. Det. Greene kindly handed her a napkin and she used it. He sat down across from her. She glanced out the window and saw Angelo getting ready to enter. For some reason, that caused a chill to go down her spine; she just never knew what kind of mood he was in. It changed like the weather.

"You need to go. Angelo is coming," she whispered, but he did not move. He looked at her, trying to figure out if she were afraid. His eyes were communicating with hers.

"Livvy, are you okay? What is going on?" he asked ready to verbally assassinate the gentleman sitting in front of her.

"I'm Det. Alan Greene; I saw Olivia come in and wanted to speak with her about her brother's death to let her know he is not forgotten and to see if she had remembered anything that would be helpful," he said watching the young man's aggression ease as he spoke. He wondered why Livvy, being so young, was not in foster care. She had no family to speak of, and it seemed to him that Angelo was somewhat controlling toward her.

"Right, but another detective came to her school like two weeks ago so nothing new has changed since then. We just left Deek's, grave and she is still upset. We just want to eat and relax. Besides, she has not remembered anything. Isn't that right Livvy?" he said.

"I don't honestly know, sir. I think I can remember his voice; it was raspy...low but aggressive. I think he was around 5'9. I'm not sure if he was a teenager or adult, and he was light skinned. I know that because he did not wear gloves. But that is all I remember," she said.

"That is a good start. Do you remember seeing tattoos on his body?" the detective asked as he pulled out his notepad and wrote vigorously on it.

"No, at least none that I can remember; he had on a doo rag, a red one, and wore sunglasses I guess to conceal his face since it was nighttime. He wore fitted jeans; I assume so he could run away after. He had on those popular tennis shoes," she said not believing she had recalled all of that. She could see his image as she closed her eyes. "I remember he wore a ring...something silver; and he had on a watch...a really nice watch," I said opening my eyes and looking at the detective. "I guess that does not matter, does it?" She felt as if she were betraying Deek for not paying close attention.

Angelo stood surprised, not believing she had seen that much of the shooter. It sent a chill down his spine. He had to eliminate him before the police found Spade, and he told them the truth. Angelo wanted to interrupt but doing so might cast suspicion on him. He would have to reprimand Livvy; she was too easily persuaded to talk to the police. He knew it was her brother, but he told her he would handle it.

"This is great. Here is my card, and if you remember anything else call me," he said as she scooted out. "As a matter of fact, call me if you need anything," he said watching Angelo watch him.

"Yes, sir; and thank you," she said.

He turned to leave, and the waitress brought out the food. Angelo sat in stone silence, sometimes looking at Livvy and then out the window. She thought he would be glad, but he seemed distracted. "Angelo, what is the matter? They might get him, and that will be a good thing. Then you won't have to worry about me all the time. I won't need protection. I can come and go," she said looking at him.

He wanted to take her face and punch her lips closed. This was not how it was supposed to go. He had to be easy. He did not want to hit her again. He was angrier at himself than at her. Sometimes looking at her, he saw Derrick. It was like her eyes knew the truth he was trying so hard to conceal. "Baby, I am going to always protect you. I just did not know you knew so much. I thought you would have told me," he said swallowing his anger and falling in sync with her eyes. Sometimes he felt like she cast a spell on him. He cared for her; all other women were disposable, but she was different. She was only a young girl; he could not expect her to understand. She loved Deek; in a way he wanted her to love him so he would not hurt her this time but warn her. BWD handled everything in house. He wanted her to love him without force or fear, but until he could he had to keep her in check.

"I didn't know I knew that. He was so kind in his speech and seemed to really care that when I relaxed, I recalled. Are you angry at me? I thought you wanted to get the guy who did this to Deek," she said.

"It's okay. You did right. You can give me that card. I should keep it," he said. There would be no communication without his knowledge; they might trick her into telling things she need not say.

**

The night air serenaded her round nose, and she was happy to at least be getting out the house. She wore a fitted purple dress that made her gray eyes pop. Her long hair was pulled back to showcase her amethyst studded earrings. She wore silver heels to finish off. Her makeup was flawless; Maria, Carlos's girlfriend, had come over to help her. She thought she looked nice.

"Yeah, that is what I am talking about. She looks hot. Come on Knockout, let's do this," Angelo said as they entered into a nightclub called Velvet Paradise. It was exclusive. Angelo held her hand tightly and told her to stay close and not speak. That was fine with her. They walked to a table where some important looking gentlemen sat. They spoke with thick accents in code, but she knew it was about drugs and delivering them. Then they started talking about people, getting girls, and prostitution. She pretended not to hear; she looked around the club and watched a group of people dancing. She would have continued ignoring what was being said, but the man asked Angelo about Livvy. She could not help but look at him, since he was talking about her.

"Nah, she belongs to me," he said somewhat offended.

"She is very beautiful; my son would love to have her," he said staring at Olivia.

"No. I can find you some others, but not this one. She is mine, forever and always," he said pulling her near to him.

She felt anger emerge within her spirit, as they talked of her like she was a horse or a plate of food. She had her own mind and thoughts. She belonged to no man. She was ready to leave. She excused herself and went to the restroom. She could not believe Angelo was actually kidnapping girls and selling them. Drugs were one thing, but people? How that was even possible? Now the dude wanted her. It was a concept way beyond her understanding. She had to do research on this. She wanted to leave, but she was sure Angelo would not allow it. She took a deep breath and walked out. She thought about just hanging at the door but thought better of it and returned to Angelo. He was now smoking a cigar and laughing and talking. "There is my beautiful lady," he said smiling at her.

"Angelo, what will it cost just to have her for one night?" the older gentleman asked, looking at Olivia lustfully.

Olivia looked at him offended and forgot Angelo's request for her to keep quiet. She had enough of the entire situation. "I am not a piece of meat, a car, or some merchandise. I am a human being, and you can't barter, negotiate, or purchase me. How dare you? That is just plain rude and unnecessary. I am not going anywhere with you ever!" she said rolling her neck. She did not care if Angelo beat her for it; the guy was out of line and she was not in the mood.

"She is feisty. I like it," the gentleman said smiling at her. Olivia was not amused. Her gray eyes burned with rage as she looked at him.

"Honestly, she is not available. I got someone else you'd like. I will contact you later; my lady is somewhat agitated, so I am going to take her home," Angelo said. He grabbed her hand and they walked out of the club, but not before he stopped and talked to Creeper and some of the other guys. When they made it outside, he asked, "You want to drive?"

He had just gotten this sports car, and he was offering to let her drive. She nodded yes, and he handed her the key. She started it up and it purred to perfection; and then she started to drive. "Angelo, what is up with those men?" She asked.

"Nothing, love; they liked the way you look, as I do. You look real sexy tonight; you look older than fifteen. You smelled so good; they just found you attractive, but they understand that you belong to me," he said.

She assumed he expected that to ease her feelings. It was time to get ghost. She did not like the way they looked at her. Angelo was dealing with outsiders who seemed to be crazier than he was. She did not reply and concentrated on driving.

"You need to trust me. I need to know you trust me," he said.

"I do," she lied.

"Good. You and I are the modern-day Bonnie and Clyde. I got you forever," he said.

She was no criminal. She lived with one, but that did not make her one. She wasn't one of those girls who are attracted to bad boys; she had enough of them before her tenth birthday. As she drove down the road, she noticed a police car do a U-turn and start to follow them. "Angelo, I think a police car is following us," she said feeling nervous.

He looked back and saw a car. "Just keep driving; there is no reason to be nervous," he said.

She kept driving and made sure to adhere to every driving law. Then another police car appeared, and she wanted to get out of the car, but Angelo said to keep driving. Then a second later, the blue lights started swirling and she was in full fear mode. She started screaming what to do, and Angelo said to keep going. He pressed his foot on top of hers and floored the gas. She was thankful that a lot of cars were not on the road. She drove, and he told her to turn. Once she did, he let off the gas and told her to hit the brakes; and then he ran. He left her there alone. She saw him as he disappeared in the darkness. She didn't know what to do. She heard the sirens getting closer so she turned off the car, but her legs would not move. Fear and betrayal held her hostage, and when the officer arrived, she just put her hands up. They shouted orders, just like on the show Cops, and she obeyed. She felt her body shaking; she knew this was not what Deek wanted for her. In that moment, she saw her life slipping away. She felt the cold, steel, cuffs kiss her baby soft skin; she was defeated. They asked her what she was hiding and why did she do it, but she said nothing. They asked if there were drugs in the car, and she shook her head no. They asked if another person was in the car, and she said no. She sat there and watched as a drug sniffing dog circulated the car and he began to bark. They found drugs, like blocks hidden in parts of the car. She did not know that. It was all clear now; Angelo knew, and he left her to take the fall. They placed her inside the patrol car, but tears would not fall. She was too angry to cry; to broken to be pieced back together; betrayed too many times to care. The cop tried to coax her to tell, but she had her own rules to abide by and she said nothing. They pulled up at the police station, and after that it was all a blur; her mind blacked out, and she went blank. At some point, she was seated in a room—a cold, soulless room—that she was sure had some kind of camera recording. The table was less than impressive...stained from the tears and betrayal of others who sat before her. She waited as she assumed, they were trying to figure out which would enter into the room to be good cop and bad cop. It did not matter; she would never talk. To her surprise, Det. Alan Greene entered. She thought he was a homicide detective; what was he doing here? He was followed by another man, who looked to be around twenty-six or so. He had a baby face, and he was soft spoken. She watched them as they watched her and tried to read them, but to no avail; behind them was a female who was an advocate. Olivia's senses were off, and her heart was in mourning. She just wanted to be anywhere but there. Deek would be so disappointed in her for falling victim to Angelo.

"Hey, Olivia. How are you?" Det. Greene asked.

She thought that a stupid question and did not answer. If this was the tactic, he was using to solve her brother's murder, it would go unsolved forever.

"Tell me about the drugs in the car," he said.

Ah, now we get to the truth. She was not about to let him think he knew her. "Tell me about investigation into my brother's murder," she countered, enraged that he had the audacity to attempt to size her up and then pounce. He did not know her, and they were not friends. If he thought it was a slam dunk, he was sadly mistaken. She had enough of men assuming and using her. If they wanted to know about the drugs, he'd have to investigate; that was supposed to be his job.

"I am still looking into some leads. I need to know what happened tonight, so that I can help you. I know a young girl like you could not be into drug trafficking," he said, somewhat softer and more fatherly. The young man who, she found out, was named Paul Davis, eyed her suspiciously. He had this air and attitude like he had something to prove.

"Miss Morris, we just want to help you. If you help us, you can walk away from all this," he said.

She was fifteen. What was the worst they could do? She had never been in trouble; she would walk anyway, she hoped. "I don't know anything. I had no idea drugs were in the car. I just got my license and jumped at the chance to drive a car," she said.

They looked at her, trying to read her, to see if she were lying. She too knew body language; she did a report on it in Criminal Justice class and got an A. She looked at them both square in the eye. She was not afraid of what they would do, because they had limits; Angelo did not. She was mad at him, but she was not stupid.

"Listen, honey. This is big. We need to know what you know," Det. Davis said showing his impatience.

"Listen, sir. My name isn't honey, and my brother's death is big to me. I need to know what you know," she said sternly. He did not frighten her; men had done horrible things to her; his threats made no impact. She was angry that Angelo had allowed this to even happen. She folded her arms refusing to yield.

"Olivia, you can walk from this if you just tell us who is selling drugs. Does this have something to do with BWD? I am doing all I can to find out who murdered your brother. I am sure it is gang related. These drugs are too, so just tell me who they belong too. Who is the supplier?" Det. Greene asked taking the lead knowing that she was not fond of Det. Davis.

"I don't know," she said.

"Okay, how did you get into a nightclub that is for twenty-one and older when you are fifteen?" he asked.

"I knew the guy at the door, and he let me in," she said lying. She got in because of Angelo, but only a fool would tell the truth.

"We have surveillance saying otherwise," Davis interjected.

"Well then, why ask me if you know?" she said with an irritated tone.

Det. Davis rolled his eyes and let out a sigh. Then he violently hit the table, as a tactic to make her scared. He only hurt his hand; she lived with Angelo. This was rated G. "Sir, there is no need for that. All you are going to do is hurt yourself. I don't know anything. We can sit here for hours, and it will be the same. Det. Greene, I will not talk to this guy. He's a bit rude," she said not looking at Davis. He had angered her.

"Det. Davis, will you leave us alone for a moment," Det. Greene said. He unwillingly left. There was anger in his eyes because he could not break her.

"I don't know. I really don't. Even if I did, I can't talk, and you know that. There are rules on the street, and they will kill me just as easy as anyone else. I just want to know about Deek," she said.

"No one is talking; no one is talking at all about that night. I know you are living with Angelo, and I know who he is. Did he make you do this?" Det. Greene asked.

"I had no idea drugs were in the car. I honestly did not; I would have stopped, but I got scared. There was no one but me. I don't know anything else. Arrest me if that is what you have to do, but I can't tell you what I don't know," she said. "I won't talk anymore. I want a lawyer."

Det. Alan Greene left, and there she was only hearing the buzz the camera made.

"I think we should let her go, and just follow to see if we can catch Angelo. She's just a kid, and she needs a break. Her mother overdosed, her brother died in her arms, and I have no idea where the father is. She got tossed into something she could not get out of. She isn't a bad kid. She's an honor roll student and a cheerleader, not a drug dealer. Just let her go," Det. Greene said.

Det. Davis was not hearing it. He wanted the supplier, and if she wanted to play hardball then he'd play. "We're going to lock her up. One night inside, and she'll start talking," he said.

Det. Greene shook his head. The ignorance of youth, he thought as he looked at Det. Davis. He walked away and hoped that Olivia would fold.

**

The sound of the cage shutting made her shudder, but it was better than looking down the barrel of a gun or feeling Angelo's fist pounding her face. She said nothing and waited. A few hours later, someone had made bail for her and she was back in the free world; still angry, still hurt, and still feeling betrayed. Carlos came to get her. He drove her back to his house, where she saw Angelo sitting and smoking a cigarette and sipping a Corona. "What happened to you?" he asked. He thought she was right behind him, but when he stopped running, he noticed that she was not there.

"What happened to you?" she said in a smart tone. He had pissed her off. She had to sit for hours being interrogated, and he asked her that stupid question. Had there not been overcrowding, they might have left her locked up forever.

"Be easy, Livvy. Just be easy," Carlos warned, trying to diffuse the tense situation. It was too late; Angelo jumped up and slapped her. Olivia, being angry still from his betrayal, popped back up and slapped him back. He stood still, as stunned as was she. She stung him hard, but she instantly regretted it. Carlos pushed him back, telling him to cool off. She was relieved. He could have easily beaten her if he wanted. "I'm tired. I just sat there and was interrogated about drugs in a car—not just dime bags, but blocks. You left me. I took the blame...all of it. I am probably going to prison. You hit me, really. I am doing this to save your ass, and you hit me...typical," she said speaking boldly and sharply, not able to control or contain her tongue. Something else was taking over; hate, hurt, malice; she had no idea what it was, but what she was feeling was stronger than her fear of Angelo.

Carlos looked scared for her. Angelo side stepped him and jerked Olivia's arm so violently that she thought he had ripped it from her body. She had to look at it to make sure it was still attached. Her entire arm was burning with an intense pain.

"Ace, she's a kid...just a kid...don't do nothing you going to regret," Carlos said, but Angelo was not listening.

Angelo did not like defiance. He killed people for defying him, and she hit him in front of Carlos. Had she lost her mind? Twilight twisted rage took over his mind, and he could envision beating her until she could no longer move. But he silenced it. Though her rage had incited a vicious yearning inside of him, it also eased him. There was sorrow in her eyes...those eyes he loved. "What is wrong with you? Do you know who you are talking to? Do you know what I can do to you?" he asked, taking his hands and pushing her hard on the ground. When she bumped the ground, it felt like her soul had left her body. It was a hard landing. He sat on top of her, his powerful hands squeezing her face. His eyes were narrowing with anger and acrimony; she could see the hate inside of him, and his smoked breath penetrated her nostrils like snake venom. "Don't make me have to hurt you. I am pissed off enough at Leah. She the one that put me on blast like that. She called the police and tipped them off. Tell me word for word what you said," he demanded, his index finger pointing at her and his cigarette butt flying angrily. He slapped her with the back of his hand. His knuckles penetrated her cheeks, and she felt her lips separate. He had busted her lip, again, and the copper taste of blood kissed her tongue.

"Get to talking now!" he shouted.

She shook off the sting of the burn that his betrayals left. She hated him so badly because he placed her in harm's way; he was supposed to protect her. In that moment, she could have killed him; if she were stronger, she would have tortured him the way he had her. She did what she was supposed to do for him, but he refused her the same loyalty. She felt a rage she had not felt before; the violent thoughts that polluted her mind in that moment would have made the devil blush. Who was Angelo to demand of her? What right had he to be angry and belittle her with the force of his hand? She felt the wrath of anger take hold of her mouth. "Don't hit me anymore. I have been good to you. I do what you ask. I did not tell the police anything. I asked for a lawyer. They tried every which way to make me snitch on you, and I didn't. I am not Leah; I am Livvy, and you aren't going to beat me because you can't beat her. Why, Angelo? I thought you cared," she said crying, shaking, and collapsing in pain from his abuse. All she wanted was to be loved...just for someone to give and not take. Why was she always the one suffering...never the one gaining? Didn't he understand that she was tired of being a victim? She just wanted peace, she wanted to rest, and she wanted to be loved. Once again, he denied her love and offered her the back of his hand. It was a disgusting taste...bitter and bland.

Her honesty hit him harder than her slap. He instantly hated himself for mistreating her. She was right. He should not beat her because he could not get Leah. She trusted him, and he had left her. "Go...just go and stay out of my sight," he said. The guilt had gotten to him. He sat back down and glared in anger. Leah had to be dealt with. She was messing up everything. He had played with her enough. The hit squad would be notified. Wherever she was, he would have her hunted down like the dastard she was, tortured mercilessly, and then murdered. He would show the state of Georgia who was in charge, and he would show Leah what disloyalty looks like. He would make Livvy understand; this would be her last time acting out as well. Things were going to have to change. He rested his head, opened another beer, and drank it. Hoping that some clarity would come to his head when there was emptiness in the bottle, he almost cried at the thought of how all of this had occurred. If only Derrick had not gone to church, found God, and decided he wanted to be inactive in the gang so he could serve God and his sister. Although he himself was no longer a biblical man, he knew that no man could serve two masters; he refused to be second to anyone. This situation was making him crazy. He could not concentrate when things seemed to be falling apart around him. He should have never messed with Leah. Deek told him to be wary of her. She was too easy, and too available to give. Her loyalty was nonexistent, and now she was going to be nonexistent as well.

The next morning, Olivia awoke feeling terrible. Her body ached from the beating she had received from Angelo. She wanted to get out of the bed, but she had not the strength to pull herself up. Her arm still burned. She lay back down and, as her head hit the pillow, Angelo walked in. She turned her back to him. It hurt to do so, but it hurt worse to look at him.

"Knockout, baby, please just look at me," Angelo said.

She did not yield to his command. So, he walked around to the other side of the bed. She could not turn away because her arm hurt too badly. Her entire body was black, blue, and purple. He sat down on the bed and apologized to her and caressed her hair and kissed her cheek. "I was so wrong. I just lost it last night, and I am sorry. Do you forgive me? Please tell me you do. I will take care of this whole thing. You won't get any time; you have no record. Come here and let me hold you," he requested.

"I can't move. You beat my ass pretty bad last night," she said as tartly as possible.

Her aggressive reply surprised him.

"Livvy, you are too pretty to use that kind of language. I'll let it pass this time, but don't say things like that. I said I was sorry. We both got out of hand last night. No matter what, you know I love you," he said leaning over to kiss her lips.

Livvy moved away. "You hurt me, Angelo. I can go to jail. I protected you, and you repaid my loyalty by attacking me. How can you say you love me, but then you do this?" she said pointing out her bruises.

He nodded and kissed each one slowly and tenderly, and then he rested his head on her stomach. "Just tell me what you want me to do. I can't stand you being angry with me. I do love you, Livvy. I am so sorry for hitting you. You are right; my anger is with Leah, not you. Hold me, please," he said.

She wanted to be angry and hurt him, but he looked so sad and so full of pain that she could do nothing. "You'll take care of this?" she asked.

"I will. I promise you I will," he said.

CHAPTER 6

Not Guilty

"Guilty!" The word came like a massive storm, rolling off the tongue of the judge like thunder breaking through the skyline. She could not move; she became numb by what she heard and in fear of what it meant. Now with no family, she would be owned by the state. Well, she thought, at least now she knew where she stood with Angelo. What did she care anyway? The streets had taken her brother, the drugs had taken her mother, life had stolen her innocence, and only God knew who her father was. Now she was truly alone and forced to live with another set of criminals. Anger flooded her bloodstream once the numbness left, reminding her of that horrible day when her brother was murdered right in front of her. She shot a look full of venom at the villain who had sentenced her for a crime she did not commit. He was harsh; she had never been in trouble with the law. She was simply at the wrong place. She had been used because Angelo needed someone to take the fall, and it was her. He too was a liar. He promised her brother while he lay bleeding in the street that he was going to look out for her. He promised her he would take care of this. She, naïve and stupid, thought that he was telling the truth. But he never cared for her. He, like all the rest of the men who came in and out of her life, wanted to use her.

The police officer escorted her back through the closed doors. No longer could prying eyes see her. She wanted to scream she was innocent; she wanted to run to the double doors that were shut behind her. But there was no need. There was no Angelo, no Carlos, nobody; they had left her. She would be here for as long as they thought necessary. But maybe that was a good thing. Behind bars, Angelo and his madness were kept at bay...or at least that is what she hoped. She rested her head on the steel bench and—though she hated what was occurring—she could not cry. She was mad. Anger consumed her. She knew the only way to survive juvenile detention was to be hard, violent, and mean; something changed in her that night she stood up to Angelo. She wanted revenge.

As she waited, she closed her eyes and wondered how it had all led to this. Why did God give her life only to let one bad thing after another continue to occur in it? If she ever made it to heaven, she would ask. She recalled it all. It all began back in 2000. She was playing with a doll that her mom had bought her from Goodwill. She called her Ruby, because of her red dress. She was five years old. She and Ruby were in the kitchen playing with pans. Her brother was named Derrick, but she fondly called him Deek. When she was younger, she could not pronounce his name, and Deek just stuck. He had just left to ride bikes with his friends. She wanted to go, but he said she was too little and would get in the way. So, she was left behind; she seemed to always be left behind. Her mom was supposed to be fixing her a snack, but her new boyfriend had arrived, and they went back to her room and closed the door. At five, she had seen so many men coming in and out that Livvy knew that meant for her to stay out of the way. She and Ruby were hungry, so she pulled the step stool to the cabinet in search of a meal. Pushing past the family of roaches, she found some saltine crackers. She grabbed them and stepped down off the cheap chair. Then she reached into the refrigerator and got cheese and a box Hi-C to drink. She washed her hands, reached for a napkin, said grace like they had taught her in Sunday school at the Missionary Baptist Church, and began to eat. The crackers were stale, so she threw them away and just ate the cheese. Another fifteen minutes went by, and her mom came out of the room with her boyfriend. She remembered it so well; she could still smell the cocaine and see her mother zipping up her pants. She was snuggling closely to this man, but who was he? Just another nameless face she found, who would use her and make her cry. He would feed her drugs and liquor. Then when he had enough, he would leave her.

Olivia scooted closer to the cabinet, not wanting her mother to see what she was eating. This time she ignored her and followed her boyfriend to the television. He said he wanted something to eat, so she turned around and pushed Livvy out of the way. Her mother told her to go play, but her boyfriend said to let her stay. He picked Livvy up and sat her on his lap. For a while he was nice to Livvy; she remembered he had a wicked smile and deep-set brown eyes. She felt at ease with him. He took Ruby and played with her, and then he started to tickle Livvy. She liked the attention. The only attention her mother gave her was negative, if she paid any attention at all. Olivia liked that someone finally noticed her. They played until her mother called him to eat his salmon patties and grits. He picked Livvy up and sat her on his lap, and they shared his meal. She eagerly accepted, as she was almost starving. They never ate regular like other families; they ate when Nene felt like it. But Deek would always have something for her, even if just a little bit. Their momma sold their EBT assistance so she could buy drugs; it was a vicious cycle. The attention he gave Livvy

53

irritated her momma; even at the age of five, she noticed her mother's rage against her. So many times, she wanted to be adopted into another family.

"Stop that. She can sit down on her own chair. You are going to spoil her rotten," Momma said pulling Livvy off his lap and placing her back on the floor.

"Nah, Nene. Leave the child alone. We was bonding. She ain't hurting nothing. Me and her goin' be good friends; besides she's so pretty," he said smiling at Olivia and pulling at her long pig tails. He reached down and picked her back up and placed her back on his lap. "We gone sit here and chill. You can go and get what I told you to get," he said peering at momma.

"You goin' to watch her why I go make this money?" she asked him.

"Yeah, I said I was, didn't I? Me and baby girl goin' just sit here and have us a good time, and you can go make me some money. Here, take the phone. Call me if something go down. I need you to bring me like five hundred and don't come back till you get it," he said.

She shook her head in obedience and left the house, leaving them alone. This was not the first time she would be left alone with one of Nene's boyfriend pimps. She never thought twice about leaving Livvy with anyone, and her irresponsible ways made Livvy an abuse victim before she even knew what abuse was. In the background, she could hear the Smurfs music playing, her favorite show. She pushed herself off his lap and ran to the television.

"So, little Livvy likes the Smurfs," he said throwing his dishes into the sink and walking toward her.

She nodded her head in agreement. He smiled at her and picked her up again. He placed her in front of him so now her back was to the television. He smiled and tickled her over and over. She loved it. Then he tickled a little lower and lower until his large hands were under her dress removing her Barbie underwear. She didn't know what he was doing, but she knew it felt different. She had seen many men touch her mother in that way, and she liked it; but Livvy didn't. It felt unnatural.

"Little Livvy, we just playing a game. You are my special girl, and this is what special friends like us do," he said.

She was silent. His touches were at times painful and then playful. She was confused. He picked her up and gently laid her down. He was sweating. She remembered because his sweat dripped on her face. It was hot. Her body shook with shame as she recalled what had occurred.

"Morris, let's go," the CO said interrupting her thoughts. He walked toward her and led her to the van.

Jeremy was a tall lanky guy. He wore black glasses that sat crookedly on his nose. He didn't say much; she guessed there was not much to say. They had nothing in common. She grew up a poverty stricken, molested bastard—at least that is what her momma love to say. She wondered where she was now. Livvy knew her mother was dead, but was her soul in heaven or hell? She did some really horrible things; things that made Livvy think living life was hell. Oh well, she never cared about what happened to her; and Livvy guessed she should not fret over her dead mother either. Her mind went back to her brother. Losing Deek broke her heart. All she had in this world was Deek. She followed the path that Jeremy led her to enter the van, closed her eyes again, and soon fell back into when she was five.

Her mama's boyfriend—or her pimp—had grown attached to Olivia. She was his favorite; he liked her more than her momma, and more than her brother. He always bought her toys, tugged softly at her ponytails, and stared long into her pleasant gray eyes. She feared him; she hated to be alone with him and would beg her brother to stay close to her. She didn't know how to tell anyone what he was doing to her; all she knew was that he was not what he seemed. He molested her for one year, and the only reason he stopped was because he went to jail. She wished that was the end of her drama, of the men who used her, but her mother was a weak woman. She could not function unless she had a man in her life and, because of her need, Olivia suffered. She always found those kinds of men who were abusers and molesters.

Olivia did not like the darkness or the silence because it made her remember all of the bad things...especially that she basically had no one in the world...she was alone. She had told herself she had cried her last tear a long time ago; she betrayed herself because the tears flowed like a waterfall down her torn face. She surrendered; she wished it were her that had gotten shot down and not Deek. Oh, how she needed him now. He was her protector and her best friend. He raised her. Without him, she had no direction and no knowledge of what to do. Who would guide her now? She did not know.

***

The first month was extremely difficult for Olivia; her thoughts alternated between her past abuse and her brother. It seemed the alone time she had allowed her past miseries to attack her mind. She had missed opportunities to run because fear made her stay with Angelo. It had now been five months since the death of her brother, and still she was tormented by it. She could not understand how one person could lose so much. She did not mourn for her mother. She had no care for her father because she had never known him. But Deek was her heart and soul. Now she was condemned to be forever lonely; being imprisoned made it even worse. She felt it deeper now because she had nothing else to think of—no school, no cheerleading practice, and no access to her books. Worst of all, she could not visit Deek's grave. She did not care about life anymore. She watched how others interacted and how they bonded, but she refused to let anyone in; Angelo would be the last to betray her. She knew how that would end. She watched as the new correctional officers came and went; a new group had come in with her. There were three women and one guy. He was the opposite of Jeremy. He was tall but well built. She had lived in a neighborhood that had a mixture of Black and Latino, so she could tell that he was probably of Dominican or Puerto Rican descent. He had dark skin, amber eyes, and soft onyx short hair that was well-kept and maintained. He was neat and smelled heavenly.

She noticed him because he looked out of place in the pod, but she said nothing. Some of the girls were calling out to him saying improper things, but she turned her attention back to the book she was holding and only glanced at him when she thought he was not looking. The third time she attempted to do so, he was looking at her. His gaze, though not harmful, made her feel uneasy and she dropped her head and did not move again until she had to. She could not understand why she felt drawn to him. He reminded her of someone, but she could not place him.

"What are you reading?" he asked walking unnoticed up to her.

She kept quiet; when she looked up at him, she could see the other girls watching. She showed him her book so he could see for himself. "I see you are a quiet one. You like Christian fiction?" he asked politely.

She nodded her head and said nothing more. She loved reading; it all started when she attended Missionary Baptist Church. After Big Bo, she didn't attend church anymore. She could not see a difference between saved and unsaved. When she thought about God and church, she always thought of him. She thought if that was how Christians acted, then she wanted no part of their religion. The CO stood a moment longer and then drifted back to his post, and she was relieved. Olivia did not want to seem friendly with him. That could cause her trouble, inside and out. She did not need that. The fact was that she belonged to Angelo. Although she was not a gang member, he had chosen her to be his girl; it was not a position she wanted but he wanted. If it got out that she was being friendly with a CO, he'd remind her why she shouldn't. In her world, submission meant survival. She went back to her book and thought no more about the CO. She had a lot of time to do and being friendly would only make it longer and harder. For a person who did not care, she guessed she cared a little bit. She had to stay strong and focus; she had to.

***

Music was blasting loudly as Angelo pulled up in his Cadillac Escalade. In his hood he was the king; he ran this area, but he had dreams of running the state and spreading the BWD as far as the map extended. He would do what his father could not. His uncle was counting on him. That large loss of drugs was a blow, but they would bounce back. He looked at his homies as all being loyal as they rallied behind Knockout. He felt guilty for not being at the trial, but she was tough. She was the only one who had found a way to his heart. She was kind and sweet, loyal and submissive—the way he liked his women. She showed how it was done, accepting charges that should have been his. He would reward her for it. She would be his queen, he thought as he exited the car and threw up his gang symbol to his homies.

"Yo, Ace. Where you been? We 'bout to ride out and hang down in 3rd and see what is popping with the homies," Carlos said.

Let's ride!" he said to his homies and they all jumped inside. When you live in the hood, all streets look alike. That was why it was not safe for outsiders. They got lost and ended up being statistics. Angelo patrolled his streets like a lion protecting his pride. He knew every car and every neighbor. Nothing occurred without his knowledge. He only had a tenth-grade education, but that did not stop him from being able to control an entire neighborhood. If he felt threatened, he eliminated any and all competition. If his own members got loose, he would rule them too. Deek died because he wanted to leave BWD, and no one left...blood in and die out. He got his freedom, but it cost him his life. He could not figure out why Avery killed him. That was the lingering question for which he had no answer. Olivia thought it was some rival gang, but that could not be. It clearly was Avery and he was not working both sides; something went wrong, and he could not find Avery to find out what. As much he tried to pretend otherwise, losing Deek was like losing another brother. It was affecting him deeply. His days were spent the same: workout in the morning, business in the afternoon, party all night long. That was the life of a boss, and he was a boss.

"Angelo, have you heard from Leah? Since Olivia is locked up, I thought she might come back around," Carlos said.

"Nope and, if she knows what is good, she won't come around me. She almost got me locked up. I would have gone down if Livvy wasn't in the car. I know she was jealous and mad I dropped her, but she knew she was a revolving door. It wasn't like she had my baby. We ain't married, and she don't own me. I put out the word she needs to disappear. If she reappears, then that is SOS—shoot on sight. On second thought, I might need to upgrade that to a BIB—bullet in brain. She messed up my money and my chica. She got the police snooping around. She better stay low," he said.

"Aiight boss," Carlos said and turned his attention back to the music. They arrived at the party, and it was in full swing. Cats were all over drinking, dancing, and eating. Angelo sat down in the nearest corner and watched as the ladies came in droves. Usually this was his favorite part. He could have any woman he wanted anytime he wanted. But right now, he was craving Livvy, and she was locked up. He knew he was going to have to find some little thing to occupy his time; she was going to be locked up for a while—too long for him to remain faithful. He would take care of her and whatever she needed; it was the least he could do for what she had done for him. She was more a ride or die chick then Leah ever was. If he ever saw Leah again, he would take care of her permanently.

CHAPTER 7

Living In Lockup

After five months locked up, Olivia started to get into the swing of things. She found solace in reading books, doing her class assignments, and keeping a journal. She began thinking again of going to college; she promised her brother that she would make something of herself. She only wished she could avoid being locked up. Her brother thought she was a genius; in fact, that was his pet name for her. She called him heart. Her heart was gone...killed by some senseless gang violence...and for what? What did they gain by killing him? She lost everything. She could still smell the blood, feel his pulse slipping away, and hear him gasping for air. She remembered telling him to hold on and Angelo telling him that he would take care of her. Deek was gone before the ambulance could arrive; his death was haunting. Months later, they locked her up for a crime she did not commit. But they never found the guy who killed her brother. Angelo lied; he said he would keep her safe and that he would take care of this. He left her; he did not even show up at the trial. Det. Greene lied because he pretended to know who had murdered her brother. They wanted to arrest Angelo, and they tried to use her to do it. She did not even see how dangerous Angelo was until it was too late. She was his girl, he said. Supposedly that was a safe place to be, but she had rather he ignored her; being ignored would have kept her from being imprisoned or maybe not. Deek did not want this for her; he knew that men had preyed on her in the past, and he did not want her to suffer again. But because of Angelo, she suffered daily. Deek knew about some of their mama's pimps violating her. When she died, he promised Olivia that she would never suffer like that again. For a while she was safe, but he got killed and she got Angelo. She guessed in some ways Leah was to blame too; it was her jealousy that tipped the police off. They charged Livvy and sentenced her to three years. That angered her. Why would Angelo let that happen? The rumor was he knew what Leah was up too. She wanted him back that badly. But by getting at Livvy, she also put Angelo at risk of getting arrested. That angered him.

Livvy wrote in her journal, trying to figure out how and why she was here. Leah's plan, though it got her arrested and out of the picture, might have been her death warrant. Angelo was dangerous. Livvy had never seen him kill anyone. She watched him beat them badly and put hits out. But never did she see him do an actual killing; she knew he was capable, and that scared her. Lockup in some ways was better than living with Angelo, but his hands still could reach her. She had to be careful not to speak too much; that is near impossible for an emotional, frightened, fifteen-year-old seeking comfort. Angelo knew she would never say anything to the police. So, he entrusted her with things that no one knew...or maybe she should say tortured her with things...things she wished that she did not know. These horrible things made her have nightmares...even in the daytime...as if her own life was not scary enough. Angelo was ruthless, violent, and heartless. When she got out, he would probably be waiting; that was a scary thought. She had no idea what he wanted from her. There were plenty of woman who wanted him: his attention, his money, his heart. They were older and more mature than Livvy, but he wanted her. She never understood that. Did he look at her like the men who had molested and raped her in the past? What was it about her that made predators prey on her? She wished she knew; she would wipe it off.

"Is anyone sitting here?" a voice said interrupting her thoughts.

"No," she replied as she watched the young girl sit down in front of her. Olivia quickly closed the journal. She wrote in invisible ink but still; somehow lockup was making her just as paranoid as Angelo. The young woman sitting in front of her was tall and cute. She had long raven silky hair and a kind smile. Olivia introduced herself; there was no need to be rude. Besides, after five months of solitude, she longed to converse with someone...to hear another voice besides her own. "I'm Olivia, but on the streets, they call me Knockout. You can call me Livvy," she said emotionless. She did not want to seem needy for companionship, though she was. She hoped saying her name on the streets made her sound tougher then she felt.

"I'm Lillian, but everyone calls me Lill-kill. You can call me Lilly. So, I hear they got you on drug trafficking; I am in for manslaughter. I killed my stepfather after he had been raping me for years; I just snapped, you know." She said this as if this was normal conversation, speaking with ease and not even flinching.

Her honesty shocked Olivia, but she guessed it was not a big deal around here. Everyone was a criminal. "Oh, okay," she said trying to be cool. She had not known of a girl who had murdered someone before; she seemed so innocent and sweet.

"So, tell me your story; you don't really deal with anyone here, and I see that no one comes to visit you. So, what is your story?" she asked.

Olivia thought that was a bit aggressive, since Lilly had no idea who she was. Olivia looked at her, and she seemed to have trustful eyes. "I don't tell my business; I don't know you like that," Olivia responded and prepared to leave because spies were everywhere. She had no idea who would snitch anything to Angelo or one of his affiliates.

"I'm sorry, don't go. Please forgive me for my lack of manners, but that is how we talk to each other. I can tell you about me, and if you feel like it, you can tell me about you. Like I said, I killed my stepfather—hence the nickname Lill-kill—because of abuse. My dad left me and my mom on my second birthday. He said he was going to get candles, but he never came back. I think he ran off with another woman—some chick he met at work. This destroyed my mother; she, of course, ran wildly and blindly into anyone who would have her. She met Dylan, and I just really disliked him. He was mean to my mom sometimes, but she just excused his behavior. He had an older son who came to live with us in the summer. He is the one that first caught his dad touching me. I thought he would help me, but he started to rape me too. They took turns; they watched one other and then critiqued each other. I told my mom, and she slapped me and said I was lying.

"This all started at the age of eight. By fifteen, I was fed up. His son was five years older than me, so he finally went off to college. But his dad was still coming in my room whenever he wanted; and I knew my mom had to have a clue. So, one day he was drunk and had a bat in his hand with the intent to use it on me, but I was not going to let it happen. I had told God I was ending this today. He came at me, and I took out my knife and stabbed him. Then I grabbed the bat and hit him until I was numb. I waited; I wanted to make sure they could not bring him back. So, once I knew he was dead, I called 911 and waited some more. My mom got home before them; I must have been a sight.

"My entire body was colored with his blood; she thought I was bleeding, but I wasn't. The first responders came and said he was dead, and I felt peace for a moment. I told them what happened and why I killed him. When I said that I was pregnant, my mom looked shocked. So, I had my baby in here, but they took him from me. I wanted him to be adopted and not raised by my mom; she would destroy him like she did me. So, he has a good family. I just hope he won't be like his father; you know? I don't want him being a pedophile," she said tearing up.

Olivia's heart hurt for her; goodness, the things men did. She felt sorry for Lilly being abused by her own stepfather. It was gross what a sick old man and her brother had done. It didn't matter that they were "step"; that was wrong. She could not imagine that occurring. She would lose her mind; although, she guessed in some ways they were alike. She too was a victim of her mother's ignorance. But her brother protected her as well as he could, whereas Lilly's did not.

"I'm sorry, Lilly. That is horrible, but I know sort of what happened to you. My dad left my family before I even knew him. My mom was a drunken, crack head prostitute who died from an overdose when I was ten. My brother took care of me until...well he got killed a few months ago and then Angelo came along and said he would take care of me. It seems like I keep on losing. My mom's pimps used to molest and rape me. Mama was always jealous of me because they would say how pretty I was. So, she said she would make me ugly; she used to beat me, but my brother would try to protect me.

"When he found out I was being abused, he beat Bo down. After that, my mom became a heavy user of drugs until she killed herself. It was just me and Deek and his gang; they were his so-called family, and they let him die," she said looking at Lilly and shaking her head. She had wanted to say those things a long time ago and tell someone her story; she just wanted to be listened to. Angelo had denied her that; he had denied her a lot of things. Because of him, she was no longer at school. She loved school; she missed it so much. He could have gotten her a good lawyer too; instead she got Steve. This was punishment for her slapping him the night she had gotten arrested. She had to escape from his grasp, or she would end up six feet under.

Lilly shook her head in agreement. She had known the same pain; now she felt like she had just met her soul mate—a sister. She had been so lonely herself and longed for a friend. "Well, Livvy, it seems all we have is each other. So, from here on out, we are sisters. You need a family, especially around here, so we will watch out for one another. You can trust me; seems like we have a similar path. How did you get a drug charge?"

"Angelo, he's the leader of Blanco Wild Deuces, he told my bother while he lay in my arms bleeding to death that he would look out for me," she said it in a whisper.

"What?" she whispered back looking around the recreation room. "That is the craziest, wildest gang in the area; shoot, even the police are afraid of them. They kill just to see blood, and your brother was one of them. No wonder no one is talking to you; they are scared," she said as if she was even a little afraid herself.

Indeed, it was the situation, but why she had no idea. Olivia was just a fifteen-year-old with nowhere to go. Angelo offered her a bed when she had nowhere to sleep. Of course, that bed came with an occupant. "He's not that bad all the time; I mean he would not let anyone hurt me or come near me, but... "she said and then she stopped. "Hey, we'll talk later," she said. She felt like a walking contradiction. Angelo was that bad. She felt like he was mentally tormenting her, even though he was not present. She wanted to get all the mess off her chest, but she wanted to protect him as well. How could she feel loyalty to a person who had betrayed her continuously?

"Yeah," she said, and then she nodded and changed the subject. They watched as the lucky kids got to go see loved ones, and Olivia knew no one would come see her. She was on my own...well at least she had Lilly now.

"Morris, you got a visitor," the new guard said. Livvy glanced at him but did not move; he must mean someone else. She had no one; she was forgotten and unimportant to the rest of the world invisible.

"Olivia, are you coming?" he asked.

She had no idea he knew who she was since he was new. She got up and followed.

"Are you sure you meant me? I don't have any family, so I think you might have mixed me up with someone else," she said.

"Look, I know I am new, but I am sure I have the right person," Miguel said. His smile was perfect, his teeth were spotless, and he smelled good. He smelled like that store in the mall. Olivia tried not to stare too long. She walked in silence. When she looked around the corner, there sat Angelo. Her heart skipped a beat. Had someone heard her talking to Lilly? Was he mad at her? That could not be good; his anger was violent. He smiled at her, and that scared her even more. She sat down, and Miguel turned to leave. She said nothing as she looked out the window. She would give anything to walk out of here, just to visit her brother's grave and to be near him. He would tell her what to do.

"Livvy, how are they treating you? You still look beautiful. You know you have my heart. You took that charge like a gangster, and I like it. I knew you were down for me. When you get out, you know I'll be here for you. Do you need anything?" he asked winking at her and looking longingly into her gray eyes.

She turned her attention back to him and away from the window; she shook her head no to his question. She would have rather had no visitor than to have him. She knew not to bad mouth him. The last time she did that, he responded violently; but she guessed it was her fault. Carlos had warned her to be easy, but she was so angry that her immaturity showed, and he checked her. She had to be really careful around Lilly and not allow her real feelings to show. He would know, and the consequences could be lethal.

"Talk to me; you don't call, and you won't write me. The least you can do is talk to me when I come to see you. I told you I get paranoid when you act like that. You're my girl. Ain't nothing changed, right?" he asked trying to connect.

Of course, things had changed; she was doing Angelo's time. If he said she was his girl, then she was...whether she wanted to be or not. It was not up to her, but him. "Yeah, nothing has changed," she said dryly.

He looked at her, momentarily bewildered by her reply. It was evident she had not forgiven him for not being there, but the block was hot. "Well if that is the case, then why are you acting nonchalant? Why are you being standoffish to me?" he gently demanded.

She let out an annoyed sigh. "I am caged; I have lived my whole life belonging to someone. I just want to be free. I miss Deek. He would not allow me to be in here if he was alive; he would have fought for me, but no one cares anymore. So, I don't either," she said, her immaturity showing. She knew better than to smart off at him. The last time she did that, she felt his wrath. Had they been on the outside, he would have slapped her for that outburst. He could not physically touch her here unless he wanted to go to prison too. She knew that.

The smile that was on his face quickly faded. His eyes narrowed. "Livvy, I take care of you. Don't be so unappreciative. You are just a little blue. Lockup is an adjustment; I've been behind these walls and look at me. At least you got someone to come see you. I'll expect some letters since ain't nothing changed. Let me know what you doing, and I will visit when I can. You don't have that long. You getting out of here in a year or two. All you have to do is keep your mouth shut; ain't nobody goin' to mess with you cause of me, so just chill. I love you, and I will see you soon," he said.

"Ok," she said looking down. Who cared about BWD; she was not down, nor did she want to be? She wanted to be done with the lifestyle. She wanted a life like the ones she read about in books, but there were no fairy tales in the hood. He was not even there for her trial because, if he was, he would have known she had three years.

"Livvy, I said I love you," he said and cleared his throat.

She looked up at him and forced herself to lie. "I love you also." With that he was gone, and reality was back. She waited for Miguel to come in and walk her back toward the dorms as they are called, but it was a cell to her. She was told when to do it, what to do, and how much of it she could do. This was supposed to be a place to rehabilitate, but they could have done that before locking her up.

Miguel had observed this entire conversation but pretended that he had seen nothing. It was obvious that this guy—a known gangster that seemed to never get his hand caught in the cookie jar—was controlling Olivia. He was new to the system, but he was not new to the story. He had some kind of gall to come into the detention center as if he was untouchable. "Olivia, what is a man like that doing here talking to you?" Miguel asked. Normally, he did not get involved, but she was young, smart, and pretty. She just did not belong here. Something about her penetrated his heart.

"He's my friend," she said.

"Okay, but he seems a bit old to be your friend," he replied wondering what had led her to this place. She had outstanding grades; she read books like Iliad and Odyssey, and she stayed out of trouble. Her good behavior had been noted. She was more than what she appeared to be.

There was nothing else to say; she knew that if Angelo wanted, he could find out what she was up to, and she did not want to start any trouble. She went back to her cell and started to write letters. She did not like doing it. But if that was what she had to do to keep him happy, she would. She hoped he would not come to visit again. She nestled herself in her bed and begin to read. It kept her from losing her mind. When they had some free time, Lillian and she talked. It was almost like they were kids in high school and not lockup, but they were in prison.

She was somewhat annoyed and angry that Angelo had come to see her. She wondered what that appearance was for. She really disliked him now for leaving her in this predicament. If the roles were reversed, he would not do this for her. He would have sold her to the highest bidder. Those thoughts swirled in her head as she rested in bed. There was a love-hate relationship between them. She had thought he cared about her, even loved her once when Deek had died and he took her in. She thought she was among friends, but Angelo had a different kind of mental thinking. He used people to get what he wanted. Love was probably something that he was incapable of. He rarely showed emotion unless it was to hurt someone. Though there were times when he was good to her, he had gotten violent when she broke the rules and mouthed off. If she did not have Angelo, where would she be? Where would she go? Who would look after her? She wanted to be done with him, but she also felt connected to him. He understood her life, and he knew her brother. Maybe he thought being imprisoned was a good thing—to toughen her up and to teach her a lesson. She did not know. She was worried and nervous all the time. His visiting after five months of her being locked up seemed more like a warning then an "I miss you."

CHAPTER 8

New Friends

Olivia was sitting quietly at the table in the library. Even being locked up, her thirst for knowledge would not be imprisoned. She was reading a book on mathematics and working through some of the problems, just for fun and to help pass the time. She felt as if someone was watching her, so she looked around but did not notice anyone. There were not a lot of people inside the library. Most of them preferred to watch television, play cards, or just gossip. She liked quiet; she liked to be with her own thoughts especially at a time like this. The visit from Angelo had her shook and extra paranoid. She thought it possible for him to have eyes on her, so she constantly watched her surroundings. She hoped she could trust Lilly, but you never know. She went back to solving the problem when she heard soft footsteps coming toward her. She looked up and there was Miguel...well, Officer Castillo. They all called him by his first name in conversation because he was so dreamy.

It seemed like every female in lock up had a crush on him. He was very handsome; his face seemed familiar, but she still could not place it; he had very pleasant soft face. He was inviting.

They both looked at one another, not speaking a word. She was not sure if he was sizing her up or contemplating what to say. He always tried, but she shut him down for fear of what Angelo would do to him or even her. Even though no one seemed to care about her, she cared about others. People thought she was rude—she was sure of it—but they had to understand that she knew Angelo. He would eliminate any problem with violence. Life meant very little to him, especially after his brother died in a police chase. Besides CO Castillo was a police officer and, in her world, they did not mix. They were like oil and water. Deek told Olivia long ago to be suspicious because men are weak and will give into lust, even those who are sworn to serve and protect. He went on to say that having a badge did not mean that they could be trusted. She believed him because he knew of dirty cops who wanted to make some extra on the side; it was how he managed to never get arrested as well as Angelo. In their world, everyone had a price. She was not sure if Miguel was good or corrupt, so she turned her attention back to the task at hand.

"Olivia, what are you up too?" he asked her curiously. He had been watching her closely. She liked to come to the library while everyone else watched television, talked and gossip, but she never participated in those things. He wondered about her.

"I'm doing these math problems. The class here is not demanding enough to stimulate my intellectual curiosity, so I had to find something a little more challenging," she said not looking at him.

"Interesting that the class does not stimulate your intellectual curiosity. Wow, I don't see a lot of young people like you. You read, do math problems, and write all the time. You are indeed a puzzle to me," he said, now relaxed and sitting down near her.

This caused Olivia alarm. She had no idea why he thought it necessary to make her life difficult. He knew very well who Angelo was—all law enforcement knew—and he knew how paranoid and unpredictable he could be. Why was he sitting near her? He was making her a target. "Officer Castillo, please leave. You are going to cause me to have some real issues," she said placing her pencil down and staring at him.

"Why? I talk to everyone else. I am just here to help not hurt," he said gently.

"You know why. You know better than I do," she said.

"No, I don't. I just wanted to see what you were doing and offer a few suggestions to you," he said attempting to read her eyes.

"Offer and then leave, because the longer you sit here the more people will speculate. I don't want any trouble," she said.

"I don't follow," he said.

"You do. You know who visited me. You know his organization. If those detectives have put you in here just to butter me up, what they want won't happen. You might be handsome, well-spoken, and educated, but I am no fool. I am not talking; I told them, and I will tell you, I don't know anything. So, leave me alone!" she said sternly.

He smiled. "You think I am handsome, well-spoken and educated? Thank you for the compliment," he said.

She looked at him somewhat confused. She smiled also, not wanting to but not being able to help herself. When he grinned like that, he reminded her of someone in her past. For the life of her, she could not place him.

"Livvy, you need to move the 2 to the left," he said looking at her equation.

She looked over her work and found her error; he was right. "Thank you," she mumbled.

"You know I am not a bad guy. I am not looking to cause you any trouble or ask you any questions. I think you don't belong here. I think you are innocent. You are just a victim of circumstances, not a danger to society. I see you reading a lot of books, but never the most important one," he said seriously but still compassionate in his tone.

She looked at him waiting for him to tell her. "Well are you going to tell me so I can? What are your few suggestions besides correcting my mistake?" she asked.

"The Bible; you read that and study it like you do math, and I think all your problems will no longer be problems. You'll learn from those words those you can trust and those you can't," he said and with that he walked away.

She watched him go, now wishing he would sit just a moment longer. He reminded her of Deek...always saying something but never really saying it...and leaving it up to her to figure it out. All this time she had been avoiding him, but he seemed genuine. None of the others had spoken indifferently or harshly about him, and maybe she was too rash in her decision to brush him off. Anyone who could solve a math equation was worth giving a second chance. She was neither ready, nor willing, to read the Bible; it scared her. She knew the scriptures because, once you learn them, they are embedded in your heart. She was top in her Sunday school class for verse memorization. She and God were in two different and distant places.

In the days of her youth, she was innocent and had no fear of confessing. But now at fifteen, she had secrets and sins. She had walked away from God. Her lifestyle now conflicted with His word, and she could not understand how demons were allowed in the church to abuse, to hurt, and to endanger children like her. God was good; she believed that. She believed in the Holy Trinity. But she also believed that—because she was damaged goods that was made to blossom before her time—she was of no use to God and therefore condemned.

She erased the thought and went back to work, but Miguel was not to be erased. Something about him was alluring, honest, and true. She felt it the first time she saw him. But, unable to clearly define the feeling, she ignored it. She gathered her things and retreated; she was allowing kindness to cloud her judgment. All the detectives needed were for her to slip up. She had to regain self-control and control her neediness. Angelo would not like the way she was behaving. She could not help herself; she longed for companionship.

A few days passed by, and she went over to talk to Lilly. She was reading her Bible, so Olivia waited. She recalled a memory of how she had loved to read the Bible. The best stories, the greatest proverbs, the best poems, and the greatest epistles ever written were stored in the Bible. But she had not opened those pages since she was ten years old. Fear kept her from wanting to open the Bible but fear also kept the words bound to her heart; God cannot be denied. She could not understand how a person like Bo could read those words and think it godly to touch her when her mother was asleep, and her brother was gone. How could her mother attend the church and not know that doing drugs, as well as beating and hating her daughter, was against God's will? Lastly how could God, knowing her life story before she was born, allow such suffering? What had she done at five to deserve to be molested? What did she do in fifteen years to be falsely imprisoned, be lied to and on, and be held captive by a mad man that she cared for and despised all at once? Why would God take Deek only to give her Angelo? She shook the thoughts and returned back to Lilly who had now finished her reading; she looked up and smiled at her.

"What are you up to?" she asked.

"Nothing. I just thought I would come and visit. What are you up to?" Olivia asked sitting down across from her.

"Reading the Bible; Miguel has started a Bible study for us. He has a lady from his church come, and she teaches us. You should come. It could have a positive impact on your sentence," she said cheerfully.

"I'll think about it," Olivia replied. "If you want to continue reading, I can just go to the library."

"Well, we can go together. I would like to go," she said gathering her things and following Livvy.

"Lilly, can I ask you something?" Olivia said as they reached the doors and walked in.

"Sure," Livvy replied walking closer to Olivia in order to hear.

"How have you survived this so long? You have been here for a year without getting visitors daily. I mean, how do you survive? I am in a constant battle between my past and present. I get angry, but you seem to have a balance," she said.

Lilly nodded as Livvy spoke and motioned for her to follow her to the back away from prying eyes and nosy ears. "I was like you at first. I was scared and angry. I felt betrayed. I also was pregnant, and I wanted my baby to be all that I wasn't. My love for him is greater than my anger about the past. I want him to have a good family that will allow me to be in his life. I found a good Christian family that has been good to him and me. They live down in Florida, but they write me twice a month. They told me when I get out, I can come live with them too. They visit twice a year. They would come more, but I don't want to stress them. They are good people, and that made me want to be good. They gave me this Bible on Mother's Day, and it has been the best gift. It helps. It can help you too," she said.

Olivia nodded and told her to follow her back to the table. She did some of her schoolwork, and Lilly did her Bible study work. They sat together, content with one another, and then Miguel entered. Olivia watched him as he spoke to everyone and then came to their table. Lilly asked him to help her find an answer to one of the questions naming the twelve disciples and how they died. That was an easy one, and Olivia knew the answer.

"The twelve disciples are Peter, who was crucified upside down; James, who was beheaded; John, who died by natural causes; Andrew, who was put to death on an X shaped cross; Philip, who was crucified; Bartholomew, who was skinned alive and beheaded; Matthew and Thomas, who were stabbed to death; James, who was stoned and crucified; Jude and Simon, who were crucified; and Paul, who as beheaded. You know what happened to Judas Iscariot. Then Jesus said in John 15:20: "If they persecute me, they'll persecute you," Olivia. Lilly and Miguel looked at her in astonishment.

"What?" Olivia asked as they stared at her like she was an alien. Olivia knew scripture; she did not fully understand it all, but she listened when she went to Sunday school and Sunday and Wednesday services. She did the same Bible study when she was around nine, and she excelled in it. She thought the disciples were the greatest heroes ever. She remembered how she thought that was the bravest thing to do—to die for God. She would have continued her Bible study if not for Bo. Bo made her fear ever walking into church. Not attending church made it easy for her not to read the Bible. She had no checks and balances anymore. She was just in this world.

"How do you know all that?" Lilly asked still stunned.

"I used to go to church," she said turning her attention back to her studies.

Miguel watched this and wondered why she used to go and was not attending anymore. Even he had not known all of that. How did a fifteen-year-old who seems so quiet and confused—so guarded and yet so in need of affection—have such knowledge and still be enslaved by another. She intrigued him. "We have church service here every Sunday and every Tuesday; Alexi from my church comes and does Bible study with the girls. You are welcome to attend," he said.

"Lilly told me about it. I don't go to church anymore, and I don't read the Bible," she said.

"Why? Are you an atheist?" he asked confused.

"No. I believe in God. But from my experience, the church is no different from the world. So why should I sit around people who think they are perfect, but as soon as they walk out the doors are no different from nonbelievers? The church I once thought was a safe haven, but demons prey pretending to pray there too. I don't feel it's for me," she said looking at him. Lilly still sat there somewhat in shock; Olivia presumed.

Miguel sat down not believing his ears. "What happened to you there?" he asked. If he knew, maybe he could help bring her back. It was obvious that she needed guidance. She was gifted and did not even know it.

"Nothing, and I don't want to talk about it. You should help Lilly with her work. I am going somewhere quieter." She got up and left. She hated that he made her say

69

things that should be private...forever forgotten. She almost felt normal—like any regular girl—but she was not normal. Her entire family was deceased. She belonged to a lethal manic. She was stuck in detention, not sure who was friend or foe. For all she knew, this was all a set up concocted by Angelo. She had to stop seeking friendship, and she had to distance herself and remember that danger lurked. She must fight against becoming vulnerable. She hated herself for being unable to keep her mouth shut. She never talked as much as she had been doing lately, and it was going to cost her if she did not regain control.

Miguel watched until she was out of sight, and his heart cried for her. She wanted to be rescued. She needed to be, but she did not know how to ask for help. He would not give up. Someone had planted the seed of God in her; she just needed it to be watered so it could grow. He recalled when he was hardheaded and stubborn because he thought he knew more than anyone else, but God brought him to his knees, and he had to yield. This was his chance to honor God. He had to penetrate the wall she had built up. She wanted someone to care. He had to undo the damage that so many had inflicted and show her that he was worthy of her trust and that she was worthy of God's love. He could tell from the sadness in her eyes that all she wanted was rest. He promised he would do all he could to help her, and then he turned his attention back to Lilly and finished helping her with the Bible study questions.

CHAPTER 9

Haunted

Being incarcerated was hard, especially when the lights were turned off; in the silence, Olivia's past rushed at her like a wave, knocking her back into time. Even being here so long could not stop the attacks that nighttime brought.

It was a time she had wanted to bury; a time she had grown to hate. She remembered the month leading up to her momma's death, and it made her body shake. By now, Deek knew she had been molested by momma's men; when she told him, his heart was broken. After that he never left her alone if he could help it, but he had obligations to his gang. He had dropped out of high school after his sophomore year to become full time active, but he made her promise to finish. Unlike him, Olivia loved school because she got to be free from the prison her momma had created. Nene had started beating Livvy on a regular basis; it started when she was six. Nene walked in on her new pimp kissing Livvy, and not in a sweet way. Him she remembered...his name was Celester; Celester the child molester, as her brother later called him. Nene blamed her, and for three years they were at war. Olivia kept getting prettier and, due to the drugs, her mother got uglier. Nene never touched Livvy when her brother was around, but if he left, she descended on her with ruthless precision. Deek ran off Lester, but after him came Bo, Big Bo. His name still made Olivia shudder with fear. He was the worst and most brutal, even worse than Angelo. He fooled Olivia; she thought he was different. Livvy was nine when Bo entered their life. He was a big guy, weighing 255 and standing 6'2; his skin was dark, and his voice was deep but pleasant. He did not look like the rest; he was well dressed always smelled pleasant. His smile was not a devious smile but a sweet one. He had kind and trusting eyes. Livvy thought he respected their momma; even Deek liked him. He never called their mama out of her name and never said anything mean at first. He pretended to be a man of God; he carried a Bible and spit off verses one after the other. Momma had met him at Missionary Baptist Church when she went. Livvy went every Sunday; her mother went when she was not high or drunk, which was once a month. Livvy thought if he were a man of God then he was good and would be good for momma. After six weeks of being with him, it started. He had violent rages. Nene was meaner because of him and called Livvy names, but she was her momma and she would not let a man beat her if she could help it. One day, she came home from school; Deek was doing his gang business so she had to walk home alone. Livvy opened the door and there was a trail of blood. She heard weeping and then shouting. She walked with caution to her momma's bedroom, and there she lay on her blood-soaked sheets with Big Bo standing over her holding a belt. Then not knowing that she was there, he spat on Nene. The sight infuriated her with an anger she did not know was possible; she ran and punched him with all her might. She hit him for her mama and for herself. She hated him coming into her room at night or watching her shower. He was a sick man.

"Leave her alone! You leave momma alone!" she demanded. He threw Olivia to the ground like he was flicking lint off his shirt; she was no match for him.

"This is grown folks' business. You be gone back in the front room, little girl. It ain't your time," he said. Instead of being kind, his eyes now held the fire of the devil. His sweet smile was replaced by an evil grin. His gentleness had changed to cruelty. He was a beast. She had been hit before; she had been violated and she had been mistreated, so he did not scare her. She got up and she pushed him, but he did not move. He left her mother and launched an attack at her. She ran. She barely made it to the door of her mama's bedroom. His large hands yanked her back, and he placed her hard on the floor. He took the belt he had in his hand and hit her once...then twice. But she did not scream, so he turned it and hit her with the belt buckle on her lower back. This was a new pain. No one had done this before, and her small frame felt like it would break under his heavy beating. But at least he was not beating her momma now, she thought.

"Stop, please stop. I am sorry," she pleaded. She could not take another blow; it felt as though death was calling her name. Just when she thought he would beat her to death, her brother, Carlos, and three other friends came raging in and attacked him. She could not move due to having been severely beaten.

Her mother did not move...whether out of fear or pain, she did not move. She just lay in her blood watching the violence. Deek pulled out a gun on Big Bo, after they had beaten him nearly as badly as he had beaten Nene and Olivia; they never saw Big Bo again. Bo left, never to return. But Olivia still carried the scars of his anger across her lower back. The beating he gave her that day broke her bones. She never had a beating that bad before or after.

The doctors said it was the worst they had ever seen. She recalled the pity and sorrow in the eyes of the doctors and nurses. The imprint of the belt buckle was forever engraved in her skin; the scars of his betrayal tattooed her inner and outer body. It took her three weeks before she could sleep and a month before she could sit without pain. She was forced to miss school, so there was no escape from the misery of her mother. Nene acted as if it were Livvy's fault Bo was gone and reminded her daughter that she hated her with the back of her hand daily. In one week, she was back on the streets rocking her black eye like it was a black diamond. It was then at the tender age of nine and a half that Livvy stopped caring about Nene. She finally understood she could not be saved and that she had to let her go. Nene reminded her daily she was a bastard. All she had were her gray eyes, fair skin, and pretty hair; she said her daughter better sleep with two eyes opened because she would cut her hair and sell it. She was crazy about things like that. Deek said it was because she looked like their daddy, but she always believed it was more than that; she was jealous of Livvy—her own child. Nene loved Deek, but she hated Livvy. If her brother looked like her, therefore he must look like their daddy also...but Nene never hurt him. Olivia shook off the thought, closed her eyes, and waited for sleep to come.

The next day she awoke somewhat shaken from her reoccurring nightmares and somewhat shaken from Miguel. She felt he wanted to help, and she thought he cared, but he was a man. She could not trust herself when it came to men; they had all hurt her, and he would be no different. She wanted to exercise a little to tire her body, so that her mind would not trespass where she could not protect it. To her surprise, the day would not be as she planned.

Miguel called her, looking like he had a secret in his eyes. A side smile crept across his face, and he quickly tried to remove it. She wondered where she was going; she followed him to the visitors' area wondering who wanted to see her. Then a fear emerged; it must be Angelo. She hoped it wasn't, but who else would see her? Her family was dead. When she looked, her eyes widened, and her heartbeat increased for just a moment.

"What are you doing here? Why would you all come see me?" she asked, looking at Coach Geter and Mr. Douglas. She had not seen them in almost a year. She had forgotten them because to remember would cause a new pain. They reminded her of what she had lost. They had been so kind to her, and then she was gone. She thought they had forgotten her too...that they did not care about her.

"We would have come sooner, but no one knew you were here. I am so sorry, but it was like one day you were in class and then we did not see you anymore. I called the last known number, and no one answered. Then we went to your old address and were told you moved. Jacoby told us that you had gotten caught up in something and were here," Mr. Douglas said.

"Jacoby? But how did he know?" she asked confused. Jacoby had not spoken to her since the football incident. How would he know anything about her, and why would he care? She kept her questions to herself, though her face expressed all.

Ms. Geter spoke. "I am not for sure, but he explained that you were living with some gang members after Derrick died. We did a little investigating. If you had come to us, we would have helped you."

Livvy shook her head no. "You couldn't. No one can help me."

"We are going to talk to the judge and prosecutor on your behalf to let them know they made a grave mistake. You just stay out of trouble and away from that gang banger," Ms. Geter said in a motherly tone. "I thought he was a family member. If I had known he was a gang leader, I would have kicked him out of practices and called child protective services."

"You don't understand; he came to visit me here. I belong to him until he wants someone else. His world and your world are very different. I don't get to decide; he does. I don't want anybody else getting hurt. It is not worth it. You just forget about me. Don't waste your time. I appreciate your dedication, but he'll hurt you," she said. It felt good that someone thought she was worth saving. She could not allow any innocent people to become victims of Angelo's madness.

"We are going to help. You call us just to keep us updated. We will come to see you every week. Neither one of us is afraid of Angelo," Mr. Douglas said. "One more thing," he said with a smile spreading across his face. "I have an equation for you to solve. You see if you can have it done before my next visit."

A smiled crossed her face. "Thank you," she said unable to hold her emotions. She let a tear escape and watched it rest upon the table. "I'm not a gang member, and I did not know drugs were in that car. But Det. Davis thinks I am guilty. I just wanted justice for Deek. I don't know how it all got this messed up. I hope the two of you aren't disappointed in me," she said so quietly they had to strain to hear her.

Her soft voice penetrated their hearts. No one believed that she was capable of drug trafficking or breaking the law. "Of course not; we know you aren't like that. It is not in you. You've been betrayed by a lot of people who should have nurtured and loved you. We will be here for you," Ms. Geter said coming over to hug her. Olivia was not sure if that was permitted, but Miguel did not stop it. It was the best hug— one she longed to have from her own mother who had denied her affection until her death. She wanted Coach Geter to hold her forever. She had not had that kind of connection since her brother died, and never from a motherly figure. It was a feeling she would cherish as long as she lived. To feel hands so gentle that wanted nothing in return unleashed a powerful emotion inside of her, one she thought incapable of having. They talked a little while longer until time was up. "I have to go back," Livvy said, longing for another embrace from Ms. Geter. They smiled at her and watched as she turned away with Miguel and walked back.

"You are popular all of a sudden," he said. He now saw his opportunity to reach her because he knew that she and his brother had attended the same school. She must have been the girl who caught his eye.

"That was my math teacher and cheerleading coach," she replied.

"You are a cheerleader?" he asked a bit stunned by the confession.

"I used to be. Why? A hood chick like me can't be anything but a criminal?" she asked annoyed; he was supposed to be a Christian.

"You misunderstand; I was not judging you, just asking a question. Everybody is not an enemy. I thought you understood that last time we talked. I am just here to help," he said.

"In my world nothing is giving without receiving, and all are enemies until proven otherwise," she said and then said no more.

She had to keep her guard up; she could feel her strength leaving her. Parts of her longed-for love, affection, and attention; but the other part of her said stop, you don't need it. She didn't. She had to make herself understand that love was not for her. She had to toughen up, but it was getting harder all the time.

***

Once home Miguel attempted to wash the scent of the detention center off of his brown skin. Fresh out of college and the Police Academy, he had gotten his first assignment. He thought working with juvenile offenders would be a cake walk, but these kids had lived lives far more horrible then he could ever imagine. He only had six months to go, and then he could transfer to the gang unit. All officers had to do a year in either juvenile or adult detention; he wondered if he had chosen the wrong placement. He thought he could make a difference since he used to be one of them. He almost lost it too, but he had a strong family, his church family, and his brother Jacoby.

He let out an exhausted sigh and found his mind thinking about Olivia and her sad eyes. What would it take to get her to tell the truth? She was not a drug dealer] or a gang banger; she was a kid who got caught up with the wrong people. Angelo was a big fish that the police wanted badly, but he always stayed at least two steps ahead. He knew the law just as well if not better than any cop or attorney, and he had street rules not legal rules. He was a danger to anyone he came in contact with. How had he gotten Olivia? She was bright, intuitive, and wise far beyond her age. How come she did not see the danger? Olivia was the link; behind her eyes hid secrets, regrets, and answers. He had to earn her trust and go talk with her coach and teacher. Together they would find a way to give her back her youth. He wondered was the Jacoby they were talking about his brother or someone else. He got out of the shower, dried off, and placed his tired body on his cotton sheets. He said a prayer and drifted into a calming slumber.

***

"Lilly, come here," Olivia said motioning for her friend to come over so she could show her the magazine. They liked to read Ebony and Essence and read about what was going on in the Black community and dream...dream about getting out and living the good life. They kept up with the latest fashion, makeup, and who broke-up in Hollywood and crushed on the good-looking guys.

"Girl is that Shemar Moore?" Lilly asked.

Olivia nodded her head yes. "He is so handsome. My brother kind of favored him, except Deek had dimples." Olivia said, recalling her brother; he was handsome, smart, and loyal. Every thought always went to him. Sadly, behind bars she could not find out who had killed him, and she could not visit his grave. That was the worst punishment. She feared he thought she did not love him that she blamed him for dying but she did not. She could never do that. She wanted to write a letter to Carlos, but she was scared. She did not know if he would share it with Angelo. However, Angelo never said she could write to anyone else. Besides it was so hard to find someone to trust.

"I wished I had met him, because he would be mine," she said to me laughing.

Olivia wished he were alive too. It was lonely to have no one in the world. She hated that so bad. She missed him intensely. "Are you going to see Liam anytime soon?" Olivia asked; she had wanted to know for a while.

"I hope so. Remember I told you I get pictures. The family is really nice. You want to see?" she asked. Olivia shook her head yes. She wondered what Lilly kept in that Bible.

"Lovely...you sure gave birth to a lovely little boy," Olivia said smiling at her.

"Thank you. It's the one good thing that came out of my life. I am looking forward to getting out so I can see him, and them," She said.

"You have more good things to come. When we get out, we'll conquer the world," Olivia said. She really liked Lillian; she had a good heart. They were becoming closer. She was really a cool girl. Meeting her, one would never know what she was convicted of. She didn't seem like a murderer.

Olivia helped her with her schoolwork, and they studied together. She never talked about BWD because she feared it would place Lilly in harm's way, and she never asked. They understood each other because they both had a tortured past, a weak mother, and a lack of trust in adults. They differed in that Lilly was saved and Livvy was not. She had never been baptized. "You know what, we need to get some Debbie snacks and celebrate. I've been here almost seven months and you've been here almost two years. We might as well have a little fun," Livvy said smiling.

"I'd love too, but I don't have anything," she said.

"I have enough to get you what you want," Olivia said to her. They went and stocked up on all the sweets they could. The only good thing about being locked up was that nobody cared what they ate. Olivia was glad that she and Lilly were now cellmates. She was not sure how it happened, but she suspected it had something to do with Miguel. They were sitting down eating honey buns and looking through the rest of the magazine when Olivia heard footsteps approaching. She looked up and saw Miguel, who had some envelopes in his hand. He came over to their table and handed one to Livvy and one to Lilly.

It happened so quickly that she could not ask him what it was about. They opened the letters and read...then reread...and looked at one another. They had been selected to participate in a pilot program that allowed them to do their time on the outside. They would live with volunteer families and go to therapy twice a week. Contact was forbidden with other criminals or people associated with their crime. For Olivia that meant BWD, and she was fine with that. The program was scheduled to start in two months. It was only offered to those with long sentences that had good behavior and good grades. Olivia stayed composed, but Lilly was hopping in the air. "Chill, Lilly. You know there are spies and haters in here. Stop all that," Olivia scolded her looking around and wondering if anyone else had seen. All she needed was for this to get out, and Angelo would be all over it and her. This was her chance to escape his grasp.

"I'm sorry, but this is exciting news," she said almost unable to contain herself. Now she would be able to see Liam, Theresa, and Roberto. They were good to her and her son. Knowing that she would be able to see them outside of these walls two years earlier than she had planned made her ecstatic and overjoyed.

Lilly did not understand Olivia's fear that someone would alert Angelo. "Lilly, all I need is for Angelo to find out. Please don't tell anyone, or at least don't tell them about me. I can't have Angelo finding out. I just can't," Olivia said.

Lilly sat down and looked at her friend. "What is it? Tell me. Come on; follow me. I know a private place where we can talk," she said.

Olivia got up and followed her. No one seemed to notice because they were all concerned with other matters. There were only a few who had gotten envelopes; most just assumed it had something to do with getting out. She hoped it stayed that way. They walked to a side room and sat down.

"Tell me why you are always whispering and paranoid. It is starting to make me feel that way too," she said.

"He is dangerous. I only survive because I submit. He has beaten me before. He punched my face and busted my lip; blood just gushed. No matter how hard I tried, I could not forget the powerful punch and the aftermath of his anger. I am afraid if I do one wrong thing, he will kill me. I've seen things, Lilly; things that will make the most seasoned cop have fear. Angelo has two sides; at first, he was extra nice to me and took good care of me, and then he wanted things. He started saying I belonged to him. I don't want to belong to him anymore. I'm scared about being released from here; even if it's to a family. He will find me, and things will all worsen. I can't go back; going back means death. I won't die until I know who killed Deek. I owe him that much. I feel like Angelo knows who did it, but won't tell me," Olivia explained.

"You can't live in fear. First thing, forget Angelo and just take care of you. Deek will understand. He would not want you to suffer. If he was willing to leave his gang, knowing that doing so could cause his death, don't you think he would want you as far from that lifestyle as possible?" she said her voice low and calming.

She thought for a moment. "Lilly, are you suggesting that Deek was killed by his own gang? No one can make that call except Angelo. He loved Deek like a brother; he would not do that," she said. Olivia had never even thought that. Could Angelo really be capable of murdering her brother? But why? He had no reason to do that. Deek was loyal to him, which she thought was his only flaw.

"All I am saying is that it happens. Think about it. How is it that the police can't find who killed him? His own gang can't find out either. Streets talk to bosses like Angelo, not cops, but he had to know who did it. Can you think of a reason he would want Deek dead? Is there anyone you trust to confirm or deny?" she asked.

She shook her head no. It did not make sense, but then it did. He was nervous that day at the diner when she told Det. Greene what she remembered. He was nearer to the killer than she was, but he saw nothing and did not pull out his gun. Angelo was as paranoid as they come. He always carried a piece. Had she been sleeping with the enemy this entire time? Was he the killer or had he had Deek killed? Who would know? She shook her head; how had she missed this obvious truth. "Oh, Lilly if he knows and has hidden the truth, I am about to get a new charge. I'll blow his brains out. I will do it," she said her body shaking uncontrollably.

Lillian walked over and held her friend. "Don't say that Livvy; you don't want to kill anyone no matter the reason. I still have nightmares, and I can see his blood. He haunts my thoughts and imprisons my dreams. Don't give Angelo that kind of power. Let it go and forgive," she said holding her as her tears dampened her shirt. "It's okay, Livvy. Things are going to be okay. Look at you...how far you have come. We are sisters. We have each other's back, but you can't go to war with Angelo; you will lose," she said embracing her. Lilly knew about loss; killing her stepfather stopped the sexual abuse but not the mental. No matter how hard she tried...how much she prayed...she still saw his bloodstained eyes. The fact was that she had sinned to stop a sin. But instead of feeling free, she was imprisoned by her thoughts. Her stepbrother, though unknown to Olivia, had been sending her horrible letters. They said that he hoped she died the same way she killed his father, and that she only got what she deserved. No one deserved to be molested, raped, beaten, or abused—no one; never was that an appropriate response. His words were imprinted upon her brain. She was so mentally unstable that she thought the harshest, horrible things to do to herself to end the voices, the images, and the words. But she had to fight to be there for Livvy.

Olivia's body, mind, and emotions were not her own. It was like the devil had taken over, and all she saw was red. Her marrow filled with revenge. She wanted the truth. She suffered from the sins of her mother, her absentee father, and Angelo. She was tired of suffering; it was time for someone else to suffer. She wanted to know what Angelo knew. She was incarcerated because of him. Her brother was dead possibly because of him, and why? What was it that Deek knew that he had to be killed? She knew a lot. Would she be next? He'd die first. She meant that. "Lilly, I need a moment. I just need to clear my head," she said feeling as though the room was becoming smaller. Breathing was becoming difficult, and her heart was palpitating. Sweat kissed her brow and then began to dress her face. She was panicking. She could not see; her vision was blurring. She pushed Lilly away. She needed to think. She needed a moment to take a 360 view of the situation. "I'll be back," she said and walked away and wept silently. In the silence, her mind ran wild with ways to seek revenge on Angelo. Hate had fully matured in her heart. He would pay—a life for a life. She was capable now. She wanted him so badly that she could feel the rage pumping into her heart. If he came to visit, she would put her hands around his neck and watch as the breath seeped out of his body. She would show him that she was the one to fear; what else had she to lose now? No one had seen that side of Olivia Morris, but it was boiling and brewing, and she was going to unleash it all on him.

CHAPTER 10

Changes

Mr. Douglas and Coach Geter kept their promise and visited again, but Olivia could not find happiness in their attention. Her mind was deeply pained by a truth she could not conceive. There were two people who had insight to the truth other than Angelo. That was Carlos and Leah. She knew Leah disliked her—even loathed her—so she could not reach out to her. But Carlos she thought was a possibility. She sent him a letter requesting he come see her, but not to tell Angelo because she did not want to anger him. She thought if she wrote in a way that came across as missing him, then he would come without talking to Angelo. She waited. She sat down at the table and began to read. She had hoped to see Miguel because she wanted advice. She could not talk to Ms. Geter and Mr. D because they did not understand, and she thought it might place them in harm. She did not want to talk to Lilly because she had her own problems; problems Olivia did not quite understand. But something was weighing heavily on her mind, as something was on hers. Lilly was right; she could not continue to live in fear. Miguel had not come in for two days. She was not sure if he was sick, hurt, or just on vacation; she dared not ask the other staff. She still firmly believed that some of them were not to be trusted. Maybe he had changed shifts. She was not sure, but she wanted to talk to him. She felt a headache brewing above her brow and closed the book. Her mind was at war, and it was debilitating. She rubbed her temples trying to ease them into submission.

"Are you okay?" a voice said.

She glanced up, and there he was. He seemed like an angel, always there when she needed him even when she did not know she needed him. "Yeah just a headache, but can I talk to you?" Olivia asked him. She was so bold because everyone was gone. This was a court day and a lot of the juveniles were gone; others were at recreation time. No one was watching or paying her attention.

His eyes brightened. "Sure, what is on your mind?" he asked sitting down.

"I don't know where to start, but do you think that it is possible for my brother to have been murdered by his own gang?" she whispered.

He looked sympathetically at her. "I don't know. I would think that anything is possible," he said.

"I asked one of the guys to come visit me so that I can ask. I don't know if he'll come, but I just want the truth. I feel like if I can find out the truth, I won't feel so lost and divided all the time. Lilly thinks that BWD did it. I swear I can't think of a reason why. He was loyal to them. He only wanted to leave to take care of me. Then like that he became a statistic," she said shaking her head.

Miguel knew the street code; most gangs had a blood in die out. Becoming a gang member had a time limit of until death do you part. It was possible that his wanting to leave the gang made him a target. "I think you should not investigate on your own. Please just leave it up to the police. You are just one month away from getting out of here. Let this opportunity be your new beginning. Whoever killed your brother may be getting by, but he will not get away. God has the final judgment. All you need to do is pray and let God in your heart," he said.

"I hear you. Look I have been wondering...how did this program come about anyway?" she asked, as she was not interested in talking about God.

"It was the brainchild of your teachers, and I helped a little. I think there are some innocent children here. Some are hardcore and will never be rehabilitated, but you and Lilly aren't that kind. We talked it over with the prosecutor, and some of the officers believe this is the best thing to do. I feel like we—the police, the state of Georgia—gave you a raw deal. Your brother was your legal guardian; then, when he died, the police just let Angelo take you. Someone should have intervened. What should have been done then will be done now. Forget the past, Olivia; God has given you a second chance. Take it and separate yourself from this," he said with a caring tone. His eyes were tender; his facial expression was sympathetic.

"Okay," she replied.

"I'm serious, Olivia. People do care about you. You are not alone. Don't think that my uniform means you can't trust me. I have a higher authority to answer to. I don't care about this, but I care about Him; because I do, I will do right by each of you in here. Besides, my brother speaks highly of you," he said smiling.

Now she was shocked. "Who is your brother?" I asked.

"Jacoby Castillo...also known as Mr. Basketball...or JC, as I like to call him; he thinks you are a really special person," he said.

Olivia dropped her head. They looked so much alike. How she had missed that, she didn't know. That was why he seemed so familiar; she knew his brother. "Jacoby is your brother? You must really not like me then," she said as everything came flooding back to her. She felt awful about Angelo giving him a tough time. She wondered where he was now.

He looked hurt. "Why would you say that?" he asked.

"It was my fault what happened at the football game. I am so sorry for that. I wanted to apologize to him, but he just scattered anytime he saw me. I figured he was really angry, as he should have been. But I was trying to tell him not to talk to me. It's dangerous," she said.

"What are you talking about?" he asked.

"About when Angelo jacked him up and threatened him. He can be extremely jealous. I have never felt a blow go through my body like that one. The blood ran like a waterfall. You know what he said to me? "Don't bleed on my leather seats." I wanted to hit him back; I wanted to hurt him so badly. But I could not, so I just pretended it never happened." She was so into what she was saying that she forgot who she was speaking to, and just kept talking. "Then that night when the police chase ensued, he ran out of the car and left me there. He had the audacity to ask me when I was bailed out: what happened to you? It sent a rage through my bones. I was so angry. He slapped me, and I slapped him back. It happened before I could think or stop it. Then he gave it to me good. But I would do it all over again just to let him know I have my limits too," she said getting angrier as she recounted the story. Her fist balled up as she thought of how he had treated her.

He looked so sorrowful. "I'm sorry, Livvy. My brother doesn't blame you at all. He never even spoke of it, at least not to me," he said.

At that moment, Olivia realized what she had done. She covered her mouth. She told what she was not supposed to tell. Did he hear that part? "Miguel, I mean Officer Castillo, I misspoke. I was alone in the car," she said.

"It's okay. I know he set you up to take the fall for him," he said.

Now her headache and heartache were both full blown. It was incredibly difficult to keep secrets that she wanted to be free of. "I am so tired of this. I just want to be free. It feels like I have been imprisoned for life; ironically being in detention is the only time I have tasted freedom. I wish I had gotten shot instead of Deek. I can't do this anymore; death refuses to take me, but life continues to abuse me. I can't keep it all inside; I am suffocating," she confessed.

"Tell me so that I can help you," he offered.

"I can't. I can't say anything about that. I have said too much already, and the consequences of my stupidity will be enormous," she replied. She could almost feel the beating she would receive when Angelo found out.

He saw the battle written in tears across her face. She was struggling to release herself from the horrid torture she had grown accustomed to. "Tell me what you are comfortable with. Maybe I can help alleviate some of the burden that you are carrying," he said in a brotherly tone. His heart felt for her.

She told him about her mother, her absentee father, and her brother. She told him things that she had not told Lilly. She told him of her dreams. As she spoke of the life, she wished she had, she felt lifted. She told him how she felt guilty that she lived and Deek died; that her accepting Angelo's offer to stay in his home was an insult to her brother. She told him of her fears. He listened to her. He did not try to get her to talk about the gang. He just wanted to know about Olivia. He was gentle when he spoke to her and suggested she come to the Bible study.

She shook her head no. "I don't believe anymore. I don't want anything to do with church, Christians, and Bibles. My mama's last boyfriend Bo was a so-called Christian. He beat her nearly to death; when I tried to save her, he beat me. He had already raped me, and then he beat me. Probably the worst beating of my life occurred that day. I still carry those scars to this day. I don't need that kind of religion. I thought church was my saving place, but it was just a breeding ground full of abuser and child molesters. I don't need that. I already had years of it, so no I'm good," she said seriously.

Her confession nearly rocked him off his chair. She had been through too much, but he wanted to help her. "I promise you, the God I serve is the One and only true God. He is not a God of confusion or injustice. The Father, the Son, and the Holy Spirit does not hurt. He only heals. If a person uses scripture as a tool of evil, that person is not of God, but of the evil one; don't let the ignorance of men condemn your young soul. God loves you," he said.

"No one loves me; love died with Deek, hope died with Deek, and my soul died with Deek. That is what everyone fails to understand. He was it for me. If God loved me, my mother would not have hated me and beat me regularly; if God loved me, I would have had a father, not pimps who molested and raped me; if God loved me, Deek would be alive and instead of being the property of Angelo I would be the property of God. God doesn't want this—this broken battered heart that was so hungry for attention and love...so needy for comfort...that I caught a case for a crime I did not commit. I am not worthy of God; I am not worthy of anyone. The internal and external scars are a repellant of anything good. To attend Bible study would be a waste and only remind me of how horrible and condemned I am," she said.

Her words penetrated his heart and stung him deeply. "No, don't you ever say you are not worthy. God made you and sent His only Son to die for you. My dear, you are worthy; your worth is far above rubies. You are an heiress; all you need to do is ask Him to enter, and He will never leave. Let God in Olivia; allow him to heal your brokenness because you will not and cannot have the peace, the love, and the comfort you seek until you do. No one owns you; you are the property of God. He loves you. Please pray with me and listen to your heart. God is calling," he said.

Warm tears cascaded from her eyes as he spoke. She wanted to love God and be loved by Him, but she was a waste of creation...a mistake. Her mother had reminded her of that daily before her death. She had said she wished she had gotten an abortion; now Olivia wished it too. The last thing she said to Livvy before she died was that she hated her...that Olivia's father hated her too, and that he was smart enough to leave. She wished she had sold her for drugs instead of keeping her. It was a cruel thing to say to such a young impressionable girl.

Olivia closed her eyes and tried to concentrate on the words he spoke. Her mind wondered back into time as it did each time, she closed her eyes. As she entered into the shack, they called home, her mother's lifeless body was lying on her bed as cold as a freezer. She must have died that night; when Olivia woke in the morning, Deek got her ready and they were off. They were used to her lying in bed all morning long, so they weren't concerned; but when Olivia came from school, she knew she was gone. Livvy ran to get Deek and told him something was wrong. He checked for a pulse but found none. Olivia didn't cry for her; she felt relieved because she could not hurt her anymore.

For approximately five years, she had lived in safety, love, and comfort. Then she was incarcerated. But in a month, she and Lilly would be on the outside. But that caused her fear. Then she heard Miguel say, "In Jesus' name, Amen."

She smiled at him. He patted her back and walked away. She had some decisions to make. Maybe she still had a shot with God. If she did not, she had nothing and would fall back into a destructive life.

As Miguel walked away, he hoped her physical sorrow would ease. The heartbreak, her eyes had seen that poisoned her mind from lies, betrayals, and fear almost polluted his too. She needed someone, she needed to know love, and she needed the power of God. He hoped she would come to Bible study.

She watched him go away; he had gained her respect and trust. She leaned back on the chair and recalled her past like it was her present. She remembered hanging out on the corner. While Deek worked, she did her homework. She liked to be near him all the time. Angelo had pulled up. She was around twelve then. Angelo had just come into his leadership role. His father had started the gang and died, so he took the reins. He was even more lethal, dangerous, and violent than his father; that caused a rift between the youngsters and old school gangsters. He was nice to her. He always given Livvy whatever she wanted and told her how sweet and cute she was. She liked Angelo back then, and so did Deek. As a youngster, she did not understand what was happening. But Deek was selling drugs, and then he got promoted through the ranks. He and Carlos had become Angelo's left and right hand. He loved them; they were all best friends. So, when Deek got killed in the streets, the lack of emotions and the lack of zeal to retaliate was baffling to her.

If she had not been so stressed, shocked, and angry, she would have seen it then. She didn't know for certain if Angelo killed or had Deek killed, but she knew for certain he knew who and possibly why and would not tell her. There was a secret in his heart and guilt in his eyes. She had not seen it before, but as she recalled everything up until now his anger escalated when she talked of Deek or what she remembered from that night. She kept one thing secret. When she first talked to the police, she told them the shooter said nothing. Then when she talked one on one, she said the shooter had a raspy voice. She recalled he said, "This is for Ace—a bullet in your face." How had she forgotten something so important? It all happened so fast. Ace was what the guys sometimes referred to Angelo as, but why? Did that mean Angelo had done something and they killed her brother for it? Why not kill Angelo? He was standing nearer to the shooter. "Tell me, Deek. Tell me the truth of who killed you, and I will honor your life by taking their life," she vowed. It was time for a new Livvy to emerge.

Later that day, Lilly and Livvy sat beside one another as Miss Alexi and Miguel taught the class. She looked to be the age of Miguel—around 24. She was soft spoken and sweet. Her eyes were bubbly, her smile was wide, and she had a deep country drawl. She was very animated and passionate about Christ. She knew most of the girls and talked to them as if they were old friends. She and Miguel seemed very smitten with one another. Olivia assumed she was his girlfriend. His eyes sparkled as he watched her. She wished someone looked at her like that. Then she would know she was safe and loved. She tuned in and out, wondering if Carlos had gotten her letter and if she could trust him. She must have completely tuned them all out. When she came back to, everyone was looking at her waiting for a reply—to what she had no idea. It all made her feel uneasy. So, she excused herself and walked away. She did not get far before Miguel caught up with her with Lilly right behind him.

"What is the matter?" he asked.

"Nothing. I just don't like a big group of people. It makes me nervous," she said.

He smiled. "That isn't a problem. We are about to break up in groups. If you like, it can just be you and Lilly," he said.

She nodded in agreement and went back. She had to make an effort if she wanted God to make one. She was not sure how it was going to work, but what she had done in the past was not working. So, she had to try. It was an interesting topic—forgiving your enemies. Olivia had many, but they learned in order to be forgiven you had to forgive. She was not sure how to forgive Angelo. He had beaten her, frightened her, dishonored her, lied to her, and betrayed her; she was sure it had something to do with Derrick's death. Then she was expected to forgive her mother, her father, and all the molesters. Who did God think she was? She did not think she was capable of such a thing. "Lilly, have you forgiven your stepfather and stepbrother for assaulting you?" she asked her.

"Yes. I see it like this; they weren't saved but acting in the flesh being led by the evil one as they gave into their own selfish desires. I learned that what is not of faith is sin. I don't blame them anymore because they were victims too...victims to the world. In their minds, that justified their actions. I sinned too when I killed him, and it was wrong. Like I said, it bothers me from time to time. But I have asked God to forgive me, so I have to forgive as well," she said.

Olivia was confused. How could an adult not know his actions were wrong? She was five when that dirt bag had molested her the first time. He was twenty years older. Was he a victim? No. He was a predator. She was baffled. She could not grasp it.

"You will forgive, too. The more you read and pray and talk with God, the more you will gradually be able to forgive. It won't happen overnight, but it will happen if you let it," she said gently to Livvy.

She nodded, but she was not convinced. When it was over, they all left and said goodbye to Miguel and Alexi. Still, Olivia pondered this thing called forgiveness.

Lilly fell asleep before her, because sleep would not come to her. She wanted so badly to know the truth. She was so tired of being haunted by a past she could not change. If she did not do something, she would stay in the same place she was now. What would Deek say at a time like this? She could not figure it out. She was not an adult; she did not have all the life experiences. She tried to hush her thoughts so sleep would come. Her sleep offered little peace.

***

Miguel entered into his parents' new house. They had moved last year into a new school district so his brother could attend a more prestigious Christian high school. It was better for everyone to remove themselves as far as they could. His mother greeted him with a long hug and kiss, and his father followed. He asked where his brother was, and his father told he was in his room. Miguel walked up the steps, turned left, knocked three times, and waited for his brother to let him in.

"Miguel! I am glad to see you," Jacoby said embracing his older brother.

"I am glad to see you too," he said walking in and sitting down on his brother's chair. "JC, I need you to do me a favor. Can you tell me what you know about Olivia Morris?" he asked looking at his brother who now stood above six feet and growing every second it seemed. He had become quite the basketball player. He was sure he would attend a good college. Miguel was proud of him for not falling into some of the traps he had in his youth.

Jacoby put down his game controller and turned his attention back to his brother. "Livvy's great. I had a mad crush on her, and it took me up to last game before the championship to get the nerve to ask her out. She's smart but quiet, so I could not get a read on her. Nobody else could either. My friends told me to keep a distance because her brother is BWD and he will like kill you if you talk to his sister. I asked her out, and she was like stunned. I thought she would accept, but she came out of left field and forgot I existed." Jacoby shook his head at the thought but continued.

"I didn't know she had a boyfriend. The dude just seemed too old, but he came out of nowhere and hemmed me up. He told me in no uncertain terms that if I wanted to live then I better never look at her again. It was mad crazy too, because some of the younger BWD attend school and they are like her personal secret service. I don't even know if she knew he had her on watch like that. I wanted to check on her, but I got approached at school and was reminded not to talk to her. I didn't," he said shaking his head. But I'm glad to be out of that school. You know, I told Mr. D and Coach Geter what I knew. When she stopped coming to school, I thought he had hurt her really bad. She seemed like a real cool chick," he said looking at his brother.

Miguel shook his head in utter confusion. "Well, she asked me to tell you that she was sorry for what happened. She feels really bad about it. Do you know about her past or anything like that? I am asking because I tried to reach out to her, and she is just hard to reach," he said looking at his brother.

"No. She was silent. No one knew she was in the classroom until she started cheerleading. Then she was like normal. All I know is after her brother died, Angelo brought her to school and picked her up. He or one of his affiliates would watch cheerleading practice to make sure no one talked to her. She was on lock down. I never saw her without him. I know this because I heard the guys talking before, I left that school. Some girl named Leah used to date him, and he has a hit out on her for calling the cops about the drugs. It was mad crazy, and I knew then it was time to go," he said. He was bewildered by how they spoke so openly in school without caring who heard. They really believed themselves to be untouchable.

Miguel did not know about Leah. "Thanks. You have given me some good information. How about we play a little Madden?" he said to his brother, and he agreed.

CHAPTER 11

A Test of Faith

With the new information Miguel had learned from his brother, he went to see Det. Greene hoping to help. "Det. Greene, I got something. Listen, did you ever interview a Leah Cruz? I think she is the link you have been searching for. She can help get Angelo. We have to find her before them, because he wants her dead," Miguel said.

Det. Greene with Det. Hoover by his side looked at Miguel with conflicted eyes. "They got her first. We found her body about two days ago. Sadly, whatever she knew, she took to the grave. We have got to get Olivia to talk," he said.

Miguel let out a sigh. He wanted to find a way to protect Livvy from having to confront Angelo. "I don't know if that is possible right now. She has a lot of anger, and she doesn't trust anyone. The things she was talking about two days ago just made me feel awful for her. She knows something or she thinks she does, but she won't tell. She thinks that we are using her like Angelo, and that once we get what we want she'll be tossed aside," he confided in them. Yet he recalled his promise to her not to talk about Angelo being in the car.

"Maybe I should try and talk with her. I have a daughter her age," Det. Hoover said, recalling how pitiful her eyes looked that night when her brother died. He had met many people in his line of work; death was just as much part of his life as living. But Olivia haunted him. He never forgot her and prayed daily for her.

Miguel shook his head in disagreement. "Well I think we should wait until she starts the pilot program...when she is back in school and feels safe. After a few therapy sessions, I think she'll open up. We just have to earn her trust, as well as show her that we care and will protect her. Do you have any leads on her brother's murder? If we can solve that, then I think we can reach her," he said sipping the last of his coffee. They all nodded in agreement and left.

Two days later Olivia, was back in her room. Lilly was quiet, and she could see hurt in her eyes. Livvy was still conflicted and battling inner demons herself. Livvy did not want to be angry with her. "Lilly, I am not mad at you. I understand. It's forgotten," she said. They had a disagreement after Olivia found out that she told Miguel some things she told her in confidence.

A sweet smile of relief dressed her lovely face. "That is a relief because I was so worried," she said.

She shook her head no. Then she told her about what Miguel, and she had discussed. She offered her Bible to Olivia and said she should read it. She opened the Bible for her friend and then left her alone. She said conversations with God should be private. Olivia opened the black leather Bible NKJV to Psalms. She felt like a stranger holding the holy book and wondered if it would vanquish her like holy water did to vampires. Her heart pounded with increased agitation as she tried to read. She closed it quickly, too afraid of what it would say about a person like her. She was not worthy of God. She had no right to His forgiveness, for she was condemned...probably from birth. She was born to be a thorn; her father left, her mother died, her brother was murdered. Nothing good came from her existence. She was like an incurable deadly cancer. She rested herself on the bed and started to drift back into a time where she had known momentary bliss, but a loud screamed halted her time travel and made her enter back into reality. She leaped off the bed to see the commotion. The news was on, and there seemed to be a horrible accident; somehow an eighteen-wheeler crossed into oncoming traffic and took out a row of cars. Olivia looked at Lilly, who had been screaming. She ran to her, trying to understand what was happening. "Lilly, what is wrong?" she asked, standing by her side as well as the rest of the group. Lilly's eyes were drowning in tears and, though she spoke, her words were inaudible. She looked at Livvy as if she could understand, but she did not. Finally, she spoke clearly. "My baby, my baby. Theresa was bringing the baby to see me because my birthday is coming up, and they got hit. I know that is her car," she said showing Livvy the car in the background and the car on the news. It started to catch on fire. It looked as if the eighteen-wheeler truck was a bowling ball and the cars were pins; he bowled a strike. The death toll was climbing. Olivia wrapped her arms around Lilly. She had known this loss; she had it twice before. "It's going to be okay, Lilly. You just have to believe and hold on," she said holding her close. Lilly's body was shaking like a wet dog and sweat dripped off her body like rain. Livvy's embrace was not easing her fear, anxiety, or pain. Some correctional officers came over to attempt to calm her and then called the nurse to come and give her a sedative. It was like they had switched places; Olivia felt so horrible for harboring any anger toward her friend for even a second. Just like that, she was taken from Livvy. She wanted to make her better. She wanted to engulf all of her bad memories and pain into herself. If God is love, why did He not love her baby enough to let him live. She hoped Liam survived. Maybe if God did not care about Livvy, at least He would hear her prayer for an innocent child. Liam was still too young to understand life and death or even know sin. He was innocent...so very innocent.

Sadness had dressed the entire detention center. Several others were impacted by the tragic accident, including some of the correctional officers and offenders. But no one had lost like Lilly. She had seen her family literally die in front of her. She was not sure if Lilly were mentally strong enough to handle that loss. Olivia was not sure if anyone was. She was unable to see her, but Miguel said she was doing better, and that Alexi had gone to see her. Olivia sat down and just grieved for her only friend. She had no idea how Lilly felt, but she wanted to make it better. Her loss helped Olivia forget her issues, but that only lasted a little while. She received a letter from Carlos. He said he would come and visit tomorrow. She was somewhat elated, but also afraid. She still was not sure if it was a set up, but she would find out soon. She had to know the truth. She could deal with Angelo beating and mistreating her, but she could not deal with the knowledge that he killed her brother and did not do anything about it. He would pay even if it killed her; he'd pay with his life for taking her brother from her.

On Thursday, she stared at the clock, waiting. Then she'd glared at the door. She wanted him to hurry; she did this routine for thirty minutes. Finally, Miguel walked in and told her she had a visitor. She leaped up quickly and walked the well-known path. As she entered, Carlos sat quickly.

"Hey, thank you for coming to see me," Olivia said.

He looked uneasy and somewhat distracted. "Yeah, I would have come sooner but you know things happen. Look, I have something to give you. Deek had left me something to give to you in case anything happened to him. I know I should have given it to you months ago, but he told me not to do it around Ace. I had to respect that. I have it in the car. I can't bring anything in here," he said.

Livvy was shocked. What was it that he wanted her to have? She looked at Miguel and asked if he could keep it for her. He nodded in agreement. "Carlos, do you know what it is?" she asked.

"No, he just told me to keep it. He was like a brother to me. I have been trying to find out what happened, but I don't know. I can't talk freely in her," he said to her while giving Miguel an untrusting eye.

"No, Miguel...I mean Officer Castillo...is not like that. He's a good guy. I promise. I would not have asked you to come. Just tell me: Did Angelo have him killed?" she asked thirsting for anything that touched her brother's hands. She wanted to feel connected to him. She wanted anything that he had. She just wanted a piece of him.

"It's possible, but if he did, he didn't tell me. Only he knows. I can't believe that; we are all family. He would not do that. Don't let these police tell you any different. I got to go. I told Ace I was going to be somewhere else. Look, he has eyes on you so keep your mouth shut and your head low. I don't want anything to happen to you. You need to write him and call. He wants to hear from you. I gotta go," he said and quickly got up.

"Carlos, what about the stuff you have from Deek?" she asked.

"I'll leave it. Livvy, I am sorry. I am sorry I did not protect you like Deuce wanted me to. I just had no idea this would happen," he said and left.

She knew he placed himself in harm's way coming to see her and revealing what he did, but she was glad. She had something to look forward to when she was released. She smiled inside and went back to her cell. It gave her hope; it carried her through. But she wondered what he meant when he said Angelo had eyes on her. Who was watching, and what were they saying?

***

A week later Lilly came back, but she was not Lilly as she was before. She was sad, depressed, and distant. It had been her baby and his adoptive parents, as well as her mother. They had all come to celebrate her upcoming birthday. It was a sad tragedy; now she, like Livvy, had no one in this world. She was sixteen and on her own. Livvy tried to console her, but she rejected her friend. She did not want hugs, kind words, or company, so Olivia withdrew too. She could not reach her, so she just let her grieve. Olivia had completed the equations Mr. Douglas had been mailing her.

When Mr. D came for a visit, she was glad for the intermission from the misery and sadness. Misery had settled into their little cell; they had another roommate— death. It had driven a wedge between them, and Olivia could not reach her friend no matter how she tried. That hurt her deeply. They were all each other had, and Livvy wanted to comfort her.

The day of the funeral, she watched Lilly walk out. It was like the light in her had been blown out. Olivia wanted to hold her and tell her good things, but Lilly's mind was in another place. Olivia waited for her return, thinking it would ease the pain that had paralyzed her spirit seeing them resting in peace. When she returned, Livvy had a honey bun on her bed as well as her Bible. That seemed to comfort her, and Olivia hoped to get her friend back.

Upon her return, Livvy sat quietly and watched her look at her peace offering. She offered Livvy a smile and sat down. Lilly reached for her Bible and then looked at Livvy. Olivia missed her. She never had a friend before, and she loved having Lilly. She made life bearable. She had a kindness and strength that Deek had. She fed off her as she had off of Deek. She hoped she was coming back to her. She needed her friend, especially now. They both needed each other.

"Do you want me to leave so you can have your private time with God?" Livvy asked her. She nodded yes.

"Okay. Lilly, I really love you. I think you are the best friend anyone could have. I wish I had known you on the outside, but I am glad to have you in my life now," she said and reached over to hug her. Lilly held Olivia long—much longer than she thought she would—but Livvy guessed a week of silence did that to you. Olivia kissed her cheek and walked out. Lilly asked her friend to give her an hour. Olivia thought that was fair.

"Olivia, thank you for being my friend. I love you. You have made this time bearable. I am thankful for the eight months of knowing you," she said with a brief smile. Her eyes still seemed sad and troubled. Olivia knew she would get better. Olivia offered her another smile and left to write letters to Ms. Geter, Mr. D, and Angelo. She despised writing him, but she wanted him to think nothing had changed. As she was getting ready to seal the last letter, she heard an awful noise. Then she saw some CO's heading toward her cell, and she followed. She pushed through and there, hanging like an ornament, was her Lilly. Tears fell slowly, but fear came quickly. She was having an out of body experience. She was screaming and did not know she was...just as she had when Deek was gunned down. There was no blood...just fear.

"Noooooooooo...get her down. Lilly...Lillian Georgiana Markley...you come back to me. Please don't leave me; please. We are all we have," she shouted pushing the guards aside. She cradled her limp body in her warm arms and rocked her back and forth, whispering for her to wake up. Her lips were purple, her eyes were wide open, and her face was drenched with fallen tears. She closed Lilly's eyes, and kept rocking and whispering for her to come back. They had to conquer the world. They needed each other. "Come back, please. God, make her come back," she sobbed loudly. This was déjà vu; she had already done this with Derrick. Now she had to lose Lilly too. "Damn you, Death. You are a horrible, unkind bully. Why are you stalking me? Why are you kidnapping all those I love?" she asked inwardly.

"Olivia, you have to let her go," They said trying to remove her. But she was not going without a fight. She could not comprehend this. How dare it come so soon? What was it that Death wanted from her? It took her innocence, her happiness, her family, and her only friend; there was nothing else for it to take. "You don't touch her. She is resting; she is not dead. She would not leave me like this. No, she would not leave me. I need her; we are sisters. We are best friends. My Lilly, come back. Please just wake up," she said reaching for her. But instead of getting closer, she was getting further away. It all occurred so quickly; strangers entered in and took her away from Olivia. Death had taken Lilly, and now there were only two: Death and Livvy. "Take me...please take me too," she yelled as she watched Lilly go, and then there was nothing.

The sounds, the sobs, the panic all returned to her, and she saw that she was not alone. She wanted to be. Why had Lilly left her? What was it that Lilly needed? She would have given her all she asked. She just wanted her friend back. First Deek and now Lilly were gone. Why was she always losing those she loved? She sat on the floor defeated and deflated; she was mentally drained and physically tired. That was all she had. Her heart was broken, never to be whole again. She had no strength to get up...no will to live; she begged Death to come back and take her as well.

She went numb, just like she felt when Deek was murdered. This was hopelessness; this was the picture of defeat...the masterpiece of disaster. "Why was I ever born, Oh God, why?" she asked inwardly as she lay motionless on the floor trying to melt into it.

"There is a note in here, and it is addressed to Livvy," she heard the guard say.

She did not even move. She no longer existed. Who was Livvy? "Who was Dinah Olivia Morris? Not I. I was nobody," she asked inwardly. There was hustle and bustle all around her, but she did not move; she could not. She had hoped to become invisible. Who cared about her? She closed her eyes to try and escape, but she could not. Lilly had left; she would have never left her. Loyalty meant something to Olivia. She did not care anymore...she really did not. All that floated in her mind was her best friend hanging.

"Come on, Livvy...come on. You need to get up," she heard the voice say.

"No, leave me. Just let me die. I'm ready," she said not sure how her mouth opened. It felt like cement, as did her body. She just wanted to die.

"We are going to have to just pick her up. I think she is in shock," he said.

Olivia struggled trying to get away, and then all was darkness.

When her eyes opened, she had no idea where she was or why. She had the worst nightmare that Lilly had committed suicide. It felt so real. She looked around, trying to figure out what was happening. She saw Coach Geter and Mr. Douglas, but why was she seeing them and not her other surroundings? "Where am I?" she asked although her throat was dry and in pain.

"Peter, she is up. Go get Miguel," Lydia said to Mr. D. Then she looked at Olivia again, her eyes revealing pain. "Sweetheart, you are in the hospital," she said caressing her arms and rubbing her face.

This made no sense to her; she had no idea what was going on. "Why?" she asked. By now Mr. Douglas had returned with Miguel. He asked the others to leave for a moment so he could talk to Livvy alone. She looked at him, waiting for an explanation.

"I am glad you are up. You were asleep for a long time. Do you remember what happened?" he asked.

"No, but where is Lilly? I had a horrible nightmare. I need to talk to her," Olivia pleaded. She wanted to ensure that her best friend was okay. The nightmare was so real that she needed to see Lilly with her own eyes to make sure she was safe.

His eyes lowered, and his face grew colorless. "She is gone," he whispered.

Olivia looked perplexed at him. She must have misunderstood what he said. "What? The program already started. We never packed our things or met our host families," she said shaking her head. Lilly would never leave without telling her goodbye. What happened that she would be in the hospital anyway?

"No, it was not a nightmare. It happened. She left a note and her Bible for you," he said, tears resting at the brim of his eyes. He had hoped she would remember so that she would not have to relive the pain all over again.

She felt disconnected as she heard his words. "Lilly is gone?" she repeated.

His eyes looked into hers, and he nodded yes.

"Okay," she responded. "What else do you want to tell me?" she asked sensing there was more.

"She killed herself, because she could not deal with losing so many loved ones at one time. There is more; I have the box Carlos told you about when he came to visit, but he's gone now. I don't know where he is or what has happened to him. I'm so sorry, but I have some good news. The pilot program has started. When you leave here, you will not be returning to DJJ. You will be living with your host family," he said watching her eyes tear up. He then offered her Lilly's Bible and her letter.

She accepted Lilly's belongings, but she did not open anything. "Can I just be left alone?" she asked. There was too much to process Lilly was dead, Carlos was missing, and she was going to a family she did not know. Hell had to be better than this.

"Yes, but there will be a guard at your door. Call if you need me," he said gently and kissed her forehead. His heart ached for her.

She watched him leave, and she felt as if she was inwardly being crushed. She had lost for the last time.

CHAPTER 12

Facing Reality

The next day she awoke with an ache in her soul. Her heart was stirring as she placed her trembling fingers upon the letter. She let out a sigh and opened it. She had no expectations and no need for an explanation, for she had the same thought when Deek died. With the realization that Lilly was gone, she wanted to die too. She felt so empty...so worn from the heartaches. She slowly opened it and read the words.

My dearest Livvy and only real friend. I am so very sorry to leave you, but my heart is weeping, and I can't stop it. I wanted to and I tried to, but I can't. I went to the funeral, and I thought it would ease the pain and make me feel whole again. While I was there, I saw others. My stepbrother was there; the sight of him made me shake with fear. I saw him, Angelo, his eyes cold...his look frightening. My stepbrother said I deserved the very worst, and that he hoped I burned in hell. I want to die; I can't live with that kind of hate. I had to leave you. If I stayed, I would have died anyway—either at the hands of my stepbrother or at the hands of another. Be strong. Angelo does not want you to love or be loved. He wants you for himself. Be careful; those who are supposed to uphold the laws are breaking them. I am going home to be with my family, and I will see the Father. I want you to see Him too. Read the Bible; tell him the secrets of your soul so He can protect you. I love you. Remember Matthew 5:44: forgive and love.

Was there ever a moment when sadness, death, and pain would not be in her soul...a moment when Angelo did not win? Her empty, hollow, heart was hardened; her soul was gone. Why was she still breathing? When would death call her home? No place was safe; death could trespass anywhere at any time, and she hated it. She must be a mess; even death didn't think her worthy to take. She was left to despise how all had been stolen from her. She just wanted it all to end. Rage was pumping through her veins. He killed Lilly, and he killed Deek. She knew it; she felt it in the very core of her being. There was an incurable hate in him. His eyes abhorred anyone who cared for her. When his hands imprinted her flesh that horrible night, she knew he hated her. The first time she vocalized her dismay to him and for a moment lost herself, he crushed her. He beat her so horribly that night that she blacked out and thought she was nine again running from Bo. Then when she woke, she was back in his house in his bed. He was loving her as if nothing had occurred...whispering how sorry he was. Now he was beating her again. It was her fault for being too loose in the lips. If she took the charges and said nothing, it would all be forgiven.

She loathed him deeply because of him she lost; she lost Deek, and then Lilly. She could have avoided that loss if she had never been locked up and never known Lilly. This hole in her heart would not exist. She tried so hard to be a good girl but nothing she did could ease her mother's hate toward her. She longed for her affection. She attached herself to her brother like a leech sucking all his love because it had been denied her for so long. Now, he was gone. She thought Angelo would take care of her; she just wanted to be in a place where she was not expected to have to be an adult; she just wanted her childhood; she wanted her innocence back. Angelo betrayed her and Deek. There was no reason for his madness and hate against humanity.

She thought Lilly would be a forever friend—a kindred spirit who understood—but she had demons Olivia had not seen and Angelo played on them. Everyone had left her to fend for herself, but she could not; the water was too deep...the sharks too many. She was drowning. Who can help her now? How can one live when there is nothing to live for? What if Angelo found her here...what would he do? It was only a matter of time before he would kill her too. No one could please him because he was too paranoid...too separate from mankind to be able to love. He was his own species—an emotionless, selfish, dangerous, murderous maniac. Her pathetic life was in his hands; only death would loosen his grip.

She lay there with her mind boggled down by grief. She glanced at the Bible, but she saw no power in the pages. What was in that book that could save her? It didn't save Lilly. Olivia was not worth saving, but Lilly was; she had a family. Olivia had no one; she should have been the one hanging. She closed her eyes. She just wanted what was stolen from her, but she could never get it back. She wanted to sleep, but images of Lilly hanging became the main attraction, then Deek, then mama. She wanted people to stop dying. The phone began to ring, startling her shaken nerves. On the third ring, she answered. "Hello?" She could not understand who wanted to talk to her.

"Knockout, it's me. Are you alone?" he asked.

It was Angelo. How had he found her? "No," she lied.

"Don't speak. Just listen. I heard about your friend, and I am sorry about that...bad break. I might not be able to visit you for a while. Things are getting hot around here. I love you, and I told Carlos to look out for you. I have to go underground for a while. But you know you my girl. I want to see you, but I know I can't. I love you," he said.

She began to dry heave. He did not have that impression on her anymore. She thought Carlos was missing. What was he talking about? "Why did you kill Deek and Lilly? I want the truth. You owe me that. Why? Just tell me. Why? What did Deek do to you?" she asked not caring what the repercussions would be. She wanted to die and, if it be at his hands, so be it.

"Are you drugged up? What in the world are you talking about? Who have you been talking to? Don't be stupid. I didn't kill anybody," He said vehemently.

"Liar! You set Deek up. Why? I don't know, but you do; maybe it was because you have never been loved so you take away all the people who love me. You are a murderer. You don't scare me anymore. I have lost everything, and I have nothing left to lose. You can kill me too if you like. It would be a great gift. You know where I am. Are you coming yourself, or will you send someone else?" she said angrily.

"Olivia, the cops have been brainwashing you with foolishness. Stop talking before you really piss me off. You shut your mouth. You do your time, and when you are released you will come back to me and act like you know who you belong too. Don't test me, Olivia; you will lose," he said shocked at her attitude and angered by her directness. He knew being locked up changed people. This was ridiculous; he wanted her to toughen up, but not to the point of disrespecting him. That was just foolish.

"I don't care; I have already lost. Don't you talk to me like that, you jerk!" she said. She wanted him to come. She was ready and waiting. She wanted to know why he killed Deek.

"Dinah Olivia Morris, you don't know what I can do. You don't know the extent of my power and how money can buy loyalty. Shut-up. I am trying to be nice because I know you are fifteen and have lost a lot, but my patience is wearing thin. Things can happen in hospitals. People die there every day. You understand?" he said.

"I do. I'll be seeing you. Do you understand me, coward?" she asked irritated by his threats. Click. He hung up. She hoped he would come and finish her off. Life was not worth living. She stared aimlessly toward the door—waiting to see him come, sooner rather than later—but when it opened the police entered.

"Livvy, we got it. We will get him," Det. Davis said. He was followed by Det. Hoover, the one who was in her apartment when Deek was killed, and Det. Greene.

"I don't understand," she said almost in a whisper.

"We tapped the phone, in hopes he would call you, and he did. We traced the call," he said smiling.

Was she supposed to be relieved...excited because they were going to get him? She did not care. She was not trying to set him up. She just wanted him to kill her, so she did not have to feel, not have to be alone, and not have to live in agony each day. "I'm tired," he said, not looking at them and wishing they would leave her. There was excitement in their eyes. They wanted him. They did not care about anything else. She heard them leave, and she got up preparing to leave too. She yanked the intravenous needle out of her hand. It was painful, but she did not care. She was on a mission; she was going to run until death took her. They had unfinished business. As she walked toward the door, Miguel came in. "Where are you going?" he asked.

Her eyes glared at his. "I was just preparing to die. I told Angelo to come and do it. I thought I'd go in search of him, so it can be done," she said in a surreal tone.

He looked bewildered. Had she lost her mind? "Sit down. Have you gone mad? Tomorrow you will be with your host family; you are going away from Hollow Hill. You are upset and depressed and speaking without knowledge or understanding. Did you read like I suggested?" he asked her, as he placed his hand gently on her shoulder.

"No. I told you. I can't open that Bible. God don't want me; I don't even want me. All I do is lose. All I have loved is gone. Why won't you just let fate do as it will and let me die? I am not worth the effort," she said.

He hoped it was the medication talking. He had never heard anyone speak so harshly about themselves. "Livvy, how can you say that? God would not have given his only begotten Son if you were not worth it. You are; you are a special person— strong, intelligent, loving, and loyal. People care about you. Your teachers have gone above and beyond for you. They are the reason for this pilot program, and they did it because of you. You are worthy; God says your worth is far above rubies. I told you that before. Don't fight the promises of God...accept them. Anyone telling you different is a liar; open the Bible and read this love letter from God. You are hurting. I understand, but you can't give up. Look, I have a visitor who wants to talk to you," he said walking to the door and his brother entered.

"Hey, Livvy. I am sorry for your loss. I thought you'd need a friend right now. I would have come before, but I wasn't sure if I should. My brother said I should at least try. Maybe I can help you navigate the Bible and share with you how God has transformed me. May I pray for you?" he said so endearingly. His eyes were soft, his voice was gentle, and his touch was so warm to her cold hands. Tears escaped from her eyes and kissed his hand. He did not remove it but held her hands tighter and prayed for her. "Just ask God to come in and He will. He is knocking at the door of your heart. Don't deny him. Let God love you," he said smiling at her unchanging face. "I am not as good at this as my brother Miguel is. I want to help you. I care about you, Livvy; I really do," Jacoby said kindly.

She believed him because there was truth in his eyes. His body language said he cared, but her heart was so mangled and ripped that she was no good for anyone. "Thank you. I mean that, and I am so sorry for what Angelo said to you. But I am not worthy of your friendship. People die when they befriend me. I am a walking plague," she explained.

Jacoby smiled; she was so thoughtful and caring. He was safe; it was her they were all worried about. "I don't think so. Things happen for a reason; I don't know why you have suffered, but I do know if you endure the testing God will reward you handsomely. He is a God of truth, forgiveness, love, and compassion; don't deny Him the opportunity to love you. We can read together, or I can read to you. The book of Psalm is a really good and uplifting place to start. May I?" he asked as he reached for Lilly's Bible.

Olivia nodded yes and listened to him read. Miguel left them alone. Jacoby had a pleasant, kind voice. He seemed full of joy as he read. Love was in every part of his body as he shared the words of the Bible. She recalled how she had memorized verses when that Bible had been such a gift to her, and how Bo had not only stolen her childhood and scarred her for life, but he also stole her relationship with God. Jacoby, thank you for reading to me," she said.

"If you like, I can sit here awhile. I would like to talk to you. I never got to before," he said.

"Why? What do you want to talk about with me? I mean, you ignored me as if I never existed," she said not trying to be harsh but honest. They weren't friends.

He looked at her very kindly with calmness in his eyes. He and Miguel favored each other so much. "I was shy. You read books daily. You never communicated with anyone. You were walked to and from school by your brother and then Angelo. So, I did not know how to approach you. I am not the only one who noticed the smartest girl in class," he said smiling at her.

Blood rushed to her cheeks, and she blushed a little at his confession. He was right; her brother was very protective of her, but Angelo was also very possessive of her. It was a big difference. "Oh, I never thought anyone noticed or even cared," she said honestly.

He smiled at her confession. He cared; he cared a lot. "They do. I do; I'd like to be friends," he said.

That was the nicest thing she had heard since losing Deek. "I don't have a good track record. I'm so confused and jaded; I don't think I can be a good friend to you," she confessed.

He placed his hand gently on top of hers. "That's okay; I'll be a good friend to you. When you are ready, you can be a friend to me," Jacoby said warmly.

That smile; Jacoby had to be about the most handsome man she had ever seen. He had golden brown eyes, midnight colored hair, warm vanilla sugar skin, and a smile as lovely as Caribbean sunset. He was sweet, genuinely kind, and as sincere as a Hallmark card. He should have several girlfriends and even more friends. What did he want with her? She smiled. "You are like Miguel...determined," she said with a hint of laughter. They both had the same genteel patient demeanor. They both had kind eyes and godly smiles.

He nodded his head in agreement. "You look tired; just rest. I'll sit here and outline some verses for you. We can study them together. What I don't know, Miguel does; you are going to heal again. God loves you more than you can ever imagine," he said kindly.

She took his advice and returned to her hospital bed. She let the sheets surround her body, and she drifted into slumber. The nightmares started almost immediately. She could not wake up. There was an emotional tug of war in her brain. Why did she not see what was going to happen to Lilly? She had said she needed an hour alone with God. Lilly had held her longer because she knew it would be their last embrace. She felt compelled to tell Lilly how much she cared, but it came too late. Her love for her was not stronger than her loss or fear. "Lilly," she screamed at her. "Lilly don't do it. Please come back." She turned from Livvy and drifted into the distance, just like Deek. But where were they going? Why were they leaving her? She fought as hard as she could to open her eyes, but she could not. She felt fear, and then she remembered the words Jacoby had prayed with her, so she tried it. It stopped; a blank screen appeared. It was like she was seeing her life: the good, the bad, the unspeakable, the joys, the sadness. But it was not painful; it was triumphant for she had overcome. A soothing sensation came over her body and surged through her marrow; calmness surrounded her.

**

Sitting in the back of the Dodge Caravan, she watched as the sites went from decrepit to desolate to delightfully beautiful. It was the part of Georgia she had never seen, although it was a good distance away from where she lived. Here she saw no prostitutes, no drug dealers, no pimps, and no gang bangers. People seemed happy; they were smiling and waving at one another. If you did that in Hood Town, you'd get robbed, beaten, or even killed. This place was called Pleasantville. She had never in her entire life heard of a place called that. It fitted the town perfectly. There were manicured lawns, no litter, a neighborhood watch, soccer games, cafés, and a movie theater. There was an absence of police cruising up and down the street. She heard no gun fire, no loud music bumping, no babies crying. What was this place? This must be what Paradise looked like, and it even smelled good.

She closed her eyes and tried to imagine what it would have been like if she and Deek grew up here and not in the hood. She was dreaming. Dreams had escaped her a long time ago, but it felt so good to dream. In dreams she found hope, a will to live, and a reason to believe. She needed that to make it through, for life was not getting any easier. Her mind went back to those things she said to Angelo when she dared him to be brazen enough to enter into her hospital room to kill her. She meant it at the time, but a thirty-six hour hold in the mental ward gave her a new insight. Her outburst pushed back her delivery date to her host family. However, it was good to talk to someone who was legally bound to keep her words a secret. She did not tell too much; she only spoke of Lilly. Something about those words Angelo said about how money could buy loyalty made everyone a suspect to her.

The battle had just begun; she wondered if this family had really considered what they were doing. It felt so good to be outside—to feel wind, to feel her skin bathed by the sun, to hear birds chirping. It had all been taken away, but to feel it again made her want to live. It was so easy to be suicidal behind walls. Blank, meaningless, empty walls had drained so many hopes and dreams. They would have stolen hers if she had not been taken when she was. She was not made for prison, jail, DJJ; that was a life far beyond what her nerves could take. Lillian must have felt the same way. It had been too much to get that brief taste of freedom only to come back to a cage and be suffocated by fear, death, grief, and threats. If only she could have held on just a little longer, she too would have had this rejuvenation and wanted to live. Olivia wanted to make her proud...to do for her what she could not do for herself...to start over, rebuild what had been torn down, and learn to let go. Letting go was the hard part. She felt that if she let go—of finding out what really happened to Deek or what must have gone through Lilly's mind—that she would forget them and betray their trust. She did not want that; God knows it had happened to her over and over again, and she did not want to be the person doing it to someone else. The doctor said she needed to let go. Easy for him; it is so easy to give advice, but hard to accept advice. She only knew one side of life: pain, agony, defeat, betrayal, heartbreak, and death. In some ways, she found comfort in it because she knew it.

These feelings occurring now seemed foreign almost invasive. She hushed her thoughts as they pulled into a long driveway. At the end, a large plantation house was set. It was white, stainless, and lovely. There was a long wrap around porch that held a swing and several rocking chairs. There were no toys or swing sets sitting out front, so she figured the children had to be at least preteens. In the driveway was a Chevrolet Impala with tinted windows, a Chevrolet Silverado, a Trailblazer, and a Volkswagen Beetle. The truck was a classic black, the Trailblazer was gray like her eyes, and the bug...well it had sass and personality. She figured the owner was a girl who really loved pink and polka dots. Olivia was not told who the family was, but she grew nervous as the engine shut off. Coach Geter and Mr. Douglas had volunteered to take her. This was their brainchild; they called it Restoration. If the few who were chosen did well, it would become a permanent project. She had to do well and make a good impression because she did not want to go back. She feared what that meant for her. Angelo was still in hiding; the police were too late. He had eyes in places she did not know, and she was scared.

Mr. D opened the door for Olivia and helped her get out. As soon as her foot hit the pavement, the door opened. She wondered who she would be living with for the next few years. A woman came out first; she had a pleasant face; light-skin like Olivia's, and animated chestnut eyes. Her smile was contagious, and Livvy quickly offered one back. She never really smiled—there was no real reason to—but she could not deny her. She greeted Livvy with a hug and welcomed her home. Next her daughter came out; she looked around Livvy's age she guessed, or a little older since she had a car—assuming the pink car was hers. She had fine curly brownish gold hair, her skin was the mixture of nutmeg and vanilla, and her eyes were ginger and innocent. She was a pretty girl, and just as kind and welcoming as her mother.

"Come on inside. Daddy is just finishing cooking on the grill. I am so excited to have you here. I always wanted a sister," she said pulling Olivia into the house. She had a very bubbly personality—nothing like Livvy. She was open and inviting like Lilly. She recalled how she had approached her that day and just started talking like they had known each other forever; she longed for that moment again.

"Wait. Slow down. I don't even know your name," Olivia said in an attempt to stop her from dragging her along.

"Sorry. I was just so excited. My name is Victoria Hoover. That is my mother, Vivian Hoover. Come on. Daddy will be glad to see you," she said.

Oh no, she thought secretly. This is Det. Hoover's family. This was his family? She would have never thought he had a Black family. The craziness was she left police to live with police. They were trying to get her killed for sure. She looked back, but Coach Geter and Mr. Douglas were talking to Mrs. Hoover. She wanted to turn back, but Victoria kept pulling her until they were back outside on the patio looking at her father. The letter never said anything about the host family being law enforcement. That explained the Chevrolet Impala with tinted windows. It was a cop car. Olivia wondered what her brother would think. Det. Hoover greeted her with a kind fatherly smile; his pale blue eyes were comforting and welcoming. She dropped her head. She had not expected this; she wondered had she traded one dictator for another.

"How are you doing, Livvy. We are happy to have you," he said noticing her shyness.

"Thank you for having me, sir," she said timidly. She would be doing better if the host family was a homemaker mom and soccer coaching dad.

"Well, don't be shy. Sit down and snack a little. The rest of the bunch has not gotten here just yet." He smiled and turned his attention back to cooking.

She sat there, and Mrs. Hoover, Coach Lydia Geter, and Mr. D came in. They were all smiles and just chatting away like nothing was wrong. Olivia sat there and listened to Victoria talk. She loved to talk, so Livvy just listened.

Fifteen minutes later, Miguel, Jacoby, their parents, and Alexi entered. Then Vincent, who was Victoria's older brother, came in followed by Det. Alan Greene and his entire family—a wife and three kids ranging from 7 to 13. Olivia stayed silent, but she was watching and listening. The amount of people was overwhelming.

Jacoby noticed that Livvy was being hammered by Victoria asking her a million questions but not allowing her to answer, and he came to her rescue.

"You looked like you needed a break," he said.

"I do, but...um...did you know about this? I mean me living with the policeman that investigated my brother's murder?" she said whispering to him. She felt uncertain and uncomfortable.

His eyes glowed mischievously. "I may have had some insight, but I think it is for your safety. You are safe here. Cops live up and down this road. We live just ten minutes away. My brother is moving here in a few months; he and Alexi just got engaged," he said smiling.

She nodded. The residences of cops were up and down the entire area. It should have been called Police Paradise instead of Paradise Acres.

"You can come to my house sometimes. I need your assistance in math. I think you will be attending the same school as me, Pleasantville Christian Academy. It's private but worth it; it's a really good school that prepares you for Ivy League universities. You are going to do well," he said.

"I hope so. I have a favor to ask," she said. He looked at her waiting for her to ask him. "Can you help me find another Bible? I would like my own," she said. She loved Lilly's because it was all she had of her, but she wanted it as a keepsake. She thought it better to have her own.

A warm smile spread across his face. "Sure. I just got a car for my birthday, so you can officially be the first girl to ride in it. Well, you will be the second; my mom rode in it already," he said laughing.

"Okay. Thank you," she said somewhat timidly. She could not continue denying God. She was scared, but the worst thing that could happen would be rejection and she knew that well.

"Come on and let's eat. Mr. Hoover can grill like nobody else I know," he said.

She followed. Everyone seemed happy; they all really cared about one another. Det. Hoover hugged on his daughter and made a fuss over his son. His wife was attentive and listened to his speech. Det. Greene interacted with his children and wife. Jacoby and Miguel's parents laughed with them. Ms. Lydia and Peter were flirting and laughing; it was a perfect night for them all.

Olivia was still silent and feeling out of place. She wondered if she could walk away unnoticed. Olivia pretended she needed to use the bathroom and went to sit on the front porch. She needed a moment for herself. Tears fell from her eyes; this is what she had missed for fifteen years, and it was all overwhelming to her. There were really people who interacted like "The Walton's." She longed for a family like that for herself and Deek. It hurt her heart that she had not known it was possible to have anyone love her in that way. She rested her head on her lap. Her heart was overflowing with emotions and a new fear was emerging. She had wanted this her whole life and, now that she had seen it, she feared losing it. She did not belong to these people. She tried to erase the need to be loved...to be wanted. She felt like a walking contradiction. She wanted things she was not prepared to have. They were too generous to her; she was not worthy of this kindness. Her sins were unforgiveable.

"Livvy, what are you doing out here? We are all celebrating because of you," Miguel said as he settled himself beside her on the top step of the porch.

Tears stinging her cheek, she turned to him. "I can't do this. I don't belong here. I want to belong; I do, but I don't," she said unable to hold her feelings inside.

"Yes, you do. Det. Hoover requested that you be here. He's a good guy, and his wife is good too. They both want you here. I am sure that night when Deek died, he would have taken you in then. We all care about you, Livvy. You are a special girl. Everybody here tonight came to support you and show you that you are not alone. We love you; these are Christian people who are doing what God has done for us. We're adopting you into our family and our hearts. You deserve this: to be happy, to have a childhood, to be safe, and to be loved. You'll get that here. God has placed you where you need to be. He has heard your every cry and kept you safe," he said.

"You don't understand; I trusted the wrong people. Lilly did not just commit suicide. Angelo scared her and made her think he would kill her too. So, she chose to do it so he couldn't. It's my fault; people want to love me, but they die. You see, I am no different than Angelo; all this time I thought I was innocent, but there is blood on my hands too," she confessed showing them to him. She did not deserve to have a second chance. Angelo was using her as his own personal weapon. She allowed him to because she was afraid of him.

Miguel wondered how that could occur. He set aside that thought and gave his attention back to Livvy. He gently placed his arms securely around her. "You are innocent. We will capture Angelo, and he will never hurt you or anyone else again. It is not your fault. You did the right thing. There is no blood on your hands; you were the only innocent person it all this," he said kissing her forehead.

She shook in response to his tenderness. It reminded her of Deek. "Did Angelo have Deek killed?" she asked feeling herself ripping in two. She had cared for Angelo once. She thought he was a savior, but he was the opposite. "Who can I trust now?" she asked crying on his shoulder.

"You need to trust us...all of us. God has a plan for you. Your story is just beginning; God has something so great planned for you. I have something for you. Wait right here; I have it in the car," he said. She watched him walk quickly. She wanted it badly. She had forgotten Carlos said he had something from her brother for her. He came back to her holding a square can. She grabbed it and held it close to her heart.

"Thank you," she said.

"You are welcome. You have to wait until your birthday, which is two weeks away, right?" he said.

She nodded yes. Her birthday was a week before school started. She did not think she would live to see it. "I guess we should go back to the party," she said.

"Yeah," he said, and they walked back. She sat down and allowed herself the chance to have fun. Some of the teenagers started playing volleyball. For the first time in her life since losing Deek, she was having fun. She was interacting with people, and it lifted her up. This was the kind of life Deek wanted to provide for her. He wanted her to be safe, to be loved, and to be cared for...he did not want her to have to worry but to enjoy life. She only wished it was something they could have shared together. She would give it all up in a minute for her brother to be alive. It didn't seem worth having when she could not share it with Derrick and Lilly.

CHAPTER 13

A New Beginning

One week had changed Olivia's entire life. She just meshed well with her host family. She received more love in one week than she had ever received from her deceased mother. She found in the Old Testament a woman who bore her name: Dinah. She was violated and, like Olivia, her brothers tried to protect her honor. She didn't feel so alone anymore. She felt like Dinah, though she lived before her time; she understood her plight, and she wept for her. She told her she loved her. When you are broken like that, you need to be reminded that you are someone special to God. Olivia was learning and growing. Maybe she was worth something to God too. Maybe her tragic past had occurred for a reason.

**

She and Jacoby went to the mall. She was kind of excited, since it was just the two of them. They walked to the Christian Collection, which had an array of things. She wanted it all. It was a store owned by Mrs. Hoover, so she said Livvy could have all she wanted. She just wanted a Bible and a journal. They looked and looked until she found one that matched her personality. It was medium sized lavender Bible made for teenage girls. She opened it without hesitation or fear. She felt her fear flying away. Next, she got a new Christian startup kit for when she got baptized; she wanted to be. Wednesday night service was approaching, and she wanted to give it all to Jesus. She was seeing how He had changed the lives of the family she was living with. They woke up smiling and went to bed smiling; no one raised their voice, and they went out of their way to help each other. They read their Bibles every morning silently and then came together to pray for the entire neighborhood. Olivia was baffled, but she liked it. She wanted to feel free like that. She wanted to live a fearless life, and she wanted to care and be compassionate...no longer angry or feeling guilty. She wanted life; in the Bible she heard that with Jesus you could have eternal life...even people like her. Jesus came to serve not to be served and to save not to judge. That pierced her heart. He didn't want to condemn her but save her from condemnation. How had she missed that? She turned back to Jacoby and told the clerk who she was; she bagged her things and they left. "Thank you for being so kind to me," Olivia said.

He smiled at her. "Anytime. I am glad to be able to see you again. I was really scared for you when you went missing. I went to my brother and was like something happened to this girl in my class and I can't find her. I am just so glad you are all right," he said drawing nearer to her.

She felt her face flush. "I am glad you cared," she said shyly.

"I did and I do. I know that may not be easy for you to believe, but I like you," he said.

"Oh," she said. "Can we get some ice cream? Victoria had this huge cone, and I wanted one so badly," she said.

"Oh, yeah. We can go to the creamery. You'll love it. It's a good place to meet some new people too. I can introduce you to some of my friends...I mean if that is okay. I know how timid you are around big crowds," he said.

"I am fine as long as I am not the center of attention," she replied.

"I don't know, Livvy; you are really pretty but I'll try. People notice you," he said with a sweet smile.

"Jacoby, you are embarrassing me. I just want some ice cream and to go unnoticed so I can read," she said.

He looked at her round face and saw it had turned red. She really was not a social butterfly; it was obvious that she had lived a sheltered life. "Well, I guess I can do the drive through, but you have to come out of your shell; this place is different. People want to know you and are friendly. Just trust me; I won't let anyone bother you. I want you to have fun," he said.

She agreed. If she wanted something different, then she had to do something different. "We don't have to go to the drive through," she said and followed him out the mall.

When she returned back home, Det. Hoover was sitting in his favorite chair. She had always dreamed of her daddy being like that, but she never had a face to go with the image. Her mother had destroyed every picture of her father because he left. Victoria and Vincent were very blessed to have a loving mother and father. Olivia wished she had gotten a taste of that. She never saw her father or his picture...not even a verbal description. Deek said he looked like her, but that was not enough. She could not wait for her birthday; she wanted to open the tin he had left behind for her. She had no idea what was in it, but she longed to have it. Her fingers longed to trace his fingerprints so she could have a connection with him. So sad are the things people long for when they are taken away.

"Is that you Olivia?" Mr. Hoover's strong voice said interrupting her thoughts.

"Yes, sir," she said walking toward him. He was good to her, treating her like one of his children as did his wife. She had a curfew; driving privileges; chores, and rules—she loved it. They had planned her life before she had even arrived at their home; it made her feel special—almost like she belonged.

Mrs. Hoover signed her up for gymnastics, and she got her on the cheerleading squad. Olivia liked the neighborhood; people actually walked their dogs and went jogging in the morning and there were no bullets to dodge, no pimps to avoid and no BWD. Det. Hoover and Olivia ran two miles every other day. They talked, not about Angelo but about her past and present, as well as what she hoped to achieve in the future. She liked him; Deek would have liked him also. He did not trust the police, and she did not either because she thought they were the enemy; but they had been good to her and to Deek. His case was still a priority, and that made her feel good.

Timothy watched her lovingly as she walked into the den. "What do you have in your hands there?" he asked her as she walked over to sit down on the floor in front of him. She handed her Bible over to him.

"I like this one. We got Victoria this one as well. I am glad you are here. Next week is your birthday. Is there anything you'd like? Birthdays are big around here," he said smiling. Her face was bright, such a stark contrast of what she was when he had first met her. She had been so shy—so afraid and detached—but as soon as she arrived at his home, it was like she was the child God had created her to be. She had the most enchanting smile and infectious laughter; what father could leave such a lovely soul behind? That he could never understand. He wanted her to know how very special she was and how wonderfully made she was. God never left her. She had overcome too much and been spared when others died. God was with her. She might not fully understand that, but God was keeping her for something special. He was with her wherever she went.

"No, sir. I don't need anything. I haven't had a birthday party before. Deek use to buy me a cupcake with the works and sing to me. He allowed me one special thing to do. Besides, I don't have friends; no one would come," she said sitting Indian style and flipping through the reading material she had chosen. Now that her brother was deceased, she did not care about celebrating much. It seemed wrong to enjoy this life when his was stolen.

He was shocked by her response. She never had a birthday party, and she didn't have any friends. She was so pleasant. He was sure Jacoby was a good friend of hers. They were together a lot, and Victoria adored her. "What would be a dream party for you?" he asked.

"I guess if I must choose, I liked the cookout you all had for me when I arrived. That would be fine, if I have to have a party. I just don't like being the center of attention," she said.

He thought that strange. He never met a child that did not want a birthday party or to be the center of attention on their birthday. It seemed like a chore to her. He wondered why that was. "You should be the center of attention on your birthday. This is home for you. I don't want you to feel like a visitor; you are family now," he said tenderly.

She looked up from her book and her eyes met his. "I've only been here a little while. Do you want to keep me...like for real?" she asked. How she had loved them. The second day, all of her defenses and misjudgments had disappeared over night. She wanted to belong. It was the only thing she ever wanted. She never felt as if she belonged.

"Yes, my biggest regret was leaving you behind that night. I guess it was not time. God works in ways unknown to man, but his plan is his plan. I told Vivian all about it, and she said to bring you here. I know it may take you a little longer to adjust, but this is your home. You're as much a Hoover as any of us. The lovely thing about being a Christian and a child of God is that we are all part of one body and one family. Jesus said in John 14:18: 'I will not leave you orphans; I will come to you.' And in Hosea 14:3 it says: 'In You the orphans find mercy,'" he said with a fatherly smile.

She didn't know that. She never remembered being taught about God looking out for the orphans, but it had to be true. From her earliest memory, she recalled being sexually, physically, and mentally abused; by all accounts she should be dead. But God must have kept her. There were no other explanations. God did really value her. Her worth was far above rubies, like Miguel said. She was a girl raised in the hood, conceived in sin, and abandoned by death; she was a priceless jewel to God. She meant something to Him. "Thank you, sir; thank you so very much for making me feel so welcome here. I would like to apologize for my actions and my belief that you did not care about finding my brother's murderer. I just did not understand," she said feeling somewhat ashamed.

She reminded him of Victoria, when she looked at him that way. She was such a beautiful young lady. Her brother raised her well. "No need to be sorry. You were hurting, and I would feel the same way as you. Today is new, so let us forget all about the past and just start over today. How about we read the Bible together?" he said.

She smiled and agreed. She scooted closer to his feet and listened to him read the Bible to her. There was love in his voice as he read God's Words. She felt powerful, renewed, and worthy. She was worthy of something more than being a victim of abuse.

***

When she walked into the church on Wednesday, she had a purpose. She went right to her youth minister, Eric. He greeted her with a smile. "Pastor Eric, I want to be baptized; I want to be saved and give all my burdens to Christ. I don't want to be worldly; I want to be in the Spirit, and I want to serve others and dedicate my life to Christ," she said. It was not her speaking, but God speaking through her. She was much too bashful. She was timid and quiet; she wanted to be invisible. But since she saw how God could transform, she wanted his peace, his boldness, his wisdom.

"Thank you, Jesus. Olivia, I am so very happy for you. Come on, God would love to have you and so would this church," he said with tears flowing from his eyes. He embraced her and grabbed her hand; they walked together to get the Hoover family and Senior Pastor Elijah. The church received her and prayed over her. Sunday, the day after her birthday, she would be baptized. For the first time in her life, she felt clean. She was not afraid; she was protected now...forever protected by God. She had an Advocate and a forever friend in Jesus. He wanted her even though so many had stolen from her, betrayed her, and violated her...even though they still haunted her in her sleep. He stopped it all. She was new. She was transformed...no longer conformed to the world. She was born again. All the time she thought she was forgotten and fatherless, He was there patiently waiting for her. Det. Hoover helped her see that. God is a father to the fatherless. He was there for her preparing her for this moment. She was so moved with emotions that she could not stop praising his name and thanking him for loving her and forgiving her. It was a new beginning for Olivia. She finally understood why Lilly had forgiven her stepfather; she only wished that her love was stronger so that Angelo, being the devil, he was, had not scared her into submission. She prayed her soul was safe. God knew her heart, and only he could judge. She recalled their last Bible study: "But I say unto you, love your enemies, bless them that curse you, do good to them that hate you, and pray for them which despitefully use you and persecute you." Matthew 5:44.

Angelo had power and control because Olivia gave it to him. She hated him, but that was contrary to the new her. While sitting in class with rest of her youth group, she prayed for him openly and let it go. She did not need that anymore. She forgave Bo, Celester, and all the rest; she forgave her dead mother and her unknown father. She was really free.

All her life she had been searching and seeking. The answer was in the book she stopped reading—the book she thought had betrayed her—but that was not God, that was man. Tonight, she separated the two.

Victoria walked over to her and held her long. "I am sorry for all you lost, but what God takes he gives back better than before. You may have lost Derrick, but you have Vincent. You may have lost Lilly, but you have me. Your mother is gone, but we share one now. Your father lost out on knowing a magnificent young woman, but my daddy gets the gift of loving you every day. You belong to God, and I am so glad he is sharing you with us. This is home now, until we all go see our Father. You are not defined by the sins' others committed against you; you are not a mistake, but God's lovely showpiece of artistry carved out by His perfection. I love you sister," she said, and tears emerged in both their eyes. Olivia held her long.

Her words were so heartfelt and true; someone loved Olivia Morris and sought nothing in return. God thought her worthy to be loved by the Hoover family. She was so overwhelmed by His unfailing love. He and her family had shown her the best of humanity; God knows she had seen the worst of it. "Oh Victoria, that is the kindest thing anyone on this earth has ever said to me. All I've ever wanted was to be wanted—not abused, not left behind, not being told that I am a mistake—and just to have someone see me and love me in my brokenness so that I could be mended. Thank you for being that for me," she whispered tearfully. Then she felt more arms hugging her; it was her entire class, including Pastor Eric. She felt safe. She never wanted it to end. Now, she had a love so impenetrable that nothing, not even Angelo, could take away. It was hers. God loved her—her mother and father did not, but He did—and he was all that mattered. It was the best feeling. She could not translate it into words, but finally she felt connected. It was good.

Once back at home, Olivia went to see Det. Hoover in his study and told him she wanted to do one more thing to let go. He was perplexed at first, but she handed over everything. She kept meticulous notes in invisible ink. She told him all that she knew; she wanted to be free of Angelo and remove all that he had done and told her. She no longer needed the pollution. Nothing would ever again separate her from God.

For the first time, she slept without fear and was able to dream without terrors; it was a peaceful, loving slumber. She had no nightmares...no fears...no worries. Peace had entered her heart; she would not let hate, evil, or pain penetrate. She had a family now; she belonged. Never again would she be homeless or orphaned. She had a father; she had the Father. He knew her; he even knew the number of hairs on her head. Though her history was not one of beauty, she was still His. He does not see as men sees; he looks at the heart, and her heart was beating love Psalms to Him.
**

"Wake up, birthday girl," Olivia heard several voices say. She opened her eyes and there before her stood the entire family. "Good morning," she said gleefully. She was happy it was Saturday. She had longed to open the tin box her brother had left her.

"Well, what do you want to do today?" Mr. Hoover asked.

"Can we go bowling?" she asked. She had wanted to do that forever. She wanted to do everything she did not do before.

"Yep, we can make that happen," he said smiling.

"Good. I have one more request; may I have some French toast this morning?" she asked.

Mrs. Hoover smiled at her. "I'll go start it now. Come on, everyone. Let her have her beauty rest," she said. They all hugged and kissed her first; even Vincent came home. She liked him. He was a really cool guy. He loved football, like Deek did. She was grateful that God had thought so much of her that he gave her such good people, and she still had Coach Geter and Mr. Douglas; they were like her aunt and uncle. She was not alone at all.

She watched them leave and then turned her attention back to the tin box. She opened it slowly. It still looked new, and she wondered when he had prepared this. Inside was a letter, a thick envelope, some pictures, a pocket Bible, and another box that looked like a jewelry box. She opened the letter first.

Happy Birthday, Genius. I love you. If you are opening this, it means I did not make it. I am sorry. I never wanted to leave you I wanted to be with you forever and always. I know you stopped attending church after Bo, but I never stopped praying for you. I did some things—some illegal bad things—but I wanted to do right and be right for you. I got baptized, confessed, and accepted Christ. We need him. I told Angelo today that I can't gang bang anymore. I told him my love for God, and you were greater than my loyalty to him. He got angry but later said he understood. I love him, but I am not sure if I trust him. Just beware sister, just be aware. I know Carlos will keep you safe. Go to him. He is the only person I entrust you to. Don't cry for me; don't be sad, because I am home and we will be reunited again. Inside you will find a photo of our father. I hoped I would live long enough to take you to him. I just want you to be safe. I have left you some money; it's enough to get out of Georgia. The pocket Bible is for you to carry always. You need God; please serve Him. The necklace is an engraved cross to remind you that Christ and I are with you always; you are never alone. I told you wrong when I said not to trust anyone, especially cops. There are good and bad people all over; listen to that inner voice that speaks and follow. I love you, my dear sister. I am sorry, but know you never walk alone for He is with you even until the end of the world. Be good, and remember I am always in your heart---Love, Deek

She read it three times. She had not known he went back to church. Why did he want her to see this on her birthday? Did he think he would live until then? Did he know Angelo would hurt him? She wished she had known this all before. She pulled out the photo and saw her daddy for the first time. He did look like them...or they looked like him. It was him and a younger Deek. There were several of Olivia and Deek; they were all her favorites. She loved him even more for thinking of her. She opened the envelope and could not believe her eyes. There were several crisp hundred-dollar bills. He had thought of everything. She took the Bible out next; she could tell he had read it repeatedly. There were smudged fingerprints. He believed, and he believed that she would too. He wanted to secure her soul. Now it was safe, and she hoped that they would see one another again. Lastly, she opened the necklace; there was his birthstone, a diamond in the middle, and engraved with his favorite Bible verse: Joshua 1:9 NIV, "Have I not commanded you? Be strong and courageous. Do not be afraid; do not be discouraged, for the LORD your God will be with you wherever you go." Derrick Obadiah Morris, you are so wonderfully brilliant. I should have known you would have never left me unprepared. I love you, brother. I am all right now. Now I know you are too," she said to herself. She prayed and then went to brush her teeth and share with the Hoover family what her brother had given her. It brought tears to their eyes as it had hers. "He has been watching all this time. Even beyond his grave, he came back to make sure I was all right. I think this is the best birthday I have ever had. Thank you all for wanting me and showing me how to love and how to forgive," she said. She wanted to return to Derrick's grave and just send him her love. She wanted to return to him. She missed him so dearly.

**

"SURPRISE," Everyone yelled as they arrived back from the bowling alley. She jumped because she had not expected it. There was not one car in the driveway. Everyone from church was there: Ms. Geter and Mr. D and Det. Davis and Det. Greene and their families. She thought that was very kind of them. She hugged her new friends and finally found Jacoby back near the food. "Happy sweet 16, to the sweetest girl I know," he said kissing her cheek and handing her a rose.

She blushed and he smiled. "Come on, I get the first dance with you," he said pulling her out to dance.

"I don't dance," she said following him.

"You forget. I saw your cheerleading moves," he said smiling. "Besides there is no need to be shy; we're among family and friends."

She nodded in agreement, and two stepped.

"Where'd you get that lovely necklace?" he asked.

"I wanted to call and share it with you and Miguel. It is from Deek. I think he knew Angelo was coming after him, because he told him he loved God and me more than him. I have to show you," she said pulling him off the dance floor and to an empty table. Mrs. Hoover and Victoria had bought her an expensive handbag, a Dooney and Bourke. She had put everything her brother had given to her in it. She shared it with Jacoby. He read the letter; his eyes dampened, but he did not cry. "Your brother was a really good guy. That is love. I can't wait to meet him, you know, when the rapture occurs. You both favor your dad," he said looking through the pictures.

"Yeah, we do. My brother said that was why my mama disliked me," she said.

"No, your mom just didn't know God. It was the drugs talking, not her. You are too lovable. Do you think you are going to look for your father?" he asked. Somehow the idea of her leaving made him nervous. He finally was able to see her nearly every day; they were good friends, and he didn't want to lose her or how he felt when he was around her. He really liked Livvy.

She was still stuck on being loveable. "No, I found one right here," she said looking at Det. Hoover, who was doing the electric slide. He did it well.

Jacoby smiled. "Good, because I don't want to lose you again," he confessed.

She dropped her head in embarrassment. He placed her hand in his. "I like you, Livvy. I hope you have many more lovely birthdays and no sadder days. When you smile...when you are happy...it is magnetic and I feel good inside," he said.

"Jacoby, stop flirting with me. You are making me blush," she said. But she was still smiling.

"I can't," He said laughing. He found it funny that she blushed around him all the time; he kind of liked it. She was so cute when she was embarrassed. "Come on, I want to see you blow out the candles," he said still holding her hand. She walked over to the table, they sang, and she blew. She only wished for more days like this. "Thank you, God, for hearing my cry," she said inwardly. Olivia hoped this was the beginning of life. She finally had a family, a birthday, a place to relax, and people who she could trust. She was no longer bound to the past misery that bound her. Her brother and Lilly were now angels her eyes could not see; but her heart could feel them forever. They were together. He was there every step of the way. She found peace in that knowledge.

CHAPTER 14

The Good Life

The water felt healing as she was dipped. She knew some people got baptized and just become a wet devil, but she was a saved soul. Dinah Olivia Morris, the girl who had lost everything...at least so she thought...went from one imprisonment to another and now she was free. She belonged to the One, and he reigned in her. She liked that. She saw Mr. and Mrs. Hoover crying, as well as Mr. Douglas and Ms. Geter. She felt loved. The purifying water washed it all away. Every bad thing had been forgotten. She was ecstatic. She was home at last; it had taken her sixteen years to find a home. She was so glad to have it. Things would only get better. She would only grow stronger. This was what she wanted so long ago, and now she had it. She could not wait for life to continue because finally she was living the good life...a Christian life. It made her feel invincible and no longer invisible. She wanted everyone to see the Jesus in her! Her life was so empty and incomplete; it was by the grace of God she was here. Indeed, he had a plan for her, and she would fulfill it. Her thoughts continued even as Victoria and she chatted with excitement about going to school.

"You are going to love this school, Livvy. I mean it's like all the people we attend church with, so it's just extended family," she said smiling. Her excitement was contagious. She cleaned up the last of her food and went up to her bedroom to finish getting dressed. That was easy because they had uniforms. Friday was a free day, and as long as it was modest, they could wear any outfit they wanted. They could wear their cheerleader uniforms as long as there were pants worn underneath the skirt, and a shirt worn underneath the top; that was fine with Olivia. She did not like baring all her skin.

Victoria was in strings and played the violin. She was good. Olivia enjoyed listening to her practice. They would ride to school together. But after school Olivia had gymnastics and cheerleading, and Victoria had her music practice. She also played the harp in church. She was very musically talented. If it were up to Olivia, she would prefer walking to school; Victoria insisted they ride together.

Olivia put on her lip gloss and ran down the stairs. Mr. and Mrs. Hoover kissed and hugged them, and they were out the door. Olivia's stomach instantly felt like butterflies were flying but she did not know why. She knew most of these kids, and she had no reason to be nervous. There were no bullets, pimps, or drunks to dodge; there was no Angelo to worry about. She took a deep breath, listened to the music, and slowly her nervousness disappeared. Victoria walked her to homeroom class and then disappeared to her own. Olivia sat down in front and glanced out of the window; then she felt a tap on her shoulder. She turned around, and there was Jacoby. He smiled and sat right beside her. "I am glad you are here. I don't know some of these kids," she whispered.

"I am glad you are here, too. Let me see your schedule to see if we have any other classes," he asked.

Olivia reached in her book bag and handed it to him. He reviewed it and then handed it back. "We have all the same honors classes, except math," he said.

"Good, I will tutor you in math; next year we can have all the same classes," she said with a smile, which he returned. Then they focused back on the teacher, as the tardy bell rang. Mrs. Kirkpatrick opened up in prayer and then asked each person to introduce themselves. Olivia knew five other people besides Jacoby: Caroline, Destiny, Caleb, and David. She liked them all, so she was happy to have them in her homeroom. Classes went by smoothly. She liked all of her teachers, though her math teacher was not as cool as Mr. Douglas. She was really sweet. When she found out how much Olivia loved math, she made her an assistant. She hoped no one thought she was a teacher's pet, but numbers just made her feel felicitous.

Since Victoria had practice and she did not, Jacoby took her home. Their practices started next week. He played football in the fall and basketball in the spring. She was contemplating going out for the soccer team. She just always thought soccer players were neat. Her brother said he'd prefer she played basketball, but she did not like that sport. She like watching Jacoby and his friends play, even seeing Miguel and Det. Hoover, but it was not something she like participating in. She guessed she was a better cheerleader than actual player.

"How was your first day?" Jacoby asked as they pulled up to his house. Since Det. Hoover and Mrs. Hoover both were at work, she went to his house. His mother was home. It was one of their house rules, since no one had found Angelo yet. She did not mind. Mrs. Castillo was super sweet, and it was easy for her to tutor Jacoby. She would walk home later. She liked to walk.

"Great. You spent most of it with me...just not math. I love it. I really like the teachers. Ms. Coffer made me her assistant in math class today," she said.

He playfully rolled his eyes. "Oh no, you are a teacher's pet already. See I told you that you are just lovable," he said teasing her.

"I can't help it," she laughed.

He opened the door for her, and they walked in; the house smelled so good. Mrs. Castillo had made them an after-school snack, and Olivia started pulling out the math books. "Jacoby, I went to the library and got some of these books to help you with your math," she said spreading them on the table.

He looked at her in disbelief. She wasted no time getting down to the business. "You are a task master. Can I at least eat and drink something first?" he asked.

"Oh, sure. But you can do both. We can do math right now with those cookies," she said reaching for one.

He waved his hand to stop her. "No, please. Just let the cookies, be cookies. I will never enjoy an Oreo or Chips Ahoy again," he pretended to cry.

She giggled. "Fine, then. We will eat and then work," she said sitting down and requesting he pour her a glass of chocolate milk.

Mrs. Castillo watched this all-in amazement. She thought that Livvy was a good influence on Jacoby. He needed someone like her in his life. "Jacoby, I like Olivia. With her around, you will do your homework at a decent hour," his mother said with a smile. They all laughed.

Sitting at Jacoby's house and laughing made Olivia feel normal, and she was having a good time. It was almost unreal. She read about this in books and saw it on television. But she never thought she would ever get to live it. Finally, she was able to be a child and have a childhood; she relished every second of it.

The walk home was brief but pleasant. She declined Jacoby's offer to drive her because it was a ten-minute walk. So, he walked her home instead. She thought it was nice of him. He was a gentleman; he was sweet, like Deek.

Jacoby had something he wanted to ask Olivia. He had been tossing it over and over in his head. The last time he asked her out, his life was threatened. But at least Mr. Hoover and Vincent liked him, so he had a better shot this time. "Livvy, do you think you would like to go out with me on a date to the bowling alley Saturday night," he asked.

She smiled and looked at him. He was not shy one bit—at least not now. He was bold and confident. At least she thought so. She really had not gone out on a date, and the thought of that was exciting for her. "I would, but you have to ask Mr. or Mrs. Hoover. I think Victoria has to come. Being sixteen, the rule is group dating," she said.

"Good. I thought you were going to say I had to bring my mom or Mrs. Hoover. I can deal with Victoria," he said reaching out for her hand.

She offered it with little hesitation. "You are really sweet to me. I appreciate it," she said.

Her willingness made him smile. "Thanks. It must be you. You seem to bring out the best in me," he replied.

She giggled a little and they walked to the porch; Mrs. Hoover was sitting in the rocking chair listening to Victoria play. "There she is. Hey, sweetheart. Hello, Jacoby. Tell me, how was school?" she asked them both.

They told her, and Jacoby sat down for a few minutes. She guessed he was mustering his courage. "Mrs. Hoover, may I take Olivia out Saturday to the bowling alley?" he asked.

"Yes, you can. I speak for my husband as well. I think that is nice. Will there be a group of you?" she asked.

"Livvy explained to me that you have a rule that Victoria had to go too. But if she can't, I can have my cousin come," he said.

"That is fine with me," she said.

"Thank you, ma'am. Goodnight, y'all. I will see you tomorrow, Livvy," he said with a smile; she watched him walk back home.

"He is such a nice young man, Livvy. I like him," Mrs. Hoover said.

"I like him also," Victoria said smiling at her.

Olivia did not say anything. She just blushed and walked inside to wash up for supper.

***

Saturday came, and Victoria was kind enough to do Olivia's hair and help her find a cute outfit to wear. They spent the majority of the day in the mall getting pampered. Olivia received her first and last manicure and pedicure; it just did not seem practical to her. That was one thing that was the same in the suburbs as well as the hood; women had to get their hair, eyebrows, and nails done. She did not like it then, and she was not fond of it now. Olivia refused to let them give her false nails, but she did let them decorate her toes. After that, they headed back home to get dressed. It was an early date; he was to be at her house at 7:00 and have her back home at 10:00. They were triple dating—Jacoby and Olivia, Victoria and Phillip, and Jacoby's cousin Hector and his date Tania—but they were meeting some of their youth group as well. Olivia was happy to have somewhere to go. It did not bother her if it had to be supervised. Anything was better than being left alone or being followed by BWD and Angelo. "You look lovely," Victoria said to her.

"Thank you, and you do as well," Olivia said.

They walked down the stairs together and went into the den to show off their new outfits. "How do we look?" Olivia asked Mr. and Mrs. Hoover.

"Well, absolutely lovely. I think I am going to have to show off my gun collection today," He said with a chuckle.

They all laughed too and would have continued to chat if not for the doorbell ringing. Olivia peeked out the window and saw both Phillip and Jacoby at the door.

Det. Hoover went to answer it, and the girls were right behind. "Okay, fellows. Here are the rules. Have my girls back in this house at 10:00. There is to be no kissing, sensual physical touching, or sneaking off," he said sternly. "Do we have an understanding? I do know your fathers and where each of you lives. I am a cop, so you know how it goes," he said peering at the young men about to take his girls out.

"Yes, sir. We do. We will abide by the rules, sir," they said looking somewhat scared. He did have an extensive gun collection.

"Daddy, can we go now?" Victoria asked.

"Yes. But you both must give me a hug," he requested.

They did, and then left. He watched them go and smiled. It was good to see Olivia being a teenager. He loved to see her eyes sparkle.

***

Angelo paced back and forth as he waited for Detective Paul Davis to meet him inside the warehouse was, he was lying low. No one came to the shadows; it was a bad place to be, but Angelo was a bad man. He knew no fear. After the murder of Leah, things began to get a little rough. He had been on a rollercoaster for the past eight or nine months. It all went wrong when Avery killed Deek instead of just attacking him. It was not supposed to be a kill shot; the only good thing that happened was that it made it easier for him to get Olivia. It would have been impossible with Deek alive, but he'd rather have things as they used to be than to have Deek dead. Things went so wrong quickly after Avery got killed. Leah had to go because she took Olivia from him and almost got him arrested. She was messing with his money, his girl, and his product; she signed her own death warrant. But he broke his own rule: never kill continuously. Now in less than one year, three people had died that were linked to him; it was bringing more heat to his area. His Uncle Luis was beyond pissed off. He had to return back to Colombia soon. His boys were in disorder; he told them all to lay low. The streets had grown eerily quiet. That would remain until he lifted the order, but he had to let the rival gangs know he was still in charge. They had to talk in code and use messengers—not technology that was easy to hack. They used prepaid cell phones, sent letters in code that were then burned afterwards, and placed ads in the local newspapers to give their location. He had made sure not to leave behind any evidence to link him to anything criminal. Olivia was the only danger. But being that she had two years left on her sentence, he was not worried about her talking. The humming of an engine drew his attention, and he placed his hand on his gun as he went to investigate to see who had driven up. He peeked out the window and confirmed that it was Det. Davis. He eased his grip on the gun and walked to the door to let him enter.

"Yo, Davis...over here," he whispered.

Det. Davis eased inside unnoticed. He looked around the facility, seeing that they were not alone. He wondered if he had made the right decision. He was behind on his mortgage, and his son had become ill. He needed the money that Angelo was offering, but it felt more like he was selling his soul to the devil. How had he become this man? He loathed men who did things like this. Yet, here he was being the man he hated. It was far too late to turn back now.

"Well, Davis. Tell me what I need to know," he said.

"The police don't know where you are. We are working on a lead that says you are hiding in Texas. As far as the murders go, no one has linked you. But the general assumption is that it is gang related. The cops have you listed as a person of interest. Now is the time to flee," he said, as sweat was now kissing every part of his exposed and unexposed body; his heart and pulse were beating uncontrollably.

Angelo watched him like a hawk. He liked seeing a cop shake before him. It made him feel powerful. The things that money could buy were limitless. His Uncle Luis told him that men were easy...so very easy. Just about anyone would do anything for the right price. "All right, but what about Livvy? How is lock up treating her? After her cellmate killed herself, I thought she might lose it for a while," he said concerned.

He thought for a moment as how to respond. If he lied, he would certainly die. His throat almost closed up as he debated what to say. He was not sure if Angelo knew it or not. "Don't you know about her?" he asked.

Angelo looked at Det. Davis as if he were an idiot. He was beginning to wonder how this guy became a detective. "Nah. If I knew, I would not be asking you. Where she at?" he demanded?

Davis let out a sigh. "They released her. She is part of a pilot program that is rehabilitating offenders who are showing good behavior. She has a lot of people on her side. Everyone felt like she got a raw deal. She's living with a host family and attending school," he said.

"What?" Angelo said beginning to pace again. He received a letter from her every week. Not once had she told him about being released. This deeply concerned him. Did she talk? How had this come about? Had they turned her against him? He recalled the last time they spoke when she dared him to kill her. He should have known then that something was not right. But how had this occurred without his knowledge? He rubbed his chin as he contemplated what to do next.

"It was something her teachers worked out for her. Lillian was supposed to be released as well, but you know what she did. It had a terrible impact on Livvy. She had to be hospitalized; but you knew that," he said.

Anger erupted inside of Angelo, and he tried to restrain himself. "Davis, is she talking to the police? How long has she been in this new life? I thought she was locked up. How does that happen?" His questions were somewhat rhetorical, but his mind began to wander. What was she doing? Who was she with? He wanted her back.

"I want you to bring her to me," he demanded. There was no way he was allowing another to take what was his. Olivia belonged to him.

Angelo was asking him to do the impossible. "Angelo, I can't do that. She is living with a police family in a police neighborhood. There is no way I can just pick her up without anyone noticing," he said with more emotion than he wanted to show. He was already paranoid, and now Angelo wanted him to abduct her. That was a suicide mission.

Angelo smirked. No one told him what they could not and would not do. That was not ever a possibility. He would do it. "Davis, I pay you good money to let me know what is going on. You are just now telling me my girl is free and living with the police. You bring her to me. I don't care how you do it or who you kill; I want Olivia. I will not hesitate to kill to get her. Be gone from my sight. Dough, give this man half his money. You can get the other half when I get Knockout back," he said and ushered him out the door. The news floored him.

The idea of having to take her was beyond anything he ever thought he would have to do. He regretted getting himself involved in this. "It'll take some time. I have to earn her trust," he said as they bounced him out with only half the money. He walked swiftly back to his car and left; his mind was running fast trying to come up with some way to lure Olivia without her being suspicious.

"Make it happen," he growled and then turned his attention back to Dough. "Dough, do you hear that? They been playing me. Knockout been released, and I thought she was still imprisoned. I got to find Carlos. Man, he will not believe this," he said.

"I know, Boss. I thought he was lying at first. I mean, that is way too strange. I got an insider. I'll see what the deal is," he said.

Angelo went back to the area he had converted into a bedroom and began to think. His world seemed to be caving in around him. This was not how kings lived, and this was not how he would live. What would his Uncle Luis do in a situation like this? It was all Leah's fault; no, it was Deuce's fault. He had to go and find God. He made his choice. He still recalled the night Deek came to him and said, "I love God and my sister more than this gang. I love you like my brother, but I can't teach my sister one thing and live contrary to my own words. She needs me more than you, and all I ask is that you let me go. I have been loyal to you. I would never snitch about what we done to the police, but I need to raise Livvy right. She needs a chance to live and be a kid. Too many men had stolen from her. As her brother, I have to be the one man that does right by her. Grant me a green light so I can go." If he had allowed Deek to walk away unchecked, wouldn't the rest follow? He had given Deek everything. What had God done for Deek? God gave him a runaway father, a crack addicted abusive mother, and a sister who was passed around to her mother's boyfriends like a bowl of popcorn. Deek still chose God over him? He chose God, when it was Angelo who had given him life? He said he was loyal. It made no sense to Angelo. He stopped believing in God a long time ago. His mother had died from cancer, leaving him and his younger brother to be raised by a father who lived by the codes for the street. He was the Godfather—the founder, the Don that founded Blanco Wild Deuces—and he was tough. He loved the power his father had. Women would drop at his feet; men wanted to imitate his style and be like him. He got killed in a shootout with a rival small-time gang: the Red Hoodlums. Seeking revenge, Angelo murdered and maimed as many as he could. The rest fled or pledged alliance to his gang. Those were the ones he used as bait until they were killed out. That was the life he knew; he was his own god. He had the power to decide life and death and only him. He was not ready to leave Olivia. She was his, whether she wanted to be or not. It was never an option. He had been waiting for his time. Now having her so young, he could mold and shape her into whatever he wanted her to be. He wanted to make her the mother of his children so that the BWD would never die. He would pass it on to them. He had to for his family as his father had done for him and his brother. But a year after his dad died, so did Cesar, his brother. He was in a car chase with the police. They shot his tires; he lost control, hit a tree, got ejected, and died on the scene. The police thought it was him. They wanted Angelo, not Cesar; he was a brain, like Livvy. Cesar was not a gangster; he loathed that lifestyle. After the police killed his brother, he truly hated those ravenous pigs. They were no different from him; they were just legalized murderers, and they judged him. It irritated him how they were seen as the heroes and he was seen as the villain. He lived in the hood; he saw the tragedy and lived the life. His gang was created to protect his neighborhood and give family to those who had none. The drugs, the sex, the trafficking, the illegal activity occurred because they needed money; it was how his family maintained their empire in Colombia. He only wanted what the good ole rich had: power, respect, and money; that's all you needed in life. He had that and would maintain it by any monstrous means necessary. Everybody had a choice, and his homies chose to follow him. They liked the lifestyle, and it was a lifetime commitment—one that allowed luxuries that they had all grown accustomed to. They weren't a gang that had a negative connotation; they were family and an organization of blood brothers. That is what the FBI, CIA, ATF, DEA, government officials, and police did not understand. You have to stand for something, or you will fall for anything; his father had drilled that into him until he died. He was a teenager when he inherited his father's kingdom; and he ruled it well. Blanco Wild Deuces were advancing and multiplying from North America to South America. They would be the new world order, and Olivia would be by his side. As he soothed himself with these thoughts, he fell asleep with a smile on his face.

CHAPTER 15

Letting Go of Fear

"Three months of school down," Olivia mused as she marked off another day. Now she could not wait for the day to start because of her great core of friends; she felt safe and comfortable. It was good not to live in fear anymore; Lilly would have been very proud of her. Today was her first day of work at Mrs. Hoover's twin brother's car lot. He owed new and used car lots that were right beside one another, and he was in need of a bookkeeper. When he found out she was good with numbers, he offered her the job. Since she had school, she worked part time; but he told her she could work full time during holidays and the summer. The best part about the job was that she got to choose a car from the new lot. After Mrs. Hoover picked her up from cheerleading practice, she was talking a mile a minute about the kind of car she'd like to have. As soon as they arrived, she made a beeline for the cars. Up and down the rows she walked, looking at each of them. She stopped in front of the Camaro, and Victor quickly joined her. The Chevrolet Camaro convertible ZL1 in blue was sleek, fast, and pretty. It was a stick shift. She guessed someone was going to have to show her how to change gears. She wanted it. "Can I have this one?" she asked Victor.

A warm smile spread across his face, as he saw how animated she had become. "You have good taste. I think we can do that. Do you want it tricked out like Tori's car?" he asked.

"Um, no. I like it as is...I mean unless you think I should. I am still in shock because you are letting me have a car," she said walking around it and still in awe that this was hers. Deek would have loved this car. He would have had a thrill riding around the hood in something like this.

"I'll make sure it has all the bells and whistles you need. I will have it ready by the end of the week," he said smiling.

She nodded and followed him inside to the office to start working. It was hard for her to focus, as thoughts of having her very own car kept breaking her concentration. She could drive anywhere, and there would be no Angelo hovering over her every move. The Hoovers were so good to her, and she was happy; she felt like a child. She had people who actually cared about her. They came to see her cheerleading competitions and never missed a football game, they went to the PTO meetings, and they took care of her. She had never known what it was like to have a mother until she met Mrs. Hoover. It was the most welcoming beautiful feeling. She cried the first week because she saw what she had missed for fifteen years and what Deek had missed; love, family, discipline, wisdom...their mama and daddy had denied them everything. She hoped when he was alive that she had given him the same amount of love and joy he had given to her; it made her feel sad to think she was taking his love and not offering him her love. Now, she looked forward to waking up each morning and seeing Victoria and her parents. The weekends were especially fun when Vincent and his friends came to visit. All her life she longed for quiet and to be invisible. But now with the Hoovers, she wanted to be wherever they were. She finally had no fear—no fear of rejection, no fear of abuse, and no fear of feeling unworthy. She was thankful that God was showing her how good life is. Living with the Hoovers was inspirational.

**

"Are you ready to go?" Mrs. Hoover asked her. Olivia had just finished doing the payroll.

"Hey, I sure am. Did Victor show you the car I chose?" she asked as she picked up her book bag and followed her through the employee exit.

"He pointed it out to me. Are you comfortable driving that? It is lovely," she said smiling at her.

"I can handle it...well...as soon as you teach me how to change gears," she said with a playful smile.

"I'll let Tim teach you that. I get too nervous. He taught Vinnie and Tori. Well, we better be getting home. We are having the Castillo's over for supper tonight," she said winking at Olivia.

Everyone was teasing her about Jacoby, but they were friends. She preferred it that way, because she was not ready to have a boyfriend. Her life was so different from the life that Jacoby lived. "Cool," she said ignoring her teasing. Mrs. Hoover handed Olivia the keys and let her drive home. She dropped her book bag on her bedroom floor and quickly returned downstairs to help with preparation. She was eager to talk with Mrs. Hoover and Victoria about her idea of returning to Hollow Hill and showing her old neighborhood the goodness of God. She wanted to take what she had learned and apply it to the hood. The thing that was lacking there was hope. People needed to know that they were not forgotten and that, even in the darkest storms, the light of hope was still shining. "Mrs. Hoover, I was thinking about going back to Hollow Hill and doing a long-term mission; I'd like to transform it from hood to neighborhood again," she said with a smile.

"That is a good idea," Victoria said as she tossed the salad.

"Well, I admire you wanting to return back to Hollow Hill and share the Good News. You should share that with Timothy as well," she said with a smile.

"Okay, I will when he comes home. It should be safe now since Angelo is gone," she said placing the plates, napkins, and silverware on the table.

"I think you are brave wanting to go back. I don't think I could do it," Victoria said looking at her.

"I'm not afraid anymore. I feel I would be a coward and selfish to stay here and not give back to my community. How can I be given the gift of God's love and not share it with people who feel forgotten and are afraid to leave their home because they might get killed in the streets. I have to; I have to go back," she said.

"I love you, Livvy. You have such a good heart. I will be glad to help you," she said and walked over to give Livvy a hug. While they were embracing, they heard a key turn in the lock. Five seconds later, Det. Hoover was walking into the kitchen.

"Hey. How are my favorite ladies?" he asked as he walked over to kiss his wife and hug Victoria and Olivia.

"Tim, Olivia has a lot of things to tell you," Vivian said smiling at her.

She was so giddy. "I do. I chose a car today, a Chevrolet Camaro. But I need you to teach me how to drive a stick shift," She said with a smile, "Also I was wondering if I could go back to Hollow Hill and do a long-term mission...like open a community center for the kids.

He was impressed by her enthusiasm. She was eager to share her faith, and he loved that. She was definitely growing, and it was encouraging. "Wow. Well, that is all very exciting. I will teach you how to drive the car. Having a mission in Hollow Hill is needed. I think we should talk with your youth pastor and go for it. I will support you 100 percent in any way I can," he said smiling at her.

Olivia's head was swirling with ideas. She could not wait to start. "Awesome. I can't wait. I should probably call Pastor Eric right now and talk it over with him," she said feeling on fire.

"Honey, wait until after dinner," Mrs. Hoover said. "As a matter of fact, will you check to see if the Castillo's are out here?"

She walked to the door and saw them pulling up. She opened the door, waving at them and then greeting them with a smile and hug. She was happy to see that Miguel had come too. Alexi was not with him, but she was glad to see him all the same. She welcomed them inside and could not help but tell Jacoby about her car. She did not even allow him to sit down before she began to talk. He smiled and said he wanted to have the first ride. They all sat down and just talked about fifteen minutes until Victoria told them it was time to eat. She enjoyed eating Vivian's food. She was a good...no, great...cook. That woman could make cauliflower taste like cake. Victoria was learning how to do the same. It smelled so good. Olivia volunteered to say grace, and then they started eating. As a nice little general conversation went on amongst the adults, Olivia shared with Miguel and Jacoby her idea for Hollow Hill. They both volunteered to help in any way they could. She was thankful for their help.

***

"Boss, this is what I found out. Knockout is part of some kind of restoration program. They are supposedly rehabilitating the lesser aggressive inmates so that they can have a more productive life. If she does it successfully, they will drop all charges. I think there is like a total of five girls and three guys doing this. Also, she was really friendly with a Miguel Castillo. All I know on him is that he is a CO who is almost done with his year, and then I guess he'll go to whatever. Det. Davis was on the up with that information. I found Carlos. He's doing what you told him to do, but he said he was not sure where they took Livvy. Being the investigator, I am, I found she lives with one of those homicide detectives...uh...Hoover is his name," Dough said with pride. It had taken him a few weeks to gather that information, and he thought he had done a good job—one that would serve to promote him to more responsibility.

Angelo listened intently and began trying to think of the best way to take back his property and to leave the country. "You saw her?" he asked.

"Yeah. She attends a private school. As a matter of fact, I have some pictures. Check these out," he said placing the digital camera in front of him. He liked that neighborhood. The people there were much friendlier than residents of the Hallow.

Angelo's heart softened as he looked at her. She was thinner and leaner. She was just as beautiful—if not even more attractive—than she was the last time he had seen her. He missed her. He longed to have her in his arms. She belonged to him. He had promised Deek he would keep her close, and he never broke a promise. "Dough, she looks good, so...um...who is this guy?" he asked.

Dough bent down and looked at the guy he was pointing at. "Boss, I don't know. He looked like that dude you jacked up that time. I can't confirm," Dough said.

He shook his head disapprovingly. "It don't matter. I just need to know her schedule and see when we can get her. You talked to Det. Davis lately? I can't deal with him. He kind of makes me uneasy, like he scared or something. How you going to be hard and be scared all at once?" Angelo said.

Dough wasn't sure if he wanted an answer or not. "I don't know, Boss. Look, they hit some of the stash houses, so we working overtime trying to set-up a new location. Carlos said he would handle it. We did lose at least two. I think Leah must have told before we could hush her up. I sho' miss Deuce at times like these. He was a soldier," Dough said.

126

Angelo nodded his head in agreement. "He was. True that. I bet she did. Livvy would not tell for nothing. Look, save what you can, keep recruiting, and keep close," he said.

"It's done, Boss. What you want me to do about Knockout?" he asked.

"Nothing. I am going to address that personally. You just get with Carlos and help him in whatever he needs. Tell him to contact me. Take that chick with you; she has served her purpose," he ordered.

"Will do," he said and retreated.

Now alone, Angelo stared into the emptiness. He hated losing money and product. He felt extremely uncomfortable with Olivia living with the enemy. He felt like when he visited her the last time there was anger in her eyes toward him, but she had to understand it was for her own good. The hostility in her voice had angered him, as she suggested that he had killed Deek. That was not true. He loved him like a brother; he just wanted him to stay in the gang. Leah and Avery killed themselves. They broke the rules and knew the repercussions of violating a direct order.

He only intended to scare Lilly, but the suicide had nothing to do with him. That chick already had issues that did not pertain to him. No one was going to put extra blood on his hands. He knew what he was and was not guilty of. It angered him that she was putting ideas in Livvy's head. He did not like that. Now he had to prove to Livvy that he loved her and had not betrayed her. She was different and approaching her was different. Unlike the skanks and whores, he truly had an affinity for her. It was hard for him to show her the affection and attention she needed when he had an empire to tend to. Things would work out as soon as he could get her back and take her with him—out of the country—away from prying eyes and nosy idiots who did not understand their culture and way of life.

It was time to go back to Colombia. She would see things his way; he just had to make her remember. No matter what, he did not have Deek killed. He just wanted to scare him into submission. He too wanted to know why Deek had gotten murdered and not beaten like he had instructed, but Avery was dead before he could even question him. That bothered him, and he wondered if someone in his crew was undermining his authority. But who? Now was the time to start eliminating loose ends. He would not hesitate to kill anyone he felt threatened his empire. He sat back down and began to play some music.

He needed to calm down so that he could think more clearly. He picked up the camera and flipped through the pictures of Olivia. A warm feeling of distaste swept over him as he realized she was with Det. Timothy Hoover; the same detective that said he would have him arrested for statutory rape. He might have to pay with his life for that empty threat. There was only one boss, and that was him. No one could have Olivia except for him. He would find out everything; it was time to test Det.

Davis's loyalty and usefulness. If he failed to come through, then he would pay for his mistake with his life. It was time for him to be seen again. Angelo hid from no man, he thought to himself. He got his belongings and left the safety of the warehouse.

***

"So, Livvy. Do you really think this will look good on me?" Victoria asked looking at herself in the mirror at the department store.

"I do, and I think your dad would approve. It's stylish and modest. I think red is your color," Livvy said. It was an outfit with a lovely sweater top and nice cream pants.

"Okay. I think I am going to get the entire outfit. Are you getting anything?" she asked as she walked back into the dressing room to change her clothing.

Olivia thought for a moment. There really was not anything that she liked. Besides, they wore uniforms to school except on game days. Mrs. and Mr. Hoover had bought her Sunday outfits, and she rarely wore anything else. She liked jeans and t-shirts...nothing that caused a lot of attention. It was because of all the unwanted attention she had received in her young life. She wanted to blend in and not stand out. Guys at school and Jacoby were noticing her, and she did not like it so much. They were nice, cool guys, but they were seniors. Unlike her friends, getting attention from older guys did not give her a rush. She did not care about being noticed by the star quarterback or the soccer team captain. It was not of any interest to her. "I don't need anything, really. Your mom brought me a box of all my old clothing from Angelo's, and we went through and found out what I could keep and what I could not. So, I like doubled my wardrobe. Uncle Victor does not mind me wearing my school clothes, so I don't need anything. Once we are done, can we go to the pretzel shop?" she asked waiting for her to come out.

She popped out the door and they walked to the register. "Yeah. I think we should. I bet some of our friends will be there too," she said smiling. "Maybe we can go to a movie, too...like later tonight," she said.

"It sounds good, as long as your parents' are cool with it," Olivia said watching the sales clerk ring up the purchase and place the outfit in the bag.

"They will. They are your parents, too. Besides, I get to do a lot more now that I have a sister. Mom is not as hesitant when it is the two of us," she said smiling.

Tori just wanted to be with her boyfriend. Olivia could see the sparkle in her eyes. She did not mind. Phillip was really nice young man; Livvy liked him too. He and Jacoby were friendly as well. They headed out the store giggling and talking, until they walked to the end of the plaza to the pretzel shop. They saw Neligh and Destiny sitting at the far right. They spoke to them and then went to order. They sat back down with their friends and started to talk.

Olivia glanced out the window and did a double take. She thought she saw Angelo's Escalade, but that could not be possible. Her mind must be playing games. A lot of people purchased Escalades; there was no reason for her to assume it was Angelo. Besides the police were searching for him in another place. She shook off the thought and returned to the conversation. After a half an hour, they said goodbye and went back home. Olivia was kind of tired and wanted to lounge and finish up her presentation for helping Hallow Hood become a neighborhood. She was thinking of calling it SOS—Save Our Souls. She needed something catchy that would spark interest. Most of it was done; all she needed to do now was meet with the local churches and assign roles.

"Olivia, do you want to go to the seven o'clock showing?" Victoria asked her sister.

Olivia nodded in agreement smiled; then she ran back into her room. Livvy thought it was sweet how excited she was over Phillip. She had a good four hours to kill, and she wanted to visit her brother's grave. She walked downstairs to ask Mrs. Hoover for permission to leave. She said it was fine but asked her to stop by the station to drop off Det. Hoover's lunch. The police station was on the way. She liked being able to come and go there without being handcuffed and hauled into one of those rooms. The idea of it brought sweat to her face. She grabbed the bag, walked to her car, and drove to the station. It looked less intimidating now that she was entering of her own free will and not being directed by an officer.

"Hey, Livvy. What are you doing here?"

She turned toward the voice and then smiled. It was Miguel. "Hey. I am dropping off Mr. Hoover's lunch. Then I am going to see my brother. How are things going at DJJ?" she asked walking toward him.

"I'm done; I start working with the gang unit tomorrow. I'm excited," he said smiling.

"Congratulations!" she said hugging him.

"Thank you. Are you and my brother hanging out tonight?" he asked.

She blushed a little at his question. "I am the chaperon for Victoria and Phillip tonight. Jacoby has a busy schedule, so we won't be hanging out; we both have things to get done this weekend," she said.

He smiled at her as if he wanted to ask more. She hoped he did not. She was having mixed feelings about Jacoby and having more than just a friendship. She was not ready for a courtship. She wanted to do other things that had been denied her.

"All right. You have a good day. I will see you at church," he said offering her another hug and walking away.

She walked through the double doors, waved at Panetta, and took the elevator to the fifth floor. She saw no familiar face; she looked to make sure she was on the right floor. She walked past the first group of cubicles undetected. When she came to the second set, a young officer bumped into her. He dropped the papers he had in his hand, and she bent down to pick them up.

"Excuse me, miss. Are you alright?" he asked.

She nodded. "I am. But can you tell me where Det. Hoover is?" she asked.

"Yes, ma'am. You can follow me," he said with a kind smile. She followed him to the very back of the room, turned down a hall, and then walked to the left. There he was, sitting at his desk talking to Det. Alan Greene. The young officer knocked on the door and left her.

"Hey, sweetheart. What are you doing here?" he asked getting up from his desk. Det. Greene smiled and waved at her, and she waved back.

She smiled at them both. "I came to bring you lunch," she said.

"Thank you. Are you visiting for a while or is this a drop and go?" he asked.

"I was heading to the cemetery to visit my brother's grave," she said.

"Oh. Well is Victoria with you?" he asked looking back down the hall.

"No, sir. She is back at home. I am riding solo today," she said.

His eyes looked worried. "Honey, I have no problem with you going to see your brother or going back to Hollow Hill, but I think you shouldn't go alone. We don't have all of the high rollers in BWD, and it would be irresponsible of me to allow you to go alone," he finished.

She twisted her lower lip. She knew he was concerned, but she would be careful. "It's okay. He is buried near here not in Hollow Hill," she said, as she understood his concern. She felt safe.

"Tim, let her go. She has a cell phone, pepper spray, and a stun gun. She can take care of herself," Det. Greene chimed in.

He looked as if he really did not want to. "You call me when you get there and call me when you leave; just be careful," he said uneasily.

"Yes, sir. I will be fine," she said offering him a hug and waving goodbye.

He watched until she was out of ear shot and quickly called patrol to follow her to make sure she was safe. "Timmy, you read my mind. I was going to do the same thing as soon as you closed that door. You know, something has been bothering me. Not about Livvy—she is adjusting well—but about BWD and Davis. It seems to me that if he knew that Angelo was in Texas, he would have gotten him by now. I don't know; I just get this strange feeling he is holding back," Det. Greene said.

"I don't know, Al. He's young and aggressive. I guess he feels like this a career maker; we used to be like that. We're getting promoted; maybe he thinks it is time for him to get a promotion too, and this case will do it. It may be that he is distracted because his kid is sick. We ought not to be harsh on him," Tim said looking at his friend.

"I hear you," he said but he was not easily persuaded. He had a weird feeling about Paul Davis ever since he arrested Livvy and refused to listen to his advice. He was hiding something.

The drive to the grave was quick, but she made sure to be vigilant. She saw no one and called Mr. Hoover to let him know she had made it safely. She walked to her brother's grave and sat down. She cleaned it off and began to talk to him about everything. Thanking him for his gift, she held her necklace tightly as she spoke to him. She ended their conversation with telling him she loved him. She called Mr. Hoover to let him know she was back on her way to the house, and he told her to stay on the phone until she left the cemetery. She got a little ticked because she thought he was being overprotective. She did as requested and hung up once she was on the main road. She noticed no one except a police car, but that was not unusual since police lived throughout the community. She stopped at the convenience store to get an orange soda and Snickers bar. "Hey, Vita. How are you?" she asked the clerk.

"Hello, Olivia. I am well today. I bet you are purchasing an orange soda and Snickers bar today," she said with a smile.

Olivia nodded and smiled back. "I owe you two dollars," she said placing the cash in her hand.

"You have a good day, and I'll see you next week," she said.

"Yes, ma'am," Livvy replied. She stopped by every day after school. She liked Vita; she was pleasant and always smiling. Olivia drove back to the house and found Victoria talking on the phone with Phillip. She covered the phone and told Livvy that Jacoby had come by. Livvy nodded and walked up the street to his house. He probably needed some help with his math. Mrs. Castillo was pulling out of her driveway as she was walking up.

"Hey, Livvy. Jacoby is inside the house. I am on my way to pick up Vivian because we are going shopping," she said with a smile.

"Well, is it okay for me to go in?" she asked.

"Absolutely, there are some sandwiches in the refrigerator. You two have fun," she said and pulled out. She waved goodbye and knocked on the door. She thought Jacoby had a pickup game today, but she may have gotten the dates confused. Moments later, he opened the door with a smile on his face. She walked inside and sat down on the sofa. "Why are you smiling at me like that?" she asked.

"I'm just happy," he said sitting down in the chair adjacent from her and turning on the television.

"I saw your brother today," she said.

"I know. He called me and said he saw you. What movie are you going to see tonight?" he asked.

She was stunned that he knew. He and his brother must talk constantly. "I honestly don't know. Victoria just asked me today and did not tell me what movie it was. She just wants to be with Phillip," Livvy said.

He nodded his head and then set the remote control down to watch ESPN.

"Well, I came up here because you stopped by the house. I thought you needed something. But if you're watching television, I can go back home and finish up my work," she said getting up and preparing to leave.

"You don't have to go. I thought you might just want to hang out," he said.

"I can't. I have to finish up the presentation, contact the churches, and get everything ready for the mission I am starting at Hollow Hill. We have a cheerleading competition coming up soon. Starting this school week, I have an extra hour of practice," she said. The idea of all that made her head spin. She also loved having activities to participate in. She felt needed. It was good to be the one giving and doing and not taking. Her work in Hollow Hill was her way of atoning for allowing her brother to die. His death still hurt her heart, and she was determined to get justice for her brother.

"I understand. I guess I'll see you at church," he said feeling a little disappointed. Olivia was a great catch, and he wanted her. But she was just out of his reach. When he thought they were on the same page, she would move further from him. That was tough. He was going to have to talk to his brother about this. He would know what to do.

"Okay, well I will see you then," she said walking toward the door.

When she returned back home, Victoria was getting dressed. "Livvy, where is Jacoby?" she asked.

Livvy looked at her not understanding. "He's at home," she said.

"Why didn't you invite him to come?" she asked.

"You did not tell me to. You said you wanted to go to the movies so you could be with Phillip. I did not know that I was to invite Jacoby as well. Besides, he is at home watching ESPN," she said.

Victoria looked at her disapprovingly. "My dear sister, you are hopeless; call him and tell him to get ready and come with us," she demanded.

Livvy let out a sigh. "Do I have to? I feel silly now. You should have told me before I went to his house," she said.

"Fine. I will call him," she said and picked up the phone.

Olivia dropped her head. He probably thought she was rude. Tori looked at her with widened surprised eyes and then hung up the phone. "He declined," she said looking at her.

"I told you he was watching ESPN. It is like Lifetime for men," Livvy said packing her books in her bag. "Are we meeting Phillip at the movies?" she asked.

She nodded yes. Olivia went downstairs and outside and sat on the porch. She wondered if she had been rude to not invite Jacoby. It was not her intention. It was just that there were a lot of things she wanted to do, and she did not want to jump too soon into a relationship. Her therapist did not think she was ready for that. She was the professional, and Livvy respected her opinions. But she was not sure how to act around Jacoby knowing that he liked her. She liked him too. That was the scary part. Maybe she should just tell him what her therapist said and how she felt and what he felt. She could be worked up for no reason at all. It may all be a misunderstanding. He probably did not like her like that after all. "Come be on, Livvy. You are driving," Victoria said.

Livvy got up and started the engine. She purposely drove up to Jacoby's house and blew the horn. He opened the door, and she asked him if he was sure he did not want to come. He said he wanted to stay home. They waved goodbye and drove to the center of town where the theater was located. Phillip pulled up right beside them. Livvy smiled and waved at him, and he returned the gesture.

"Listen, Livvy. I need you to do me a huge favor. The movie starts at 7:00 but will be over in two hours. Phillip and I aren't going to watch it; we are going out. I need you to be back here at around 9:30, but you can't go home," she said.

"What?" Olivia asked. "You just made me into a liar. I don't even want to see the movie. I have homework to do."

"It's what sisters do; I'd do it for you. You can still do your homework. Go to the park or to the creamery. You can go to the movie, if you like. I just wanted some alone time with Phillip. I told you to bring Jacoby. I love you for doing this," she said and jumped out the car.

Olivia could not believe it. She watched her go and shook her head. What if she ran into Mrs. or Mr. Hoover? What was she supposed to say? Livvy picked up her cell and dialed Jacoby. He answered on the third ring. She explained the situation and he said he would come and meet her. She was grateful. At least now, they would have that conversation. She had nothing but time on her hands. She let down the top, sat on the edge of the car, and looked around as people busied themselves. She found herself angry with Victoria for being dishonest. All she had to do was just ask her mother; she would have allowed her to go out without Livvy. She was mature enough to know what to do and not do, but she hated being part of any dishonesty. She had felt ashamed for allowing herself to be part of her scheme. No good ever came out of lying. It was wrong to disobey your parents.

"Hey, Livvy. I have arrived," Jacoby said with a smile.

She turned around and smiled. "Come take a seat inside my ride, so we can talk," she said.

He looked skittish, as if he were trying to figure out what they needed to talk about. "Are you mad at me or something?" he asked. Miguel had told him that whenever a female says we need to talk that he should run the other way. When women wanted to talk, that meant you did something wrong.

"No. I am upset with Victoria. I can deal with that later," she said trying to figure out how to talk to him without scaring him off or offending him.

"Oh. Well tell me what is on your mind," he said opening the car door and settling inside relieved that he was not at fault.

"How do you feel about me? I mean, I know you like me as a friend as I do you. But do you want more than a friendship? I feel conflicted; like, I like you, but I feel I shouldn't because of my past. I have this tortuous past that haunts me, and I don't want to hurt anyone else as I try to process and deal," she said, hoping that she made some sense to him. It was not her intention to just blurt out her feelings. But since she started therapy, she was not so shy and quiet anymore. She had things to say, and she wanted to say them. Her therapist said it was better out than in.

He smiled. "It's okay. I do like you, a lot. But I can take it as slow as you want. I don't know everything that has occurred in your life, but I understand your need to be hesitant. I would be too, but you are in control. We will go at your pace," he said. His father had long ago taught him about respecting women, and his mother had a review session with him as soon as she thought that he liked Olivia.

"Really? I have been tormenting myself. That is such a relief. You want to see a movie since we are here?" she asked.

He grinned at her honesty. No one could ever call her a liar, because she said what she honestly felt. It was nice; he didn't have to guess or assume anything. She was blossoming. "We can do that. You are really cute when you are nervous," he teased.

She didn't care. She followed him into the theater and relaxed. She liked things to be easy. Jacoby bought popcorn, and they sat down to watch the movie. He placed his arms around her shoulders, and it felt nice. She liked not having to worry about what she said or felt. He was just a cool guy who accepted her. That was something new. She'd just have to study later. It was nice to be with Jacoby like this, but she and Victoria were never doing this again. She did not like disobeying the Hoovers. Tori was their biological child, but Olivia was replaceable, and she did not want to disappoint them or go back to jail.

CHAPTER 16

Kidnapped

Angelo watched closely as new visitors arrived in Hollow Hill. He heard that the new moving force was Livvy. He wanted to know what she was doing, but the police and pastors were among those coming and going from the center they were opening up. How had they turned his little Livvy into a church girl? Det. Davis had given him the intelligence he needed. He now knew Livvy's schedule as she was preparing for a cheerleading competition. The plan was for Det. Davis to pick her up from school. They were going to tamper with her car, and he would just happen to be there. He had begun to hang around so that it would not cause suspicion. He drove off and went back to his new home. It was time to prepare. This was war; the streets belonged to him and no one else. His mind drifted back to who had taken his best friend. No one knew of his plans or of Deek becoming a Christian. He had to know who among his trusted friends had become a Judas. Who had sipped from the cup and spit back venom? He would find out. No lose ends could be left behind this time. He needed to know those who were following him had loyalty.

***

Olivia rested her tired head on the sofa and stretched out her aching body. Victoria confessed to her parents what she had done and was grounded for a week. Olivia didn't know why she told because she was not going to snitch on her; but Livvy told her she was never doing that again. Tori's conscience got the better of her and she told on herself. Olivia did not get into any trouble...thank goodness for that. Things were much easier now with Jacoby too; they just talked. He never looked at her in lust but in love. He listened to her. He never made her feel afraid or stupid. She felt safe with him. He was becoming her best friend. She smiled at that thought, she never thought of any man after Deek could be a friend. She sincerely cared for

Jacoby, and she hoped she would not lose him. There was no way she could lose another friend, especially after losing Lilly.

"Are you sick?" Mr. Hoover asked as he sat down on the end of the sofa, looking anxiously at Olivia. She had been busy as of late, and they were like two ships passing.

She felt like it, but her aches came from workouts. "No. I am just tired. Today has been extremely long, with work, practice, and fixing up the center. I was glad to see so many kids come through. I hope it makes a difference," she said. It felt like the entire community was waiting for SOS. They longed for God and thirsted for His Word. It was great. They were going to start having Bible studies, movie nights, and life classes.

He smiled at her; she was so different from the girl he met in that apartment that cold night—her eyes frightened and her heart broken. "I am proud of you. I think it will make a positive difference," he said.

It made her feel good to hear feedback that was positive feedback and not negative. He was proud of her. She liked that. "It went well...better than expected. There were no BWD's present...well, some of the younger guys...but no one that would cause harm. I told you that you have been worried for nothing," she said.

A smiled crept across his face, and he gently patted her lower leg. "Parents will always worry; it's what we do," he said looking at her with his affable blue eyes.

It warmed her heart that he cared enough about her to be concerned. She fell asleep to his voice...the voice of a father she always wanted to have.

***

Cheerleading practice was becoming like basic training for the Marines; coach was becoming a drill sergeant. They were running a mile before each practice, which was fine. But the weight room workouts and then practicing the routine with only Sundays off was almost killer. Every Saturday they did an hour of cardio and then went through the routine over and over again until she dreamed of backward and forward flips. Gymnastics had turned into preparation for the cheerleading competition. Her body was slowly melting down.

"All right. Ladies, and gentlemen, this is it. Give me all you have, and I will let you all go home. But we have to nail it. I want it to be crisp and cohesive; everyone must be in sync," Coach Rivera said looking intensely at all of them.

Olivia wanted to go home to shower so that she could go to Hollow Hill to help set up for the official open house. As soon as the music began, she made sure to do her part, and she hoped her fellow teammates were ramping up their effort as well. She did not have the physical energy to continuously do this over and over again...not today...today she had other responsibilities that needed her attention.

"Yes. See you guys...I knew y'all could do it. We have one more practice before the big competition; be good, be blessed, be safe until next time," she said smiling at them.

Olivia let out a sigh of relief and went back to the locker room. She decided to shower at school and just leave school to go to the center. By the time she finished showering, her fellow teammates had all disappeared. She could not blame them; they had a tight schedule. She felt reenergized when the warm Georgia air caressed her face. She inhaled and exhaled smiling. She walked to her car, placed her bags inside, and turned the key. It would not start, so she tried again. She knew she had a full tank of gas; it was brand new so there could be no problems with it. She got out and looked under the hood. The sad thing was she had no idea what she was looking at or for. Deek had never shown her how to work on a car. Although she worked with Uncle Victor, she never saw the service side. So, she had no idea what was wrong. She stood there momentarily perplexed when a voice interrupted her thoughts. She looked up and saw Paul Davis. Her heart leaped with happiness. He would know what to do, and she had something to give him as well. "Det. Davis, I am so happy to see you. I thought you would have gone home by now, but my car won't start, and I don't know why," she said greeting him with a smile.

He smiled at her and got out of his truck. "Livvy, have you driven this car that hard already?" he asked with a chuckle.

"No, sir. I take good care of her; I promise," she replied.

He looked and began tinkering; she got back in the car waiting for him to tell her to start the engine, but it still was not working.

"Livvy, I think we are going to have to get a part. You can ride with me, and I'll show you things you need to know about cars," he said with a smile.

"Okay. But if it takes too long, you might have to drop me off because I have to be at the center soon," she said.

"It won't take that long. Come on and get into the truck. I will have you up and running in no time," he said.

She grabbed the money she had saved for him and his son, leaving behind the rest of her belongings. She followed him to his truck. She was happy to see Paul because things had been rough for him and his family. His son had become severely ill, and his medical bills were climbing. His demeanor had changed. Det. Davis, for all his aggressive interrogating practices and vehement dislike for criminals, seemed more human now with his luster gone. He was extremely kind to her, and she was considerate of him. She knew death well and hoped and prayed it would not take his son. It is a horrible thing for a parent to bury a child, and she could tell that he loved his son very much. She recalled what that loss had done to Lillian; it made her shake. It seemed so unnatural for a parent to bury a child. "Mr. Davis, I wanted to give you this. I know it is not a lot, but it's the money I saved from working and collecting at the dealership plus some extra from the cheerleading squad. I hope it helps with the medical bills," she said offering him the envelope. They had managed to collect a total of fifteen hundred dollars.

He looked at her and instantly felt shame for what he had been doing. How could he allow Angelo to take her when she was giving him money for his son? "I can't accept your hard-earned money," he said.

She knew he needed it; she overheard Mr. Hoover talking about it. "Take it, please. If you don't, my friends and I will be hurt. I want you to have it. I really do. You don't have to give anything in return; this is for your son. Mr. Hoover said it is our Christian duty to take care of each other," she replied handing it to him again.

He reluctantly accepted. She found that odd, but then again, some people were just proud. They drove a few more minutes and arrived at the store. She told Det. Davis she had to use the restroom first and then he could show her what she needed. It was getting near time for her to go to the center, and she worried the car would have to wait until later. He nodded and was about to speak, but his cell phone rang so she dashed off to the restroom.

"You got her?" Angelo asked.

"I do. But can you just forget about this? She just handed me money for my sick son. I can't violate her trust. Just go on and leave Georgia and let her be. We can call it even and just forget this," he pleaded.

"You getting soft, Davis? I can have you eliminated just as easy as anyone else. You can be replaced. Bring her to me. Then you get the rest of your money, and we never speak again. You got it? I got you under surveillance, so stick to the plan." he ordered.

Davis looked around trying to see if he could find who was tailing him. "I got it." He said regretfully. He hung up and walked into the store and found Livvy waiting for him. He pretended he could not find what he needed. "Livvy, I am going to have to drop you off and come back," he said.

"Okay, I understand. We are tight on time," she said and followed him out the door. Once in the car, it seemed like the mood had changed. She feared he had gotten some disappointing news about his son. "It's going to be all right, Mr. Davis," she said kindly.

If only she knew, he thought to himself. "I hope so, Livvy. I really do," he said looking in his review mirror and seeing a black El Comino following him. He continued to drive toward the warehouse on the outskirts of town.

Livvy looked at her watch and got nervous. She did not want to be late, and it seemed that Paul was in another place. "Det. Davis, you passed the turn," she said, assuming his mind was so focused on his son that he was not paying attention.

He knew that. It was all part of Angelo's plan, and he could not back out now. "I have to make one stop first, and then I will take you. I'd like to see the center as well," he said calmly.

"Okay. But we really have to hurry," she said looking at her watch. She wished she had grabbed her cell phone. She never liked to be late, especially at her own event. She wondered where he was going anyway. These were the shadows; no one came out here for leisure. Even her brother did not come to the shadows. He was scared of nothing. The shadows were the equivalent of the elephant graveyard in the Lion King movie. Coming here was asking for trouble.

They finally slowed down and stopped in front of a warehouse. It looked eerie, even in the daytime. She looked at Mr. Davis, waiting for a response. Surely, he would explain why he had brought her here. As she started to ask, the passenger door opened. She screamed and began to swing her arms, but to no avail. She felt someone remove her seatbelt and then drag her out. She kept kicking and screaming for Davis. When she did not hear his voice, fear engulfed her like a hail of bullets. How was his wife going to deal with a dead husband and ill son? It was too much.

Finally,...she thought to herself...finally death had come for her too. She had no idea what to think or do, but a voice told her to calm down. She saw no reason to continue to fight; she was losing anyway. She complied and was sat in a seat with her eyes covered. She calmed her breathing and started to use her other senses. It smelled musty, and there was movement; she heard several different footsteps and whispers. Then she heard footsteps that she knew; only one person walked that way: Angelo. How had he found her? Who had given him the specifics of her location? He must have seen her at the center and followed. Det. Hoover had been right. He knew something like this would happen, and she naively thought Angelo had given up on searching for her. How could she have been so foolish? But what about Det. Davis? How did they know? Did he help them? He would not do that; he was a man of honesty and integrity. He strongly disliked drug dealers, gang bangers, and anyone who made the streets unsafe. Her mind was swirling with unanswered questions. She felt a hand rest on her shoulder; she wanted to jerk away but she did not. "What is going on?" she asked not sure what direction to send the question. "Angelo, I know you are here; please just let Paul Davis and I go," she implored.

She was a smart girl, he thought inwardly. He snickered. "Davis can go as soon as he pleases, but you belong to me and you will stay right here," he said.

He had confirmed her fear. He somehow had persuaded Det. Davis to give into his demands. She grew angry with that truth. "Remove the covering from my eyes," she requested. They were removed, and she looked around. She saw them all: Creeper, Biggs, Dough, Jose, and Det. Davis. How could he betray her trust? "Davis, did you know about this? Did you set me up?" she asked with a hurt voice. It was her own fault. Hadn't Deek taught her to be wary of men who wore badges? She thought Paul

Davis was a better man then that. He said nothing. He did not even look at her. "I forgive you. I know you have to be in a tough spot to not uphold the oath you took when you became a police officer, but I do forgive you," she said. She meant that; it was Angelo who had done this. He looked at her in shock and awe. He wanted to speak but was unable. She saw his eyes began to water. Angelo made a motion, and Dough walked Davis out.

"Don't kill him, Angelo...for goodness sakes. You've done enough of that," she said boldly.

He smirked at her boldness. He looked at her wondering why she even cared what happened to Davis. It was apparent that he did not care about her. He was easy to buy off. "I won't; he'll kill himself from the guilt," he said at her. Then looking to his gang members, he said, "Fellas, finish packing up. Then leave us alone."

She watched them leave. She did not understand the gang mentality; they did not want to follow rules or the law, saying they were lawless; they had all the power, but they did whatever Angelo said. In essence, they were following rules and taking orders; so why not be productive citizens of society instead of misfits and criminals? "Untie me, please," she asked because her hands were hurting from being tied behind her back. She could not run because there was no place to go. The shadows were a bad place to be, even in daylight. She was safer in the hands of Angelo at the moment.

"You have to stay calm to keep me calm. But if you get feisty and fiery, you will not like the consequences," he said as he removed the rope. She let out a sigh of relief and massaged her burning wrists. Her thoughts were now together, and she looked at him attempting to read his eyes. Now she had him face to face, and she wanted to know why. "Why, Angelo? Why did you kill Deek and Lilly? What did either do to you?" she asked.

He rolled his eyes and threw up his arms. "For the last time, I did not kill Deek and I did not have him killed. I gave a KA order for a simple beat down because he wanted to become inactive to raise you. But then he got saved and wanted to quit the gang life altogether. That cannot happen. All I told Avery to do is beat him. I was as shocked as you were when he got murdered. I swear. Lilly...that was on you for talking to her. I told you to be quiet. She was not in any way affiliated with us; you let her tell you that I killed your brother, and you believed her over me. Leah and Avery made a choice to disobey. I never touched Avery. I could not even find him to ask him why he killed Deek; someone else got him first," he said looking her in the eyes and not flinching.

No one else wanted to harm Deek; she was not fully convinced. "Why did he say, 'This is for Ace: a bullet in the face?'" she asked.

He looked at her dumbfound. "I don't know. I did not hear anything but gunshots. When my pops and brother died, all I had were Deek and Carlos. I am Ace,

Deek was Deuce, and Carlos was Tres. That was our order: 1, 2, and 3. Don't you see? Killing Deek would be like killing myself. I loved him for real, same like I love you. I didn't have him killed. I swear that I don't know who did. We have to go," he said. It was time to get moving. He had a set plan and did not want to deviate from it. Doing that could get him caught. He was not going to prison.

She looked at him. She was stunned because there was truth in his eyes. He was sincere; it was the first time she had ever seen him show any emotion about her brother, but she was not going with him. He'd have to kill her as well. She was not going to be his slave anymore. She saw the better side of life now, and she could not go back to his life.

"I am not going with you. You murder people, and you will murder me too. Do it now, so I don't have to suffer anymore," she said without emotion.

He stopped walking and jerked Livvy so that they were face to face. "Damn it, Livvy. Would you stop with all that crap? You go move in with police and find God and think you are all holy and want to be a martyr. Chill with it right now. I have been extremely kind to you. I know about that guy and about you telling the cops about my stash houses. I have not killed you. I wouldn't because I know why you did it. I betrayed you, so you betrayed me. It's done. We can do this easy or hard, but you are going with me," he said. His eyes displaying his emotions as he pulled her near; she wondered if he would knock her out or tie her back up. "Livvy, let's go right now!" he yelled with aggravation.

She took a deep breath and forced her cemented feet to move. She wanted to fight him, but she would lose. She wanted to scream, but he would hush her. All she could think about was the last beat down he gave her. Her body was already tired from the weeks of hard practices. She had aches in places she did not think possible, and she knew starting a fight would only make matters worse. He placed a blindfold on her and grabbed her hand; she followed. They put her in a rear seat and told her to lie down. Angelo was right beside her; she could feel his hands resting on her body. The tears did not come at first; she held them off. But the burning of them was too much, and as soon as they began to move, she cried because now it was real. She wondered where Davis was and if he regretted allowing them to take her. She had no idea where they were even going. She felt hopeless. She prayed Mr. Hoover would come to save her because, if not, she had no one; she would be at the mercy of Angelo and that frightened her. Her cries must have reached his ears, because he leaned over and whispered in her ear to stay calm; his lips were kissing hers. She tried to halt the tears as much as possible. She had to cry on the inside. She didn't want to feel his kisses.

**

Det. Hoover glared at the clock on the wall and again back at his own watch. Something was not right; Olivia always called. He looked at his wife; she nervously kept looking up and down the street, but to no avail. He called her cell again, but it went right to voicemail. The waiting made him crazy, so he told his wife he would be back. He got into his car and drove to the places she had gone before. She was not at the cemetery, the bowling alley, or the theater. He drove back to her school. When he went around the back, he saw her car. The hood was raised; she must have had car trouble he thought and let out a sigh of relief. Once he walked to the car, all his alarm bells went off and he contacted dispatch. Inside her car were all her belongings, even her cell phone. He looked around, but no one was there now. Fear entered into his brain as he thought of all the horrible things that could happen to her. He began to call her coach and teachers; someone had to see something. There seemed to be no struggle. But where could she be and with whom? In less than ten minutes, he had patrol out looking for her.

"Alan, it's Tim; I think someone has abducted Livvy. Her car is here with most of her belongings, but she is nowhere to be found. She was supposed to be at the center an hour ago. I got this bad feeling that one of the BWD got her. It had to be someone she trusted, because there is no sign of struggle; I mean her keys are still in the car," he finished as he watched his friend Edward from missing persons arrive.

The news stunned him. Something had to be wrong because she was so excited about opening day. "Oh no. Well I am coming. Where are you?" Alan asked.

"I'm at her school," Tim said.

"I am on my way," he said.

Every available police officer was out looking for Olivia Morris. Mrs. Hoover was now back at home pacing. Mrs. Castillo had arrived and was attempting to soothe Vivian's shaken nerves. There was much speculation but no evidence that a crime had even occurred. She was just gone...vanished...disappeared like she never was.

"Vivian, she is a smart girl. I am sure she is fine. We just have to think the best and pray. God is watching her," Lucia said holding her friend as she wept silently.

Vivian heard her friend, but her mind was too shaken. Olivia should have been safe; things were finally coming together for her. "We were supposed to keep her safe. I have failed that child. Oh, dear God, help me," Vivian pleaded.

Vincent threw his car into park and ran into the house, almost tripping over his own shoes as he searched for answers. "Mom, what is going on? Victoria called and said to come home quickly. Where is Olivia?" Vincent asked looking around the house.

There were tears in Vivian's eyes as she looked at her son. The words she spoke nearly killed her to speak. "She's gone. Someone has taken her, and I don't know when or where. Her coach said she showered at school and, after that, she did not see her again. Someone tampered with her car and I guess must have taken her then. Your father is out looking and told me to stay here, but she has not called. I have not seen her since I kissed her and Victoria goodbye this morning," she said feeling weak and needing to sit down.

Vincent stood still. How could this happen? Police lived all through this neighborhood. Everyone knew each other. How could someone enter and exit unseen? That was not possible. He comforted his mother and then went to find Miguel. He walked outside and bumped into Jacoby. "J, have you seen Livvy?" he asked.

He shook his head, his face flushed and his body tired from running throughout the neighborhood searching for her. "No, I have been searching with my brother. I saw her at school; she was happy. She was tired though, because the practices were getting intense. She was excited because the open house was today, and she was going to give Det. Davis that money for his son Monty. I don't know where she is. She would have told me if something was wrong," he said looking lost and confused.

"Can you think of any other place?" Vincent asked wanting to help.

"I honestly don't know where to look. My fear is that Angelo returned and, after seeing us remodel the old general store, he took her. I don't know where he'd go with her," he said. Now that he no longer attended his old school, he had no idea what was going on in the streets.

Vincent collapsed into the rocking chair. He felt useless and horrible. Somewhere his sister was frightened and in danger, and there was nothing he could do. She was family now; he loved her like he loved Victoria. She had suffered so much and lost her entire family, and now they had lost her. He prayed that she would come home, soon and safe.

Det. Hoover pulled up in his driveway to find his home filled with helpful neighbors. His heart hurt as he returned without Olivia and without a clue as to where she was or who had taken her. How had he allowed it to happen? He thought he had covered all his bases. He should have never allowed his guard to be down. He had been so consumed with her safety that he had become her biggest threat. He opened the door and stepped inside; entering the house felt like it instantly drained his energy. Now he had to look at his wife, daughter, and son—their hungry eyes searching for answers he did not have. He walked slowly up each step and slowly turned the doorknob. Instead of an interrogation, he was greeted by his daughter hugging him tightly. He thought maybe Olivia had returned home...that he had acted prematurely in calling out all the law enforcement...but as he drew nearer and heard his wife praying, he knew it was not to be. He kissed Victoria and walked into his study. He needed quietness to think. He needed to look at the bigger piece of the puzzle. Everything was connected—the murders and the drug bust. Somehow Angelo knew their moves. He had to have help from the inside. But who was the traitor? Who had given up Livvy as a sacrifice? He wondered silently.

***

The car slowed down, and Dough parked. "Boss, we have made it to the safe house. You want to keep on moving or stay the night?" Dough asked.

"We'll stay here tonight. Go ahead and change cars again, because we are leaving at daybreak. You have the schedule, and I need you to burn anything that can be traced. We have enough disposable cell phones. We will lay low tonight. Let me know what the news is saying," he said.

Dough shook his head and went to work. Angelo was mentally noting the actions of those around him. None of them had the authority or even a reason to override his order. The only person who had any authority was Carlos, but he refused to believe his number three would kill his number two; however, if he did that meant he must kill Carlos too. He kept thinking about what Livvy had heard the killer saying—that this is for Ace. But she must have misunderstood; Avery could have easily said Tres. That was what Deuce was trying to tell him. He was trying to say who had shot him; he must have been saying Tres. Carlos had to be talked to and dealt with. If he did what he thought, he would eliminate him first but only after he confessed to all of them. He lifted Livvy's sleeping body out of the car and gently placed her in his bed. He removed the blindfold, and she looked peaceful. His body had missed hers. He kissed her ever so gently, not wanting to wake her. But her lips were an elixir to him, calling him to love her. He refused himself and let her rest untouched. They had to make it to South America. This would be the test to prove who was loyal to him.

"Ace, we are set up for tomorrow. Carlos is looking for you also. We need to eat. You think Livvy might cook?" Dough asked rubbing his growling stomach. He was hungry.

Angelo turned around and looked at him like he was an idiot. "She is resting. I don't want to disturb her. Order something from a restaurant; get that curb side so you won't risk being seen and back up, so the license plate isn't seen. Order enough food for everybody. When you all have eaten, we'll have a meeting. Tell Carlos to wait until then," he said. He was thinking this would be the time. He was mentally composing what he would say. As he finished his thoughts, the soft whimpers of Livvy brought him back and he walked into the bedroom. "Are you hungry?" he asked looking at her soft gray eyes; they danced frantically trying to figure out where she was.

"No, can I go home please. I won't tell a soul anything. I just want to go back home," she implored not sure where they were now. She knew she was not in Georgia because it smelled different. They were somewhere near water; the salt was polluting the air. There were no windows, so there was nothing to allow her to verify her suspicion.

"You are home; you are with me. You need to eat. Dough will return shortly. Come on and sit up," he said softly.

His gentleness frightened her; it was like the calm before the storm. She was not sure how to feel or what to say. She heard another voice say Angelo's name. It was a voice she knew well. Carlos came into the room, and instantly she felt safe. As long as Carlos was near, he would not allow Angelo to harm her...she hoped. She remembered that night Carlos tried to calm him, but he beat her anyway. Olivia was relieved to see him as she thought Angelo had murdered him for coming to see her. It was good to see him alive and well. He was safe, and she was praying she would be too.

"Carlos, I am talking to Livvy. I'll talk to you after we finish eating," he said looking angrily at Carlos.

Carlos nodded and left out the room. Olivia watched the quick interactions, and she pondered if there was an unknown battle brewing. Maybe Angelo was just paranoid again. She did not want to agitate his delicate nerves, so she played along and listened to him. Dough arrived moments later. The aroma of food made her stomach growl, awakening a hunger she didn't know she had.

They all sat around the table, and it was like she was back at Angelo's old house. There was tension; it was not because of her, but there was something else. Olivia said grace, and they began to eat. She looked at Biggs, Creeper, Dough, Jose, and Carlos, and she wondered what they were thinking. Did they not care that she had been taken away? Did they not understand the seriousness of the crime? Taking her across state lines was going to get the feds involved. They acted as if she was supposed to be there. They really believed that she belonged to Angelo.

"So, Livvy what was it like living with the enemy?" Dough asked.

Olivia looked at him completely in shock. He was the enemy. "They were good to me. They treated me like their child," she said honestly.

He nodded but wanted to know more. "I mean how did you end up there?" he asked.

"That's enough, Dough," Angelo said. "You can talk about something else."

Everyone grew silent, and all that could be heard was chewing and breathing. Olivia felt fear enter in her body; she tensed instantly. She thought they all saw her as a snitch, and this would be her last supper. She knew how brutal they could be. After they all finished eating, no one left the table. Angelo had called a mandatory meeting of the board. Since Olivia was not excused, she figured it was about her. She tried not to show any fear. Angelo got up and started to talk. "I called this meeting because it has come to my attention that there is a traitor among us. Livvy is here because she needs to hear this too. Derrick "Deek-Deuce" Morris got murdered over a year ago by Avery "Spade" Harris. I asked Avery to take a crew and KA Deek because he wanted to quit the gang. Someone told Avery to kill Deek instead. This has baffled me until now. Deek was over all the drug dealers as my number two. Carlos, also known as Tres, is over all the soldiers; he's my number three. Out of

145

those two, who would gain from overriding my word? It was not me and not Deek. Deek would not kill himself; I would not have Deek killed, no matter what he did. He was and is my brother; we have been friends since grade school. He lost like I lost, and I would not do that to Livvy. But one among us has. Someone has violated the oath of our blood brotherhood. Today is judgment day." He paused for a moment and looked into the eyes of each of his brothers, knowing who the guilty one was. For a moment, he thought of the disciples and how Jesus knew who would betray him. Sadly, Deek had no clue how disloyal Tres really was. "Carlos, I believe you found out about my orders to Avery and lied to him, telling him to kill Deuce instead." The truth of it deeply pained Angelo's heart momentarily. He quickly shook it off. "You know that treason is punishable by death. We believe in doing things in a judicious way, so you have the opportunity to defend or deny. But you can't lie," he said glaring at him and watching his brown skin turn red.

All the others looked surprised, as did Livvy. Carlos would not kill her brother; he had no reason to. She could not help herself and she spoke, "Carlos, you would not do that. You and Deek are brothers. You look out for me," she said encouragingly. Angelo was just grasping for straws.

Carlos looked at her and then back at Angelo. There was sadness in his eyes. His lip quivered, but only for a second. It happened so quickly that if you blanked you would not have noticed. He regained himself quickly. "I did what had to be done. It was for the best interest of the brotherhood; I was protecting our way of life. Deek was at my house writing a letter to Livvy about if something happened to him. He told me to look out for her, and then he proceeded to say that he wanted to leave the BWD to make a better life for her. I told Avery what to do, but he said you ordered something different. I told him you changed your mind. I did it for you, Angelo. This way Deek got out like he wanted, and you got Livvy; I got more control. It was a win-win situation," he said unable to look at the rest of the guys. At the time he thought he had done the right thing. But after seeing the suffering, the death, and the change in the entire group, it didn't seem worth it. He had nightmares right after it happened because of how deeply affected Olivia was. If he could take it back, he would. He loved Deek too. "I'm sorry; if I could do it all over again, I would have never done it," he said now talking to his hands as the rest of the board sat baffled.

Olivia felt her heart stop. Her breathing became labored. She was not hearing this; he was not confessing. She trusted him because her brother told her to. All this time, the devil was him. He was far worse than Angelo. With Angelo, she expected the worst...but not from Carlos. He had a baby, a girl who was his only family; he knew how important Deek was to her, and how important she was to Deek. "You Judas! You are a sick, manipulative, lying bastard!" she shouted getting up ready to take her bare hands and squeeze the life out of him. It all came back. He fooled Deek too. She felt hands pull her back, and she looked hatefully into Carlos's soulless black eyes. "Carlos, how could you? What on earth possessed you to take the one thing I had in this life? You were playing me all along. You played the cops too, didn't you? You set up Leah, and you put ideas in Angelo's head about Lilly. I trusted you. For all I know, you probably called the cops on me and Angelo. You did not come to visit me in DJJ because you cared; you were playing a part and seeking information. You are a heartless, soulless waste of life. You better hope I never see you again, or I will kill you and I don't care who sees me do it. Going to Hell would be too good for you. You're a penniless traitor," she swore. She was vexed...so full of venomous vexation that it was seeping through her veins and dripping down her body like sweat. "Take your hands off of me and let me shoot him like he had Deek murdered," she shouted.

"Calm down, Knockout. We got this," Creeper said, recalling how she knocked Leah out. She was not one to mess with when angry. She reminded him of Deek when he got mad, and that was a scary situation. Although she was a lightweight, she was super strong. He was having a hard time holding her back.

"Let her go," Angelo said and walked toward Olivia. "I told you, Livvy, that I didn't do it. I would never do that to you. Go back into the room and shut the door," he requested. He was feeling vindicated, but he did not want her to see what he was going to do.

She was not going to move. "But he killed Deek. He told Avery to kill him, and he lied about it," she shouted.

"Babe, go in the room and I will be there shortly. We are going to handle this," he said calmly, but he liked seeing her feisty. It was attractive.

She was too angry to move. Creeper escorted her back and locked her inside the room. She lost it; she lost her self-control...kicking, screaming, and shouting. She tried to calm herself, holding onto the necklace Deek had given her and rocking herself back and forth. She was in a trance, going mad like a rabbit dog. She was trying so hard to be in the spirit and not the flesh, but she felt like the flesh was winning. God said vengeance is mine, but at that moment she wanted to serve her own kind of vengeance.

"Ace, what are we going to do?" Dough asked still in shock from Carlos's confession.

"We can't just kill him here. We already got heat. We can't take him, or Livvy will kill him on the road. We can't leave him alive because he can't be trusted," Biggs said looking at him angrily. He was the main one with Livvy, and he killed their brother. BWD was family, and Carlos violated all the rules.

"We are going to Scarface him. Beat him, torture him, put a bullet in his brain, tie a weight around his legs, drop him in the ocean, and let him be sea food," Angelo said glaring at Carlos. He hated him now too. He knew better than to see Livvy without his consent. Indeed, he was playing two parts but now he was played out. His time was up. It was time to die.

"Please, Angelo. I am begging you not to kill me. I did it for the right reasons," Carlos said. He knew what Scarface meant and that it was a brutal way to die; it was worse than how he had Deek killed. At least his murder was fast. But to Scarface someone was a slow and painful death, only done once to the man who killed Angelo's father; it was like the plague.

"Nah, you have been playing both sides. I don't do turn coats. You made Livvy think I killed Deek. That is unforgivable. I loved you homes, but you got to go," Angelo said walking over to pick up a hammer and mash his hands. He watched with excitement as he screamed, and he hit him again just for the heck of it. Then they stuffed his mouth and walked him outside to carry out justice BWD style. Watching as the life drained from him, Angelo said, "Now you know how Deek felt lying in the puddle of blood and dying in his sister's arms. It's time to meet your maker, homie. To hell you go, homes." Angelo stood back and watched the others finish him off and dump the body. "That's how traitors die," he said laughing.

CHAPTER 17

On the Move

Olivia's nerves were still shaken after they pulled out in the early morning with one less. She had no idea where Carlos was, but she knew he was dead. She had heard his screams. His screams were worse than Livvy's. Somehow, it did not make her feel better; revenge is bitter and not sweet. She was in the company of murderers, and they acted as if nothing had occurred. She longed to be blindfolded again. She felt so horrible that her last words to Carlos were words of anger and insults. Maybe if she had been kinder and offered forgiveness and not judgment they would have spared his life. No one could save her now, and she did not deserve to be saved. She had forgiven Paul Davis but condemned Carlos. What kind of Christian was she? She felt like she was the old Livvy again. Oh, how she hated herself for having even a taste of the good life only to be thrown back into hell. She looked out the window and watched as the sky went from dark to light. She wondered where they were heading; she wondered why Angelo wanted her so badly and sought her so relentlessly. Clearly, he was obsessed. They pulled into a port. The guys quickly unloaded the bags to an awaiting big boat—it was a yacht or something...she had no idea what exactly to call it. Angelo must have planned this a long time ago. She wondered where they were going. Since they were traveling by water, she would never get rescued. If they had gone to Mexico like she had assumed, she would have stood a chance. But now she had no idea where he was going, and he was not telling her. She was quickly taken down to a room so as not to be seen, and Angelo went back up top. She sat quietly wondering where she was going. She felt so lost and angry. Her brother had been murdered by hands he trusted; Lilly was right. Olivia didn't know how to feel. Angelo had told the truth. But she still was angry with him for taking her away from a family she loved, as well as for his brutal mistreatment of her. What was she supposed to do? There was no one to trust but herself. The man driving the boat seemed familiar to her too. She had only seen him a brief moment. She put her hands in her pocket and felt her brother's Bible. She had forgotten it was there. She pulled it out and began to read. She needed something to keep her mind from violating and entrapping her. A knock at the door startled her frayed nerves. She stuffed the Bible back in her pocket, but not before Angelo saw her.

He put his hand inside of her pocket and pulled it out.

"It belonged to Deek. He gave it to me," she said wondering if she would get a slap or a verbal reprimand.

"Here," he said giving it back. "I don't mind you having it. You want something to eat?" he asked softly.

She nodded yes. He offered her a sandwich and bottled water. She took them both and thanked him.

"You don't have to act like we are strangers, Livvy. We're safe now, and you can let down your guard," he said caressing her hair and kissing her cheek.

She said nothing and continued to stare at her food. She did not want the hands that murdered to be touching her. Even if he did not kill her brother, he had killed others. She knew she was not safe; in time she too would do something to cause him to break.

"You finish eating and then take a shower. You'll feel better after a shower," he said and then left the room.

She would feel better if she were in Georgia with the Hoovers. She was not sure what day it was or how long she had been missing. Her watch had gotten broken in her attempt to get away. She knew that the police had to know she was missing. But because Davis was on the take, he probably misled them. She would never be seen or heard of again. She would be a face on the milk carton. She wondered if they had sent out an Amber Alert. It did not matter. They were in open water leaving the United States, and she had no idea where she was going now.

Momentarily accepting defeat, Olivia began to eat the sandwich and took a shower as ordered. At least he was softer and kinder to her, even knowing that she had given up some information. She suspected he knew that would occur and had already prepared for it. Considering how he did not like to be disobeyed, she should be thankful. But he was too good...too nice. She knew sooner or later—just like it was when Deek was murdered—he would begin to want and to take. She wished to have amnesia because she did not want to remember any parts of her life. The beginning had been so horrible that she hated it. She even regretted being born. But then she had seen how good life could be, only to be back at square one. She loathed her memories. She slipped down and began to cry uncontrollably. This was not supposed to happen. She was supposed to be cheering, going to the movies, hanging out with her friends—not fleeing from crime scenes and being owned by a mad man. What had she done to deserve this? There was a tug-of-war internally inside her heart; she recalled the scripture in 2 Timothy 1:7: "For God has not given us a spirit of fear, but of power and of love and of a sound mind."

"Fight, Livvy. Fight for your life," she whispered to herself. Angelo was stronger and more ruthless; there were limits to what she would do, but not him. He had no limits because he had no fear, no care, and no conscience.

"Livvy, are you still in there?" Angelo asked. She had been inside long enough, and he had longed to love her. No longer could he deny the urge to have his hands wrapped around her body. She belonged to him, and he would not be denied any longer.

The interruption of his voice sent chills throughout her veins, turning her blood iceberg cold. "I am. I am coming out now," she managed to say. She took her hand and wiped off the steamed mirror and looked at herself. She mentally asked herself when she would be brave enough to fight for her freedom. Angelo stopped knocking and slid the door open. She felt crushed before he walked inside. Her towel covered her shivering body; her eyes looked sorrowfully at him. She wanted to be left alone. Tears wanted to fall. Her soul was screaming. She wanted to jump in the water and get away. Still she was unable to get over Carlos's betrayal or the fact that he was dead. Now his child would grow up with no father, and his girlfriend had lost her love. Olivia was part of that. The knowledge of that guilt was mentally killing her. She knew what that meant. She prayed to God that Carlos's child would not suffer...that she would seek not the world but God. A child without a father is so vulnerable...so very vulnerable; Derrick and Olivia were a perfect testament to that, as was even her dead mother. Nene had no father to tell her how a man ought to treat her, so she accepted whatever she could get. If only fathers knew how important they were, they would never abandon their children.

"Come on, I have a change of clothes for you," Angelo said.

Olivia did not want to move. Angelo reached for her, but she avoided his touch by walking ahead of him back to the room. She instinctively and protectively held her own body as she mentally recalled all the unwanted attention, he had given her previously. It was as if her body was not her own but his. She was tired of people taking her body and using her to pleasure themselves.

Angelo watched her carefully, reading her body language. "You are still upset about what happened the other night. I understand. We were all affected, but at least now you know. You got to cheer up. You are with family and friends. No one is going to bother us anymore," he said gently kissing her cheek. "I've missed you. I miss waking up and seeing you, holding you, and loving you. I know you missed me as well," he said kissing her again.

She was visibly sickened by his touch. She knew it was coming; it always came. "Please, Angelo. I just want to rest," she said still holding her towel firmly around her body to protect herself from his advances. She did not miss him; she enjoyed the separation and would seek to be imprisoned again if it meant he would be kept at bay.

"You can, but I just want to hold you," he said.

Her body recoiled at his request. He wanted to do more than hold her; his eyes told the truth his tongue tried to hide. She wondered how she should handle it. If she allowed him, then she would feel guilty; if she denied him, he would take it anyway and she would feel dirty. What other option did she have? If she fought him, they could all assault her. They would do whatever he requested; she was among enemies now. His hands were dancing across her body. Then he stopped as if he thought of something. "Did you have sex with that guy from school...the one I saw you with?" he asked.

She looked at him in utter shock. "Nowhere near the amount that you had while I was locked up," she said before she could stop herself. Her quick reply shook him. He looked at her, not sure what to make of her comment.

"So, is that yes or is that no?" he asked.

"I have not had intercourse with anyone. I don't like it anyway." she said.

He looked into her eyes. "You do with me. I have never forced you. You do it because you want to please me. You are going to be the mother of my children," he said.

He loved to say that as if it were some kind of honor. "I am a child myself. I am far from ready to be a mother," she said scooting back and hoping he would lose interest and go back up top to be with his friends. "Where are we going?" she asked attempting to change the subject so he would not touch her anymore.

"It's a surprise, but you will enjoy it," he said. "Let me hold you. You have been teasing me."

"Can't we just wait?" she asked maintaining a monotone voice hoping not to upset him.

"For what? I have waited months and months. I miss you. Don't you want to show me your appreciation? You owe me some loving after accusing me of a heinous crime. If you really cared about me, you'd show me," he said without stopping his advancements.

"Not really...seeing as how you left me to rot in jail after you promised that you would take care of it. I say we are even," she said angrily.

He stopped and looked at her. "What did you say?" he asked. It seemed lockup made her speak up, and he was not sure if he liked it. Lately she had been slipping and talking to him rudely. Now he was about to be tired of her.

She did not repeat herself; she just stared at him.

"That is what I thought," he said and continued his advancement.

These were the times she hated being weaker, younger, and a girl. No woman could do that to a man...just make him submit. She thought if she gave in then he'd leave her alone for a while. At any moment, he could have taken her and had his way; but at least he was kind. She closed her eyes and waited for it to be over. She tried to think of good things and remove herself from what was occurring. It was time to go into survival mode. She would have to submit until she could find a way to get out. She hated herself for not fighting, but she could not handle an assault. Even one blow from his powerful hands felt like being struck by an army of men. He was so strong, and it looked as though he had gotten bigger since she had been away. She cried herself to sleep when he left, holding onto the necklace her brother had given her. She needed to be strong and courageous, but fear was holding her captive.

***

Two or three days passed. Olivia couldn't gauge the time for sure, as she was kept below deck. They made it to the Caribbean where they all got off. Dough and Biggs were meeting their families. It was Livvy's understanding that they were going to set up a BWD there. It would be part of Angelo's world domination. Creeper and Jose also met their girlfriends there; they were going to stay a few days and then go to Mexico. Angelo and Olivia were bound for South America. He said they could stay in the Caribbean for a few days as well before leaving. He said they all deserved a vacation. Angelo acted like he had not kidnapped Olivia. He acted like she was not underage or an unwilling participant in his activities. No one really noticed them; they just blended in. Angelo walked with his chest puffed out brazenly, bragging about how he outsmarted the police. A new fear grew inside of her as she witnessed his new attitude; if she did not find a way to escape, she was doomed to never be found again. She hoped in the eleventh hour that rescue squads would come for her. But she was the girl with no family, and this was no movie; this was real life. No one missed her. They probably all thought she had set this up. There was no telling what lies Paul Davis had told. With sadness in her eyes, she began to accept defeat. She belonged to Angelo once more. Now she was going to a country where no one knew her, and she would be buried a nomad. Maybe it would not be so bad, she tried to tell herself. At least she was in the Caribbean. If she had not been kidnapped, it would have been a great vacation. But her mind was occupied with what was really going to happen. She sat down in the sand and looked longingly at the pristine crystal blue water. She stared off into the distance looking for someone to rescue her. It was foolish. She had to give up the escape notion and just accept her fate. Angelo was not going to let her go. He never would until something else he wanted more came along; God help whoever she was.

"Babe, what are you looking at?" Angelo asked her.

She jumped at the sound of his voice; he was like a snake, slithering around and then just popping up. His venom was in his hands...those brutal horrible hands that killed and attacked at will. "Not anything. I'm just looking at the water," she responded not looking at him.

He sat down and started to play with her hair. "It is beautiful, just like you," he said.

She could not reply because she was trying hard not to cry. The tears fell anyway. Her heart longed for home; she was so homesick and so afraid of what could happen. There were so many things to fear, and now she had no one to turn to or trust. She thought about the Hoovers, but they might be on the payroll too. Didn't she always trust the wrong people? So, could Miguel and Det. Greene turn her in? How deep did the betrayal go? She had no one to turn to, and she was dying inside; her spirit was decaying. She was dying by the hands that said they loved her. This was not love; a child she might be, but she knew this was not love. She was a slave. No matter how he masqueraded it, she was his slave. She wanted to be free.

"Livvy, why are you crying?" he asked wiping her tears away.

She looked at him as bravely as she could. "I just want to go home and be normal again. I don't want to worry about being killed, getting pregnant, or making you angry. I just want my life. I want to go to school and go back to cheerleading. I want to tutor kids in math. I don't want to be forced into a lifestyle of bullets, drugs, and sex. I don't," she said hoping that words would penetrate his stone heart.

He let out an exhausted sigh. He gripped her chin and jerked her face so that she was forced to look at him. "Not this again, Livvy. I tried to be good to you and let you have some fun in the Caribbean, and all you talk about is yourself. You have to stop being selfish and start taking care of me. I am your man, so stop with the tears and woman up. You got soft after living with that police family. Where is my gangster girl? Now don't upset me when I am having fun. You need to think of a way to make it up to me," he said. "Get yourself together," he demanded and then pushed her face hard, showing his frustration. Why did she make him act this way?

She dropped her head; that was her last appeal, and he mocked her. He made it about him and could care less about her. She took a deep breath and got up. She had to find some way to leave. Her mind could not figure out a plan. It was life or death, and she had to do something.

"Where are you going?" he demanded.

"I am going to get myself together," she said.

He looked at her and smiled; then he got up to follow. That was her problem. She had no alone time. He was on her like skin; he watched her like a hawk. She had to find a way to leave him. He liked to drink. She had to get him stupid drunk and call back to the states to tell someone. She could call her youth pastor. Her mind was racing. She only had one more day, and then they would be on a flight to South America. She would probably lose her chance. She had to play his game better them he did. It was dangerous. He would not overlook her disobedience again. She felt his hand grope her body, and he pulled her near him. She did not push away, falling into sync with his stride. "You are just a little homesick. Things are going to be fine," he said.

She nodded her head in agreement.

***

Det. Hoover sat stone faced in his office; he was exhausted, angry, and leadless. He could not ignore how scarlet red and sad his wife's eyes were, as well as Victoria's. Vincent called him daily to ask if he heard anything, but he had nothing. Jacoby came by daily seeking leads and asking what he could do. No one had called in a tip in days, and they had no idea who had Olivia or where she was. It was driving him insane. He felt like a failure. He had been given a second chance to do right by her, and now she was suffering. The Amber Alert came up with nothing, as they had no idea what cars were involved. Her picture was on every television station, in every building, and on every billboard, but nothing had yielded any decent leads. She was alone and scared, and he could do nothing about it. It was killing him.

"Det. Hoover, I have a gentleman out here who wants to speak with you. He said it has to do with Livvy," Gail said pushing up her glasses.

"Bring him in," he replied, life now coming back into his body. This might be what he needed to find her. He looked at the door, expecting a young man or teenager associated with BWD who was looking for a deal. He would offer it, as long as it brought Livvy back home. An older gentleman came through the doors. He looked to be in his mid-forties. He had a youthful glow and solid gray eyes; they were eyes that he had seen before. He sat down and put out his hand. Det. Hoover shook it. "Sir, my receptionist tells me that you have some information."

"The young lady who is missing...Dinah Olivia Morris...well, I am her father," the gentleman said.

Det. Hoover looked suspiciously at the man. Olivia's biological family was deceased. "I think you are mistaken. Olivia has no living family," Det. Hoover said.

"What? She got a mother named Dinah Netanya Lee; we call her Nene. She got a brother named Derrick; he goes by Deek. I am her father, Obadiah Morris. She got eyes like mine. I was at work...sitting in the break room...when the Amber Alert came on TV. I might not have been around, but I know my own child," he said. He was not there when she was born, but he could not deny her; she looked just like him, except that she was better looking.

Tim could not believe what he was hearing. How could the man be gone this long and then appear? The gentleman was eyeing him suspiciously. "Her mother died when she was ten, and her brother died when she was fifteen. She had no idea where you were," Timothy said.

Obadiah dropped his head in shame. "How did they die?" he asked.

"The mother overdosed, and Derrick was murdered by his own gang right in front of Livvy. The leader of the gang took her in and made her take the blame for crimes he committed. She actually did some time in DJJ," he said.

The horrible news quickly penetrated his heart. His worst fear had come true. "Oh no, I should have never left them behind. Who took her?" he asked.

"We don't know. I have my suspicions, but there is nothing definitive," he replied looking at the man across from him and wondering how he could abandon his family.

Obadiah looked at the detective and wondered how he could not know. She was on all the news channels, but he seemed to have no answers. "How can you not know? I bet if she was your daughter or some rich little girl, you'd know. Since she is a little Black girl from the Hallow with a deceased family, you don't care," he said looking upset.

His allegation infuriated Det. Hoover. "Oh no, sir. You will not come into my office and attack me. You are the one that abandoned your family. I took Livvy in, and I treated her no differently than my other two children. I love Livvy as if I was her biological father. Because she is my daughter, the entire force has dedicated time and effort to finding her. I'll have you know—as you sit in my office with judgmental eyes and a slanderous tongue—that my wife is a beautiful Black woman, my children are beautifully Black, and Livvy is mine. Unlike you, color doesn't matter to me. You can either help or you can leave, but you will not make this what it isn't. Do you understand me?" Det. Hoover said getting up and glaring at the man across from him. His loud voice alerted the others, and the entire office was standing at his door looking. This was not old Georgia or the old south; he hated racism. He despised anyone who voiced it because it was disgusting and ungodly. He was a soft-spoken man who was slow to anger. But when it came to defending God and his family, he had no patience with foolishness and unfounded accusations.

Mr. Morris got up and apologized. He said nothing more and walked out as he had come in—with his head down. The crowd dispersed, and only Det. Greene remained. He walked inside and closed the door.

"We are going to find her, Timmy; you just have to be calm. Who was that guy anyway?" he asked.

"He claims to be her father. The child has buried her mother, brother, and best friend. She has been locked up for a crime she did not commit. She has been abused her entire life; and now he comes back. He did not come to help. No. He came to accuse. He suggested that I am not doing my job because she's a poor Black girl and I am white. It pissed me off because she is not that. She is an intelligent, loving, sweet little girl who loves God. All she has ever wanted is to be loved in return. I'd give my life for her—same as I would for Victoria and Vincent. I hate that she needs me, and I can't help her. I am the only father she has ever known, and I can't save her when she needs me. Do you know how that makes me feel?" he confessed and wept openly. Never had he been that impacted by any other case. But since he first met Olivia, he felt a connection to her. She was his. God brought them together, and no man was going to take her from him. She was his daughter now. He was her father. He would dedicate his life to finding her and bringing her home.

Alan felt the pain in his own heart as he saw his best friend weak and in need. He placed his hand on his shoulder. "You are too hard on yourself. We are trained for this. We are going to bring her home alive. You're an awesome dad. She knows that. You just have to focus. I've been looking at the timeline you made. I have been thinking that the only person—besides us and Miguel—who could have betrayed her is Paul Davis. I am not implying that he is a renegade, but something is fishy about him. I think we need to talk to him. Jacoby told me that Olivia had collected some money for the Davis son. But when we went to check out the car, there was no money. How is it that she left everything except fifteen hundred dollars?" Alan said placing his own paper down.

Tim wiped his eyes and began to look. "Al, do you think he would jeopardize his job, pension, and family to work both sides? He wouldn't betray her like that—not my Livvy," he said not believing what Alan was saying.

"He has massive medical bills because of Monty's illness. He is always one step behind BWD, and those he brings in are the smallest fish. Something is not right. Miguel even came to me about it. He's a bright kid. He said he thought he heard some things when Livvy was in DJJ. You remember her friend hung herself. How would Angelo know about what she said unless someone was working the inside? This might be bigger than just Paul Davis; we need to start looking at our own," he said.

Det. Hoover shook his head in disbelief. The reward was 15,000 dollars, and no one was calling. He could get a snitch to sell out for much less; maybe it was in house. "We need to treat him like a suspect. Let's talk to the higher ups about it. We got to get our Livvy back."

The two began to work quickly, only letting a few others know because they feared that more were involved.

***

Paul Davis kissed his son and tucked him in as his wife prepared to read Monty's favorite book. Regrets were occupying Paul's every thought. He did the unthinkable to save his family, and now another family was suffering because of his selfish actions. He wondered where Livvy was now and if she were all right. It had been five days, and Angelo was long gone. He could not stand to be around the Hoovers. Seeing their sadness and worry in Vivian and Tim made him nauseous. It was obvious that they loved Olivia as much as he loved his son. He could end it all and tell them what he knew, but he was not sure if what he heard was true or not. The least he could do was tell them who had taken her. When he looked at his wife and his son, he felt like the scum of the earth.

Sweet Livvy had collected all that money to help him with his son's medical bills. He betrayed her trust. Instead of anger, she offered him forgiveness—a forgiveness that felt like a sword being thrust into his heart piercing his soul. He had no right to it.

"Mary-Elisabeth, I have to go. I need to take care of some business," he said kissing his wife. He drove back to the station and got on the elevator. As each number change, a part of his manhood left. He had sold out an innocent child to save his child. He had no justification for his actions. He walked in stone silence up to Det. Hoover's door. He knocked and waited, trying to mentally prepare for the verbal and probably physical beating he was going to receive. If the roles were reversed, he would have beaten any man who harmed his family.

"He isn't here. He got a lead, and they are in Florida...something about a dead body," Gail said looking at him.

"Gail, does he have his phone? It is urgent that I speak with him," he said hoping that the dead body was not Livvy. He could not live with himself if they had murdered her.

"He does," she said and went back to her desk.

"Gail, who was the dead body? Does it have to do with Livvy?" he asked frantically.

"It's not her. The body is male, but that is all I know. We're praying for her and you too. How is your son?" she asked.

"He is better. Thanks," he said. He dashed back onto the elevator. His heart was beating loudly like the tell-tale heart; he felt like a character in a Poe story. He dialed the number frantically, but no one picked up. He took a deep breath and dialed Miguel. He answered on the second ring. He asked him to meet him at the diner because he needed to talk. Ten minutes later—disgraced and ashamed—Paul Davis was telling Miguel everything. Though he knew it meant he'd lose everything, he needed to ease his soul and bring Olivia Morris back home. Miguel listened without interruption. He felt sick to his stomach as he heard how they dragged Livvy out of the car and Paul did nothing. Then he felt admiration for her when she told Davis that she forgave him. Why? Why did he do this to Livvy? Hadn't she suffered enough from those she thought she could trust? "Where is she?" Miguel asked annoyed. He was holding back his anger. If he did not need information from Paul, he would have beaten him.

"I don't know for sure. I heard them say something about Mexico, but they found a dead body in Florida. So, I don't know where they are right now. I guess it's some Spanish speaking country," Det. Davis said.

"They probably said that to throw you off. If they went to Florida, they are probably on the water sailing somewhere. Does he have family in Mexico, Cuba, or anywhere in Central or South America?" Miguel asked.

"He isn't Mexican; I asked him, and he got offended. I don't know his family history because his mother, father, and brother are all dead," he said.

It was almost comical what he said, except it wasn't because Livvy's life was in danger.

"I work in the gang unit. I can get that information," he said calling his superior and asking him to run all they had on Angelo and his family background. As soon as he got the information, he texted Det. Hoover and Greene. "Davis, you need to talk to your wife and then your superior and apologize to the Hoover family," Miguel said.

"I know and I feel horrible," he said.

"You should. Livvy trusted you. I am going to Florida to find her. I suggest you go to your family," Miguel said. He got up and left. Immediately his phone began to ring. He answered it thinking it was Tim or Alan, but it was Eric the youth pastor. "Hello?"

"Miguel, it's Eric. I am calling because I received a call from Livvy. It was very short. She said Caribbean and then something about South America. Then she hung up. I don't know what is wrong or if she got caught, but you have to save her," Eric said still in a panic and mentally praying. She had come too far in her journey with God for it to end like this. "Please keep me informed," he requested.

"I will. Call my mom and tell her so she can be with Mrs. Hoover. I am on my way to get a flight," he said and hung up. He called Lt. Hoover and told him what Eric had told him. Tim told him what Vita said she saw, which were a black El Comino and some strange young men driving around the area. Miguel then contacted the FBI to pass on all the information he had, telling them that they had to be swift. He was not sure how much danger Livvy was in, but if Angelo knew she was calling home he could kill her.

***

Her heart finally stopped pounding out of her chest. She had made the call and prayed that someone would come before Angelo took her away. It was not easy to outsmart him. But once he had a few drinks and started dancing, he let his guard down. She pretended to be sick. But he wanted to party more, so he allowed her to walk alone. She unplugged the phone and patted water on her face, so she looked as though she had been sweating and jumped in the bed. She turned out all the lights and waited. Early in the morning, she heard the door creep open. She was at ease now; at least she stood a chance of surviving.

"Babe, baby, are you up?" he asked gently shaking Olivia.

"I am," she said breathing easy and staring at him. She saw his arm reach for the lamp and the dark room was dark no more. She blinked her eyes several times to adjust and looked at him. This was the time to play it up. She reached her hand out to caress his face.

"Did you have fun?" she asked.

"I did. We need to go," he said.

"Why? It's barely morning, and I am tired," she said trying not to show her alarm.

"I am feeling paranoid. We have been here too long, and I want to go," he said.

She had just made the call a few hours ago. That was not enough time to save her. "Can we wait until morning?" she asked.

"No," he said and pulled her out of bed. She did not fight; she put on her clothes and followed him out. It was so dark. She was so frightened. She may have misjudged. He probably was playing her, and now she was going to be fish food like Carlos. They made it back to the boat and took off. He walked her below in silence.

"Angelo, tell me what is wrong. You are scaring me," she said frantically.

"The less you know the better. Now chill out and go to bed," he ordered.

So that is how it was. The kindness wore off like fake gold on a tarnished chain. "What about the others?" she asked.

"They are following the plan as it was laid out. Why are you concerned about them? You need to be concerned about me?" he said.

Olivia felt destroyed once more. Who would find her now? She sat on the edge of the bed feeling deflated. She had no other wonderful ideas. She would just have to make the best out of a bad situation.

"Olivia, get in the bed with me," he demanded. His nerves were still shaken. Something did not feel right.

She dropped her head and rested beside him. She felt so tired. But her mind would not hush, keeping sleep at bay. She didn't know if she had the stamina to deal with him another minute, let alone another day. He pulled her closer to him and held her tightly. It was uncomfortable. They stared in silence at one another. She could not understand how someone so handsome was so horrible. He was kind, but cruel. Finally, he fell asleep. She continued to stare at him. He was vulnerable now. She could easily take her pillow and end it all now, but that was evil; a sin for a sin was not right. She recalled Lilly telling her that. That was how Dinah's brothers handled her violation; they killed all the men. Her brother was dead; no one could defend her honor. She erased the thought from her head. She touched him to make sure he was sound asleep. She had to get away for a while before she gave into her murderous thoughts. She got up and tip toed to the upper deck. It was beautiful watching the sun come alive. It looked like the water was its blanket, and it was just getting out of bed. There was something so lovely and so innocent about it. She was spellbound by its beauty, wishing she were the sun.

"It's lovely, ain't it?" the captain said to her.

"Yes, sir. It is. Where are we going?" she asked unaware that he had been watching her.

"I ain't supposed to say. You are far from home. I can tell you that. I hope you know how to speak Spanish, because you are headed that way," he said puffing on his cigar.

She knew Spanish and Portuguese very well; her school offered several languages as each student was to do an international Christian mission their junior or senior year. She wanted to go to Brazil, so she chose to learn Portuguese. She liked learning about other cultures as much as she liked numbers. She kept that to herself. The less Angelo knew the better.

"Where is Angelo?" he asked eyeing the young woman lustfully.

"He is sleeping," she said still looking at the water and the sky. It was a bewitching sight that captured her attention. It would not let go mainly because it had freedom and she longed for it. She glanced at the captain and then back at the water. She remembered him now. He was with the gentlemen—or should she say thugs—that night at the club. He was, she guessed, an errand boy.

"You want to try to drive? It is fun," he said still admiring how lovely she looked. Angelo said she was off limits. The others he could have, but not her. He wondered why she was so special. The fact that she was forbidden made him long for a taste all the more.

"No, sir. I better not do that. I'd rather look at the scenery," she said.

"You must be really special to Angelo. I move a lot of girls for him back and forth. You know, it's good money—human trafficking—but you are the first girl I seen him take to. He looks out for you," he said as his mind danced with impure thoughts.

Something about how he said it made Olivia feel uncomfortable. "He and my brother were good friends," she said.

"Oh. You aren't for sell then," he said with a chuckle.

"No, she ain't. She belongs to me," Angelo's voice boomed.

Olivia closed her eyes and did not look back. He sounded angry, and it was too early in the morning to feel his wrath. "Livvy, come here," he ordered.

She did not want to. She feared what would await her. She turned around and walked toward him. He reached out for her hand and walked her back below as if she were some toddler lost in the store. "What were you doing out of bed?" he asked trying to contain his annoyance.

It was simple; she was uncomfortable, and she wanted to stretch out her legs. "I just wanted to see the scenery. I thought it was okay since you were sound asleep," she said.

He shook his head. "You can't just wander, not even on this boat. You go where I tell you, and I told you to go to bed," he said.

She walked toward the room, but he pulled her back. "Why do you seek to make it harder on yourself? I will break you and you will submit," he said.

She knew what that meant, but she was already broken. "You don't have to hit me. I won't do it again," she said.

"I think you have been spoiled and used to getting your way. I have to remind you," he said shaking his head in disapproval.

"You don't; I remember well enough. I am sorry and it won't happen again," she fearfully implored.

He did anyway. He did not hit her in the face this time; instead it was body blows. He took off his belt and stripped her down, leaving just her undergarments; he hit her over and over again, and she could feel her flesh separating as the leather and metal spikes penetrated her skin. He beat her until she did not even feel him hitting her. She only knew he was hitting her because she saw his arms moving. He grew tired and began to use his left hand; it was like he was in a trance. He was shouting insults in Spanish. She crawled up in a ball and waited for him to finish. Tears mixed with blood penetrated and painted the floor, but she remained hushed; she was in such indescribable agony. She should have never gotten out of the bed, but she just wanted to see the sea and be away from him. She had no other intention besides to calm her mind. She should have killed him in his sleep.

He jerked her up violently and threw her onto the bed. She turned her back to him; his face made her hurt and her body shook at will. She could not control it; blood stained the sheets. She bled like a waterfall. The numbness was wearing off, and the pain returned. She reached for her brother's Bible, held it near her heart, and started quoting the scripture her brother loved.

Hours later Angelo returned. He sat down on the bed and offered her something to eat, but she declined. He offered an apology, but she did not accept. She did not move. She just started saying the Lord's Prayer and ignored him. He did not like that she was not talking to him, so he physically turned her over. "I am talking to you," he said.

It was so painful when his fingers penetrated her open wounds. She could not cry, for her tears had turned to dust. "Can I have some bandages please?" she asked. Her knuckles were white from gripping the pocket Bible. Her body was still spilling blood, and the pain grew more intense each second. She felt so cold. Her body was freezing; she hoped death was taking her.

"I'm sorry, Livvy, for having to whoop you like that. But I had too. You make me crazy sometimes. I just love you so much; I had to do it to bring you back for your own good." He said her body looked like a wall full of push pin holes. The sight of her bloodied body was heinous, and he wondered how he could have inflicted that kind of beating on her. This was why she feared him. If she only obeyed, this would have been avoided.

"Can I have some bandages, please?" she again requested. He got up and brought back the first aid kit. She did not know where to start because she had so many lacerations. She looked like a tiger. It reminded her of Bo. Angelo took the cream from her hand and tried to help. "I can do it," she mumbled.

"Livvy, don't be stubborn. You can't reach it, so let me help," he said.

She did not fight him. She had no reason to. He had broken her all the way down. She was so tired that she went to sleep while he was cleaning her wounds. She had strange and painful dreams that tormented her; even in her slumber he haunted her.

***

Olivia awoke in a strange bed. She was no longer on the boat, but she could not tell where she was or how she got there. She did not move; pulling her knees to her chest, she began to pray. She was not sure what day of the week it was or how long it had been since she was taken from Georgia. It seemed like a lifetime. She heard the door open. She looked and saw a petite older woman come into the room. She watched her methodically but quietly. She asked her nothing, and she spoke no words. The lady worked swiftly, placing food and drink down and then tending to Olivia's wounds. On instinct she jerked back, but the elderly lady smiled kindly and in broken English explained she was cleaning Olivia's wounds. Olivia responded in Spanish; she looked surprised but relieved and began to converse with her. Olivia wondered where Angelo was. He had to be near and, if so, she would not move. Her body was still hurting and burning from the horrible beating she had endured. The old lady told her she had been asleep for a few days. She had been sick with fever, but she was better now. However, she needed to eat to regain her strength. Olivia thanked her but did not touch the food. Where had Angelo taken her to? She did not know, but she hoped soon someone would find her. She wanted to shower, but she was too scared to move.

"Olivia, you are up finally. I see you met Abuela. She has been tending to you night and day. Come, you can shower and change clothes. Then you can meet my uncle," Angelo said smiling as if nothing had ever occurred.

Olivia did not think he had any family alive. She got up slowly because her body was stiff. Then she showered. It was a nice house—much nicer than what he had back in Georgia. It was huge with Colombian style architecture, and it was well taken care of. There were armed guards walking around the perimeter of the house. There was a long driveway that ended with a gate that surrounded the entire house. It looked like something out of a Mafia movie. Livvy quickly walked into the bathroom. The water was a welcome distraction, but her body was still sore. She washed her scarred skin with the most delicate touch. She looked in the mirror and did not recognize herself. She only knew it was her by her eyes. She had lost weight and looked like a board full of push pins. Angelo had done a number on her this time. She wondered how he explained that to his grandmother.

Olivia put on the clothes laid out for her, and she walked out of the bathroom. Angelo greeted her with a hug, but she did not hug him back. How dare he take her from her home and forced her to be in his? She loathed him. He grabbed her hand and escorted her downstairs to see his family. They seemed so kind and civilized—nothing at all like Angelo. His Uncle Luis smiled and greeted her kindly. She responded respectfully. She wondered if he knew that Angelo was on the run. Did Uncle Luis know she had been kidnapped and that Carlos was murdered? Was he part of the human trafficking? Was Olivia in the lions' den? She did not know; but what she knew was they were Angelo's family and not hers. She may be young, but she was not dumb; she watched and listened. This was a family business. Angelo's father did not just out the blue create BWD; they were part of something bigger. That was what those conversations were about—family business. She thought it was all code. But it was more than that—so much more than she had ever thought. It was over now; she was officially in too deep. She excused herself, went back to her bedroom, and wept silently.

CHAPTER 18

Saving Olivia

"Vivian, we were too late. But people have seen them. They said she looked good and was in good spirits. We just have to keep looking. You keep praying, and I am going to bring her home," he said.

"Okay. Victoria wants to speak with you," she said handing her daughter the phone. Four weeks had gone by—four weeks of wonder, worry, and fear. Every time a lead came it in, it was too late.

"I love you, Tori. You take care of your mother, and I will be home soon," he said hanging up the phone.

"Tim, we need to go home and let the FBI handle this," Alan said.

"I am not leaving without her. I don't care who does not like it. She is in South America somewhere, and I will search each inch until I find her. I don't care if it takes years." he said.

"You are right. Let's go." he said. The two were taken to the airport determined to bring Olivia back home.

***

Olivia's stomach felt like it was in knots. She thought they said she was getting better. She sat on the bed holding the trashcan vomiting. She wanted to go home. How she missed Mrs. Hoover, wishing she was there to bring her tea. She missed them all. Her mind went to Jacoby, and she wondered how he was doing. Had they won the cheerleading competition? How was the center going? How were Caroline, Destiny, Mr. D, Coach Geter, Victoria, Phillip, and Vincent? She had to let go of those memories; they brought more pain then joy. She just hoped they were enjoying life far more than she was.

"Babe, are you feeling any better?" Angelo asked as he poked his head inside.

She shook her head no and started vomiting again.

"I don't understand why you are throwing up. You don't eat anything," he said walking near her. "The doctor is coming; he can figure it out."

She just looked at him and said nothing; he turned to leave. The doctor arrived within an hour. He did all the usual and asked her to take a pregnancy test. Olivia refused, but he insisted. Then Angelo heard the commotion and ordered her to do what the doctor said. She did, and they waited. The doctor went to check and told her it was positive. She was pregnant. Now she was forever linked to him, whether she wanted to be or not. Angelo went running through the house in excitement. Olivia was not having a baby in a country other than her own. She was deeply depressed to be pregnant. She got up and walked down the stairs. Angelo was distracted and she asked the doctor to call her family and handed him a note she had addressed; if he didn't call, she hoped he sent them the letter. She implored him and hoped she could trust him. He said he would, but she was not sure. Olivia knew now that Angelo would not allow her out of his sight. "Livvy come back inside. You need your rest," he said,

She walked back inside, and he lifted her up and carried her back to the bed. She cried herself into a fitful slumber. How was she supposed to raise a child? She was still a child. What life would this child have? Would the child be born out of rape? Was it rape if she did not fight him? It did not matter; she would never get justice, but God knows she could not raise a child in Angelo's chaotic world.

The week passed with no news from the States, but Olivia did find out that they found Carlos's body...or some pieces of it. Angelo was gone often with his Uncle Luis. His aunt and cousins were gone on vacation. That left Livvy alone with Angelo's grandmother.

Olivia was happy; his grandmother was a kind gentle soul. Olivia also confirmed while walking the grounds with Helena that Angelo's family was a notorious crime family. All this time, she thought he was just a bum fumble; but it was a sham. He really was connected and rich. They were King Pins and had their hand in every kind of crime: from extortion to murder, from human to drug trafficking, from dog fighting to buying police and politicians. It frightened Olivia even more that she was carrying his child inside of her. The child would inherit this illegal kingdom built off the blood of innocence. She wrote another letter and had Helena drive her to the post office to ensure it was sent. She guessed Angelo felt safe around his own family because he allowed her some freedom; she did what she wanted when he was away. She read books mostly. But when no one was watching, she stole paper and envelopes; she sent letters to church, to Miguel, to any address she could remember. She wondered if they even made it to them. She prayed daily that her child would be like her and not Angelo. She would not forgive herself if she screwed up his or her life before it began. Before she found out she was pregnant, she contemplated suicide. But her baby was making her stronger. She hoped that the Hoovers would find her, or at least that Miguel would. He had to. There is nothing a mother would not do to protect her child. She would not be the mother, her mother was. She would not blame her child for the sins of his or her father. This child was the blessing out of the burdens. She sat down in the garden rubbing her belly.

"Olivia, come inside my dear. You don't need to be outside so much," Abuela said.

Olivia smiled at her and got up. She was not as delicate as they treated her, and the pregnancy was early. She was just a few weeks. There was no need for the alarm. She honestly did not feel like she was pregnant; but, then again, she was not sure how she was supposed to feel. Maybe all that movement did not start until months later.

**

"Tim, Tim, come here. I have a letter from Livvy," Vivian said screaming and running all at once. She handed it to her husband.

It was her handwriting. It was from Colombia. She was a smart girl. She was in South America. Now they had an address. He contacted Jeff the FBI contact and related the information. After he hung up, he received a call from the church saying Livvy had sent them a letter. She was alive, and that was all that mattered.

"Tim, will you be able to bring her back?" Vivian asked overjoyed to hear from her.

"We have an address; I am bringing our girl home," he said.

There was a reserved calm as Tim Hoover sat on the plane to South America for a second time. Finally, she would be coming home where she belonged. He still could not believe that Det. Davis had sold her out. But he was not alone; two correctional officers had fallen victim too. Now three law enforcers were being locked up. The thought of it angered him and hurt him so deeply. How frightened Livvy must be in a foreign country without anyone. "God, keep my daughter safe until I can reach her; please keep her safe," he said.

***

Olivia sat down and pulled out her brother's Bible and read: "Let not your heart be troubled; you believe in God, believe also in Me....I am the way, the truth, and the life. No one comes to the Father except though Me." John 14:1, 6. She just had to be faithful to God. He was protecting her. At least being pregnant meant no beatings. Angelo's family would not allow it. For now, she was safe. She was frightened what they would do if she gave birth to a son. They would train him to be like them, but she did not want that. Angelo and Uncle Luis hoped it to be a boy; Angelo was the only male in the family since his father and brother had died. Luis only had two daughters. Olivia had eight months to get out, and she would find a way.

"Hey, Livvy," Angelo said rubbing her stomach and kissing it. It sent a chill up her spine. She did not like him to touch her. Although she tried to hide her dismay, it showed. He looked at her, not sure how to react. "Did you eat today?" he asked in an attempt to ignore her discontent with him. He had been brutal in the past, but he was trying to control his rages. However, he would not react that way if she did not push him. Didn't she understand his love for her?

She shook her head yes, which irritated him.

"Livvy, what did I tell you about that? I hate it when you do that. Just say yes or no," he said eyeing her distastefully.

His tone irritated her immensely. "Yes. I ate today, master," she said tartly.

"Go upstairs," he ordered with his finger pointed toward her. His face was reddening as the words came off his tongue.

Olivia got up and walked slowly. Maybe she had gone too far. What would he do now? She opened the bedroom door and sat down on the puffy Victorian style chair. "Are you going to beat me?" she asked coldly.

"I have not decided yet," he said walking past her and opening the drawer where she stashed the stolen paper. "Have you been writing? I heard the maid took you to the post office. Why would you need to go there when we are all here?" he asked annoyed. She was trying his patience. He asked for obedience, and she gave his disobedience. He tried to be sweet, but she wanted to be tart. How were things going to get better if she continued to act this way?

She showed no emotion but looked at him right in the eye. "She was going, and I wanted to ride. You don't take me anywhere. I went to the store with her yesterday as well. Did you hear about that?" she asked insolently.

"Are you trying to mock me? Just because you carry my child does not give you the authority to do as you wish; if anything, you should be more careful. This is not Georgia; this is Colombia. There is a different set of rules here. There are people here who are ruthless, and little girls trying to be cute get killed. I don't take you places because it is not safe for you," he said walking back toward her.

She swallowed hard, and he hovered around her.

"I didn't know," she said. She did not want to go anywhere with him anyway. She just wanted to go home, and the only way she could leave was to see the layout. She was well aware that escape was nearly impossible because she had no idea where the airport was. She had no passport or any other identification; all those things were back in Georgia. She was not going back on a boat either. She was stuck until someone came to rescue her.

"I know, and that is why I am telling you. You have got to listen to me. I might not do the right thing all the time, but I do care about you. I don't want anything to happen to you. I'd rather I hit you then some stranger. They'll gang rape you, beat you, torture you, and kill you. It would be a way for them to hurt me and my family.

We aren't the only families in this line of work. You are carrying something so dear to me. I am not going to lose either of you. I'll be better, I promise; but you have to listen. I think we should get married before the baby comes. Things will be as they should," he said kissing her lips tenderly. He started to walk out the room then said, "I'll work on my temper. If we get married, we are bound forever."

Tears fell from her eyes, washing her lips to remove the stain of him. She did not want to be married...not to him. She thought being locked up—and losing her entire family and best friend—was as bad as it could get, but this had to be the worst.

She got up and walked to the door but removed her hand. She stood there transfixed and finally went to take a shower. This would be her life now: no school, no dreams, ND no life. She would be confined to these walls by her dictator. She put on her nightgown and hummed herself a lullaby. The door opened slowly, and Angelo returned and walked up to her.

"Did you contact anyone from back home?" he asked calmly.

She thought about lying, but he already knew the truth. "Yes. I wanted to let them know I was okay. You never said I could not contact them," she said.

He looked annoyed. She knew he wanted to hurt her, so she braced herself. It did not come. Instead, he paced back and forth as if he were thinking. His eyes glanced at hers occasionally, and then he stopped and motioned for her to come to him. She was hesitant, but she finally walked to him. He slapped her. She thought about slapping him back, but instead she ran to the door to leave. He was faster and used all his strength to keep the door from being opened. "Please, just let me go," she said.

"No. You have my child. You aren't going anywhere," he said.

"You don't care about me or this baby. You just slapped me for contacting the only family that I have left. You have denied me kindness, courtesy, respect, and love. I was good to you. I stayed true to you, and you left me to get arrested. You beat me for no reason at all. That is not love, it is hate; you are just like my mother. You kidnapped me and forced me to have sex with you; you play mind games constantly with me. Why? Who is it that you see when you look at me? Who do you hate so much that you make me pay for their sin? What have I ever done to you? Is it not enough that I lost my virginity at five? Do you care about the scars I have carried or how deeply saddened I was when Deek died and then Lilly? I have nothing, and the little I had you took. You are still taking; if you hate me so much, then you should kill me. I am slowly dying anyway. All I ever wanted was to be loved and have a family. I have been denied it over and over again.

"Living with the Hoover family was my last chance, and you took me away from them. I sent them a letter of gratitude, and I told them that I was okay. They deserve to know that. I have been faithful and loyal to you, even though you have not been to me. I could have learned to love you if you had just backed off, but you keep pushing.

I will not allow this child to be like you. I don't care what you do to me; my child will know God, love, and kindness. I had forgiven you, Angelo; and then you do this. You beat me with a belt because I wanted to see the ocean and clear my head. I prayed for you with the same compassion I prayed for my brother, but that is not enough for you. If you touch me again in a violent way or force me to have sex with you, I will kill myself. I will do it to save me and my child...so help me. You let me out of this room," she said with all the courage she could muster. She glared at him and did not blink. She meant her words. God forgive her, but she would rather die at her hands than at his; she understood why Lilly did it.

He looked at her like she had lost her mind. She felt like she had. Olivia was tired of being a punching bag; all her life, someone was taking from her. She would not be a victim anymore. His face tightened as he ground his teeth. He wanted to take his hands and beat her, but he could not. They were at a stalemate, but she had two and he only had one. She was in no mood to bargain.

"You are mad; you have just completely lost your mind. I can't believe you just said that to me. Fine. You win. I'll do whatever you want. Just don't hurt yourself or the baby. I'm sorry I hit you. It won't happen again. I do love you, Livvy. In the way I understand love, I love you," he said taking his hand off the door. Her truth penetrated his heart. He had pushed her too far; maybe he should have backed off and let love come instead of trying force it.

She looked at him. "You need to read 1 Corinthians, chapter 13, and learn how it defines love. This is not love. If you loved me, you would have been honest about Deek. You would have never kidnapped me. You would have left me alone. Your lust led you to this. You are mean and cold. You hurt and you hate. You need to talk to God. We have nothing to say to one another," she said and walked out the bedroom slamming the door as hard as she could. She walked downstairs in search of Abuela. She found her sitting in her chair knitting. She looked at Olivia's face and shook her head. She let Livvy cry on her shoulder. "Why does he hate me?" Olivia asked her.

"Shush, child. He does not hate you. He hates himself. He has many demons, and now he has to face them," she said. "He can't hit you. You are in a delicate state and so young. You could miscarry. I will talk to him," she said getting up and walking her to the kitchen. She offered Olivia something warm to drink, and an hour later she walked her back to bed. She tucked Livvy in, and she fell asleep instantly.

***

The doctor did as she had asked; he called the number and told what he knew. He learned—as he had suspected—she was being held against her will. He had been there many times before. At least she was not really pregnant. He would not tell anyone. He had to let them believe that she was until help could arrive. He set back in his office chair alarmed by what had transpired. For too long that family had been taking innocent girls and tricking them out. He had grown tired of it himself. He dialed a trusted friend, told him what he had seen, and asked for his help. Two days later, the Calvary had arrived in the darkness with Agent Chris, Jeff, and Tim. The doctor again told what he knew and explained that the Gaviria family was a dangerous family. "You have to enter with caution. You understand they have cameras, armed guards, and a kill mentality. If you are going to strike their compound, you have to attack in early morning and know exactly where she is. She is allowed a walk in the morning, and she spends her time reading in the library; but that is all I know," the doctor said looking at the three gentlemen before him.

They listened without interruption.

Timothy let out a sigh; he knew it would not be easy, but he had no idea it was this serious. They had arrested Dough and Biggs with ease, but they refused to talk about anything. "Thank you, sir," he said to the doctor. Then he turned his attention back to the agents. "I thought he was just some local punk. He's part of the Gaviria drug cartel, and my daughter is in there. We have to get her out soon," Det. Hoover said.

"We have to do more surveillance. We want to bring her out safe, and we have to take our time," Chris said

Det. Hoover dropped his head in his hands. It got more complicated the closer he got to her.

"Senor, I will help in any way I can. They trust me, and I have access to every part of the house. I assure you she is fine. She is a little underfed and she has been battling a stomach virus; but she will be fine," he said in an assuring tone. They talked more and then departed, hopeful that Olivia would be home soon.

CHAPTER 19

Understanding

Olivia walked to the garden to rest her head and contain her thoughts. It was evident that she was not returning to Georgia. She was so tired of battling Angelo and living in fear. She recalled what she had said in anger about killing herself. It was probably the only way out. She pulled her knees to her chest and let the sun cook her skin. She just did not have the will power to fight anymore. She could not understand what turned Angelo into an animal. What made him hate? Despite her sixteen years on this earth, she did not understand why some men thought it was their right to hurt another. He had no argument with here; he had no reason to place his hands on her. At times, she loathed him; other times, she longed for him. The conflicting feelings were making her hate herself; if there was a child growing inside of her, it was part of him as well. She had to find a way to work; didn't she? There was no textbook for this; nothing in her classes prepared her for how to live this way of life. She felt so lonely; nothing was familiar to her. This was not her country, not her home, and not her heritage. She did not belong here, but she did not belong anywhere. She was a wanderer. It was selfish of her to burden innocent people because she wanted to be saved. The Hoovers had done enough; she should not expect more. Angelo and his family were not going to allow her to leave. It was a truth she was going to have to accept. God was not limited as she was; God she had no matter where she was. She had to hold on that truth. God said I am with you wherever you go.

"Livvy? Livvy? Are you out here?" she heard Angelo's voice. She did not answer. She just looked toward his voice. He walked up to her, his eyes affable and his voice so gentle. "I was looking for you all over. It's hot out today. Maybe you ought to come inside," he said reaching his hand out to hers.

"I'd like to stay a little longer," she said.

"Okay. You feel like talking to me. I know I have not been a good boyfriend to you. I have been treating you like an enemy, but I love you. It's different with you. You aren't like other people," he said taking his hand and playing with her hair.

"Why have you been so mean to me?" she asked looking intensely into his eyes.

He looked as though he was searching trying to find the right answer. "I don't know. I do what I know. My dad hit my mom, and she allowed it. He said you have to keep a woman in check. It's how you show your manhood. Then she died. It changed me. After my pops and brother died, I died too. I was a child not older than you when you lost your mother. I hated her for dying and leaving me behind. I just didn't care about anything but money, power, and respect. It's all that I have known, especially after my mother died. My uncle looked to me to carry on the legacy. As far as you are concerned, I wanted you to love me like you loved Deek. I wanted someone to look at me like you looked at him. You idolized him, but you fear me," he said.

"My brother never took from me. He loved me and gave me everything he could. You give, then take, and then hurt. I never know what Angelo I am getting. You can be kind and sweet. You told me I was beautiful after seeing my scars. I liked that you. You changed. I can't deal with that. You have killed people. You killed Carlos, and you said you loved him like a brother. Why should I believe you won't do the same to me?" she asked.

He let out a sigh and dropped his head. "Olivia, I'm sorry. I can't change the past. Abuela and Uncle Luis have had a serious heart to heart with me. We are who we are. My family is different; loyalty and honesty are key to our survival. I had to kill Carlos. He would have killed me sooner or later. It's the world we live in. I know you; I trust you and I love you. I don't want to hit you, and I don't want you to be afraid. It was wrong of me to take you, but I didn't know what else to do. It was getting hot for me in Georgia, and my family wanted me to come home," he said.

"My family wants me home too. Please just let me go back," she requested.

"I can't, Livvy. You'll learn to love it here. You'll adjust well," he said leaning over to kiss her forehead.

She dropped her head. She was not going home. "Okay," she said getting up and preparing to walk back to the house.

"Come on, Livvy. My family loves you. I love you; we will get married, and things will work as they should. You know I will protect you with my life," he said.

She followed listening to him but wondering who was going to protect her from him. Her face still held his hand imprint on her cheek. She held her stomach and worried. Once inside, she walked to the library; it was the only room in the house that was unused, except by her. Her mind was still trying to unlock the confessions that Angelo had made. She understood that they both had suffered in life; it was why he and Deek were so inseparable until her brother chose God over gang. She sat down on the plum oval shaped chair and opened her brother's Bible. It was her way of communicating with him and seeking his advice. She knew there was power in the pages, for God had brought her through every trial; she could not give up now. She felt weak and forgotten in the past—even somewhat now—but survival would no longer be submitting. When she cowered in front of Angelo, it fed into his mindset of power; but when she expressed herself nonviolently, it halted him and made him think. She was weaker physically, but she was stronger spiritually. She had something he did not; she had God. She had her brother's Bible to navigate her through. Physically, her brother was gone, but he had left behind an invaluable gift that she had not thought of before; his Bible was an extension of him and her only defense in this new world. She prayed silently, moving her lips and asking God for guidance. She opened the Bible, not looking for a particular verse but letting God lead her to what he needed her to know. She found herself reading second Timothy, which made her remember the Hoovers. Timothy Hoover was too good a man, too honest a person, too in love with God to violate her trust. She had a bond and, no matter what lie Paul Davis told, he would know the truth; he would find her. She just had to endure for a while. As she read from chapter one to chapter four, she found power and inspiration. Maybe instead of looking at this situation as horrible, she should use it as a time of ministry. Angelo had tormented her because he was tormented, but he was God's child too. She could not allow her fleshly mind to consume her; if she did, she was no different than him. Christians were different; they are the light and the salt, loving when others hate, praying for those who seek to punish. Christians love God and serve Him no matter the situation. She would not yield to man, but she would yield to the Creator of man. She had more than herself to think of. This child, though not conceived as she had hoped, would not be like them; this child would be better. The purpose of second Timothy was Paul preparing Timothy, and now God was preparing her. As a Christian, she had to avoid disputes and quarrels. She must show Angelo why Deek left the gang for God. Maybe...just maybe...he would find God too. If God could change her brother and her, why could He not change Angelo too? All things happen for a reason, she thought silently to herself. God does not make mistakes. He is the Master who is all knowing, and He is devoid of any wrong; He is always right. That was why Lilly forgave her stepfather and stepbrother; she only wished she had forgiven herself. "Tell me what to do, Lord; tell me how to help him see. Please, Father. Just allow the seed to be planted and unhardened his heart so he can see as you see. I ask it in Jesus's name, Amen." Angelo was like Pharaoh, and he refused to let her go. God, when he had enough, would part any sea to bring her home. She would wait on God. She began to pray the prayer of David in Psalm 142:

1 I cry out to the Lord; I plead for the Lord's mercy. 2 I pour out my complaints before him and tell him all my troubles. 3 When I am overwhelmed, you alone know the way I should turn.

Wherever I go, my enemies have set traps for me. 4 I look for someone to come and help me, but no one gives me a passing thought!

No one will help me; no one cares a bit what happens to me. 5 Then I pray to you, O Lord. I say, "You are my place of refuge. You are all I really want in life.

6 Hear my cry, for I am very low. Rescue me from my persecutors, for they are too strong for me.7 Bring me out of prison so I can thank you.

The godly will crowd around me, for you are good to me."

"Who are you talking to?" Angelo asked finally making himself known; he had been standing there for the last ten minutes, watching and wondering what she was doing. Why did she spend so much of her day surrounded by books and reading the Bible? Or was she writing another letter pleading for someone to come for her? No one would come...not here. He would make her see. She was probably carrying a son; he had wanted one for so long. To be the father to his son that he did not have. To teach him the things he had never known. His father, though he loved him, was not a man to become. He wanted more for the child that Livvy was carrying.

His voice did not startle her; she was not afraid anymore of him. She turned slowly to see him walking near her. Hours had passed since their last conversation in the gardens. She wondered what thoughts lurked behind his ebony eyes. Had he grown angry or gentle? She could not tell. It was almost as if he were devoid of thought, for there were no tell-tale signs written on his face.

"I was talking to God, praying for understanding and for you," she said.

He looked at her surprised and then moved forward so now he was right beside her. She could feel his breath on the top of her head. He lingered and then sat beside her on the chair. "You pray for me? What did you pray about," he asked?

She looked at him and tried to imagine a time in his life when he was good. How had she been through such a struggle and turned out so differently? She guessed because of Deek. Her brother kept her from being Angelo. He was once a child who knew no wrong and was innocent. His life was destroyed by trying to please his earthly father. She had wanted to please her earthly mother, but Nene never loved or cared for her. But God loved her before she knew who He was. He knew and knows her entire life story. "I prayed that you would change. There is something still human, still good, and still salvageable if you just ask God for forgiveness and accept him into your life. Deek did not betray you; he was trying to save you. His love for you did not stop because he found God; he was hoping that you would find him too. Deek was the most selfless person I knew. If you don't come to the truth and accept Christ into your life, you will die. You will burn for all eternity; you don't have to if you just do the right thing. Kidnapping, killing, selling drugs, and selling women might give you temporary joy. But after a while, it fades. It fades because it is of the world and not of God; the Father never fades. He keeps every promise, and He protects His children. You must be a lover of God and not a lover of the pleasures of this world," she said placing her hands-on top of his. She thought maybe he'd feel it as she had with Miguel and Jacoby.

He looked into her eyes, trying to figure out why. What was this power that consumed Deek and now her? His father had taught him that a man takes what he wants. To depend on another is weak and stupid. His mother, Angela, believed in God. As a young boy, he watched his mother shrink right before his eyes while still holding her Bible and talking about God. He made his decision never to love a God who took mothers. God killed his mother, he allowed her to get cancer, and he allowed them to have to stay in a place that was not good because his Uncle Luis and Pops quarreled about how the family should run the business and separated. His father died without making it right with his brother. Now Livvy wanted him to accept God. God destroyed his family. God left him behind, taking the people he loved the most. He was his god. He decided who died and who lived; he controlled what would and would not happen, and only him. It was the only way to live; it was how his father lived. "Don't waste your prayers on me. I am the master of my fate, and I do as I please. If you want to read and pray, that is fine. I will not take that from you. I can't serve your God because he betrayed me too many times," he said getting up and starting to walk away.

"Angelo, it does not have to be that way. If you accept Christ, then you wouldn't feel the need to hit when you are angry. You would love God more than yourself, and you would love others more than your own pleasures. You have to, Angelo. You will hit me again; you will get upset over something simple and attack me...maybe even kill me. You might even hurt the baby. You are capable of anything. I am just saying that if I have to be here and I have to raise a child with you, don't you think that child should have the best parents? You can't be a good father if you don't know the Father," she said looking at him. Her heart was pleading with his because she was more worried about their child than she was for herself.

He turned around and walked back to her. She thought it was maybe to hit her, but she was prepared.

"Stop. You make me lose my temper; you just push me and push me until I can't do anything but express myself physically. I will not kill you...never. I will not hurt our child. I know what it's like to be without a mother. I would never deny the baby that. I know what it's like to have your father abuse you. I want him or her to be like you. You remind me of my mother. No matter what I did or how bad I was, she loved me; then she left me. She died, and I could not save her or help her. She was just gone...like my brother and pops...like Deek. I loved Deuce and cherished our friendship; he was my blood brother. I never wanted him to die. I already buried a brother, and I lost it when Deek was killed. Listen, Livvy. I know there is a God; I know because my Madre told me so, but I don't love Him, and He doesn't love me. I was condemned to hell from birth. Your prayers won't save me; I can't be saved," he said.

Now, she understood. He blamed God, as she had, for his misfortune; he thought God did not love him, which is what she had thought. They were so different, but yet so much alike. They were both longing for what was taken; they were both seeking ways to fill that emptiness. God had given her earthly angels: her brother, Lilly, Miguel and his family, the Hoovers, Vita, Det. Alan, and her church family. They had all in some way offered her hope from God through their kindness and love for God. Angelo needed that too; all of BWD did. She hoped that Hollow Hill would have a revival—an awakening of the soul—to see that God was still in control.

"I will pray for you. I will pray as long as it takes, because I don't believe God is finished with you. You will struggle, you will fall, and you will lose it all; then when you are so low—the lowest you can possibly get—you will look up and God will be there. I may have a piece of you growing in me and I may never leave this place until I die, but I won't marry anyone who does not serve the God I serve. Do what you will as long as you want, but I will pray until I can't anymore. I will love God in this life and the next. You have no power over me. All power is in God. He is who I serve; He has my loyalty, my heart, my life," she said standing up. She felt stronger as each word lifted from her lips...as if she was empowered by the Holy Spirit.

He let out a grunt but said nothing more. There was nothing to say. She watched him leave and then reclined back onto the chair. She rubbed her stomach; it ached so badly. She did not like eating the food that Helena cooked. It tasted good, but it did not agree with her or the baby. She was now only eating broth. She did not like that either. Maybe it was because she felt anxious and nervous that her stomach kept doing flip-flop. She held it tightly and made a decision: as long as she had Jesus, she was impenetrable. No matter what Angelo did from this day forward, he was not in charge anymore; God was, is, and always will be.

   **

She awoke feeling refreshed with her mind replaying the conversation that Angelo and she had. Her body relaxed as the warm water cascaded down her back, and it was like the stress was all gone. She felt an inner peace that only God could give, and she knew it would be all right. This was just her flesh—her earthly body— so let come what may; but her spiritual body was strong. "God, I will not question you. I will not blame you, for I know that you will give me a hope and a future. You've carried me this long and loved me when I rejected you. So, Father, I will wait; I will praise you," she whispered to herself. As she turned off the water and got out, she took her hand and rubbed her stomach. She hoped she would be a better mother to her child than what she had. She tried to imagine how she'd look in the coming months; she still had not gained much weight. She looked like she was losing; she hoped the baby was all right. She walked downstairs and heard male voices speaking. They stopped when she made it to the last step. It was Angelo, his Uncle Luis, and two men she had not seen before. Olivia walked into the kitchen and sat down at the table. Angelo excused himself and followed her. "You need anything?" he asked so soft and with ease. There was something different in his eyes that was almost human. After their talk in the library, he had made himself invisible. She hoped God was changing him. But the fact still remained that he would not allow her to return to Georgia.

"I'd like to go walking," she said.

"All right. Do you need me to assist you?" he asked.

She shook her head no. He turned to leave but turned back around and gently kissed her. "I am sorry; I know I said it before, but I am. I'll do better," he said.

She nodded, and he caressed her cheek and kissed where he had hit her. Then he turned to leave with the men; she heard the door close and the car start. She assumed they were off to take care of business. Olivia attempted to get up to walk, but her stomach was doing something weird and she was not sure if she could move. Her face became distorted, alarming Helena. She ran to call the doctor. She told Helena she was fine, but Helena insisted she not move. The doctor came immediately, but Olivia told him she was fine. He said she needed to go to the hospital. Abuela held her hand as they took her to the hospital. Olivia held her stomach. They were speaking in Spanish quicker than her ear could pick up, but she could make out the doctor asking if she had been stressed. If he lived with Angelo, she wondered how stressed he would be. Plus, she was kidnapped and forced to live with a family she did not know. She thought anyone would be stressed. Because she was pregnant at sixteen by a man who she did not love but feared, stressed was an understatement. She was depressed, scared, panicked, extremely anxious, and homesick. She wanted to be back in Georgia. Hollow Hill was Disney Land compared to Colombia. Her blood pressure began to rise, and she blacked out. She fell into a deep dream, or maybe it was real. She could hear voices but not see faces.

"Where is she?" Angelo asked walking toward Helena.

"Senor Gaviria, she is with the doctor. She had some cramping after you left. Her blood pressure shot up, and I called the doctor. He said she must come here. I don't know anymore," she said looking worried.

He collapsed on the waiting room chair. This was karma. It was his fault for being so angry with her and hitting her; he had caused this catastrophe. He never wanted this. He rested his throbbing head into his hands and cried. Helena tried unsuccessfully to comfort him. His grandmother had already angrily chastised him, as did his uncle; they were right, family was first and he had no right to put his hands on her. Deek would never hit her. How could he? He would never be the man Derrick was; he could not force love, and he could not earn her love. The words Olivia spoke were like daggers in his heart. He confessed he was wrong, but she looked so sad; all she wanted was to go home. Her words penetrated to his soul. He had no right or reason, but his father had treated his mother that way. She allowed it; he hated her for letting his father mistreat her and them. Yet he was repeating his father's mistakes. At times he loved his father; at other times he feared him. Livvy would never love him or respect him. Now he could lose his child and Livvy too. He did what he had never before done and prayed quietly to God...a God he had mocked and disrespected...a God he had loathed because of the death of his mother...a God he had blamed for every bad thing that ever happened to him. The person to blame was himself. He had been the devil's advocate. He had slaughtered innocent people because he lusted for power. But being number one was lonely. The top was not what it seemed to be.

He wanted to confess; he would give his life to protect her and his child. He wandered aimlessly, searching for a chapel where he could pray, confess, and save his burning soul. Like following a luminous light, he found the hospital chapel. Opening the doors was like walking into God's arms. He walked until he was upfront and looking upward. He searched the depths of his soul; his talk with Livvy had loosened his hardened heart. The Chaplin saw him enter and came in behind him; he had seen this many times...a family member of a dying patient seeking solace and refuge in God's house. "Son, can I be of assistance?" he asked walking toward Angelo.

"Father, can God hear the prayers of a condemned man who has mocked Him and done so much wrong he can't find a way to do right? I am a horrible person...a beast. I have killed and lied. I have committed every sin God asked a man not to do. Now my girlfriend and unborn child are fighting to survive. No one will tell me anything, and I think God is punishing me for my sins. I did them; He should take his revenge on me, not them," he said crying; rarely had he cried. The last time was his mother's funeral, and his father slapped him for being weak. The tears that fell were for his brother, his father, Deek, Livvy, his baby, and himself. He thought he would drown in them. He understood; he understood how Livvy felt after Deek bled to death in her arms. Now he had to feel it too. "I am not strong enough. God I cannot do this anymore. I can't carry these burdens anymore," he confessed.

"Son, calm down and sit with me. God loves you. He can't deny Himself. God is love. My son, this is not punishment, it is not revenge; it is God telling you to come home. I will listen to all you need to confess, and I will pray the prayer of salvation with you. Receive the Son, for Jesus is the only way to God. He will wash away your sins and make them as white as snow. There is nothing so bad or so big that God can't fix it. You, my son, have to allow him to do so; you must leave the flesh, the pleasure, and the world to become a humble servant of God. You must be willing to give it all up so you can have all the promises He has for you. You are an heir to His riches, His love, and His forgiveness. With man these things are impossible, but with God all things are possible," the Chaplin said.

"But Father, I am evil in its purest form. I followed my earthly father and not the Father. I walked away; I forgot. I blamed God and took credit for things that now bring me shame. I have only taken; I have never given. How can he love me?" he asked.

"He is God, and God is love. Give yourself to Him today; that is all He wants. He wants you as you are. If you are broken, he will mend. If you are angry, he will calm. If you are hurt, he will heal. If you take, he will give. If you lie, he is the truth. When you are in darkness, he is the everlasting light. Receive him, Angelo. Listen to your heart and let him in," he said resting his arm on his back. Together they prayed, and Angelo asked for forgiveness. When he opened his eyes, the Chaplin was gone. He searched for him but could not find him. He left in search of the doctor so he could see Livvy and ask her forgiveness too.

Agent Jeff and his counterparts had seen all this and were preparing to take Olivia. The doctor stayed true to his word and kept everyone out of the room so that he could set up his female agent as a nurse to go into the room and remove her. She entered inside undetected and gently.

Olivia heard soft footsteps, and she opened her eyes. The nurse gently touched her hair and whispered she was here to help. Olivia looked at her dumbfounded. She did not understand what she meant. She was too tired to ask; she drifted back to sleep.

Agent Martinez whispered in her microphone, letting them know that they could take her. The family had gone to eat, and now was the best time to move. They moved swiftly and quietly. They removed her as if she were never there, slipped her into an awaiting car, and drove off. Olivia was sound asleep. Now they had to get her on a plane and back to the states before Angelo figured out what was happening.

***

Olivia woke up. Looking around the room, she wondered if Angelo was near and if he would blame her. She could feel the beating, but she did not see him. She saw a man with his back turned. He did not look like the doctor, but maybe they had changed. It could have been one of the bodyguards that worked for the family. She had no idea what was going on. All she knew was that she felt exhausted.

"Excuse me," she whispered. She was so thirsty and hungry. He turned around slowly, and she saw those blue eyes. She knew those eyes. "Det. Hoover, is that you? Or is it a figment of my imagination?" she asked believing her eyes were playing a trick on her. She missed him so much that she thought she saw him.

"It's Lt. Hoover these days, sweetie. Livvy, it's me. I am here, darling. We missed you," he said coming to her side and holding her hands. It had been a long three months. Now he had her back.

"My baby! Did I lose the baby?" she asked shaking.

He shook his head no. He was grateful that she was not with child; she was still a child herself. "No, you were not pregnant. The doctor said that so he could get you out of there. Your vomiting and stomach cramps were from a virus and because you were not eating enough food. You must have caught something being in another country. The doctor said he knew something was wrong because when you first arrived you had welts, lacerations, and bruises all over your body. It looked like you had been severely beaten," he said and for a moment he stopped talking as he thought of Angelo beating a defenseless girl. Then he let out a breath and smiled warmly and continued speaking. "Then when you handed him the letter and asked him to call, it all made sense to him. You were so very smart and brave," he said as he caressed her hair.

She was just delighted to hear she was not pregnant. She would have loved her child, but she was not prepared for marriage and motherhood. "Can I have something to eat and drink?" she asked; she was starving.

He nodded and called a nurse.

"Am I still in South America?" she asked.

He looked at her frantic eyes and wanted to calm them. "No, you are in South Florida. When you are stronger, we are going back to Georgia. Vivian, Uncle Victor, Victoria, Vincent, and Uncle Alan, as well as the Castillo family, are on their way here. They can't wait to see you," he said.

She could not wait to see them either. God knew she loved each and every one of them. They were a blessing to her and a salvation in her time of trouble. Then she thought about her capture. "What about Angelo?" she asked afraid.

At the sound of his name, Tim's face changed. He disliked Angelo with a great passion. "He won't be an issue," he said.

With that knowledge, Livvy felt comfortable to share with Tim the things she had faced. "His family is a drug cartel. Like for real. I thought I was going to be stuck with him forever. They killed Carlos because he had Deek killed. It was Carlos the entire time. He was playing both sides," she said still hurting from that truth, and the tears started to flow. The gang life was no family. Families did not kill one another. Carlos had her brother murdered; he then looked in her face and lied daily to her, as well as to everyone else.

"So were a lot of other people; like Davis, Rhodes, and Richards. They were on Angelo's payroll," he said. Their betrayal enraged him.

Livvy was not surprised. Money had a way of making people do ungodly things. "Don't blame them. I am sure they did it because they were financially stressed, especially Paul Davis. He just wanted to keep his house and take care of his family. I don't blame him. I forgave him completely. I forgive the others as well. If you have never been in that place of loneliness and confusion, it is easy to judge and to look down on them. But Angelo is a master at reading people, finding their weaknesses, and playing them. He did it to me all the time. I fell for it, and so did you and Det. Alan when you first met me. Remember how smooth he talked? It is what he does. He preys on people. Don't look at Det. Davis like a bad guy or be angry with him. He allowed his weakness to be shown, and Angelo used it against him. I hope he has not been imprisoned. God knows having to deal with his actions is prison enough. He needs to be at home with his wife and son; growing up without a daddy is a terrible thing for any child to endure. Besides, he and the rest including Angelo need our prayers. I know how it feels not to have a father; forgive him, Mr. Hoover. We have to forgive and love them," she finished looking at Tim and trying to eat the food the nurse had brought in.

He smiled at her and rubbed her dry hand. His eyes softened and one tear escaped his eye. "My, how you have changed and grown. I must confess, I was very angry with Paul; I am ashamed to say that I had to be physically retrained because I wanted to harm him for what he had done to you. He violated your trust and allowed us to suffer four days before he told what he knew. Lt. Greene said something was not right, but I could not believe that one of our own could do that. I felt so guilty for not being there and for not seeing it. Please forgive me; I tried so hard to protect you that I placed you in harm's way," he said resting his hand on her hand.

She did not see it that way. She saw a man who did not know her open his heart and home to her. He loved her instantly even though she had been raised completely different from his children. He did not judge her or think unkindly of her. He showed her how a father was supposed to be. It was his generosity and love for God that had given her the hope and belief that she would survive. It was his voice she heard reading scripture when Angelo was hitting or hurting her. The seed of God that he and Miguel planted in her heart shielded her when she needed it the most. How could she ever think him responsible for what occurred? "Mr. Hoover, please don't feel guilty. You have nothing to be ashamed about. You offered me love without looking for anything in return. You offered me safety even knowing that doing so could place your own family at risk. You have been the father I have always wanted. Your wife has been the mother I never had. I only survived because of your prayers, your love, and your kindness. You don't need my forgiveness because you have done nothing against me and everything for me. You brought me back home. I feared you would give up, but you did not. You did for me what you would do for Victoria and Vincent, and I am thankful for that. I love you. I love you so much for seeing what I can be, for looking past my past, and for seeing the person God created me to be. I felt worthless for so long. So many men have taken from me and abused me that I thought that was what I was. Living with you and your family, attending church, and serving others has given me a joy I can never describe. I owe you so much more than I can say. I am just sorry for what you and the family had to go through. You saved my life. Everyone—from Miguel and his family to the church, the school, and my new friends—saved my life. I would have given up if you had not come to me and opened your heart and home to me. You see, you have protected me just as a father should," she said taking her other hand and placing it on top of his. She felt in that moment that they were connected. She wondered if this was how daughters felt about their daddies. She had lost a family. But Victoria was right. What God takes; He gives back double. She was so blessed. The good always outweighed the bad. Angelo was a distant memory that was so far from her now. Mr. Hoover smiled, and they prayed together. It was the most heartfelt prayer she had ever heard. He called Olivia his. He called her his daughter. That stirred up emotions inside of her that she had never before felt. When she was born, she was sinless and perfect. But her father left the family anyway. He never knew her. He had never seen her. But he hated her enough to leave her and her brother behind. Here was this man—who knew her history, her sins, and imperfections—but still chose her. He did not care that she was born a bastard, molested, raped, beaten, and associated with a gang. He just loved her—Dinah Olivia Morris—the girl whose mother said she wished she had gotten an abortion and the girl who shared the pain of Dinah in the Bible. God called her His. God gave her a new family, real friends, and another chance at life. She would honor God in all that she did because—even in her loneliest hour—the Father heard her cry. He brought her from devastation to deliverance.

CHAPTER 20

Reflection

When Olivia returned home, it was like she had never left. She had such an outpouring of love that it covered the time she had been away and healed the unseen wounds that Angelo, Bo, Celester, her mother, and father had inflicted. She missed Lilly and Deek. She wanted them to be part of her homecoming. She guessed in a way they were, because she still had her memories. Sometimes she closed her eyes, recalling something funny Deek said or how Lilly and she had the same celebrity crushes. She felt like they were there with her. She didn't hate death anymore; for some, life was too hard. All people have a different level of strength, and God knows exactly what a person can handle. But sometimes you just grow weary and tired, and God allows you rest. Deek and Lilly needed to rest. They had suffered their entire lives and found peace in the scripture of God. She understood her anger was not with the villains who had slain them or God; it was with herself. She was upset with herself, upset that she didn't do enough. After therapy, she found that she blamed herself for what happened to her mother, brother, father, and Lilly; she thought it was because of her that Death found them. Once she admitted it wasn't anything that she did wrong; she was able to breathe and grieve the right way. God does not—cannot—make mistakes. He is neither a God of confusion nor a God of hurt; He is love. He used the circumstances in her life to show her He was in charge—not Angelo and not her other tormentors, but just God alone. When she reflected upon how her life turned out, she could see the pieces come together. It helped her to serve the children and families of Hollow Hill. She was using her life experiences to minister to the forgotten of society. People think that—because your skin is darker, your language is different, your financial situation is unstable— outside appearances define your character and worth. They fail to see that we are all part of one body. The Bible says we each have different jobs in that body, but all are needed—not just rich, not just white, not just intelligent—all people. That is what she wanted to teach Hollow Hill. Now it's called Victory Hills; two years later, it is transformed from hood to neighborhood. Missionary Baptist Church is the center in which everything goes around; it is the heart of town. God is the focus as it should be. Olivia sat back holding Victoria's hand as she recalled it all; they were sitting at their graduation. She could feel Derrick and Lilly because the sun was shining right on her. It was welcomed. God never had forsaken her. He was with her every second and every minute of each day; now she was graduating from high school. Goodness! The miracles God can produce when we start praising His name! He saved her; He delivered her from her devastation. Victoria held her a little tighter as Principal Summers began to give his speech. The Hoover family, the Greene family, the Castillo family, and Mr. and Mrs. Douglas (Coach Geter got married) were sitting together, with Miguel and Vincent videotaping their graduation. It was good to be ending this chapter of her life. She made it, and she knew Derrick was proud of her. The angels were singing in heaven.

"It is the first time it has occurred in our history that we have two valedictorians. Please join me in welcoming Tabitha Victoria Hoover and Dinah Olivia Morris-Hoover, as well as our Salutatorian Jacoby Elías Garcia-Castillo, and the rest of the class of 2012," Principal Eli Summers' said. He wore a warm and enduring smile as he hugged each of us. "These kids are my heroes because they represent what Pleasantville is about: serving others and glorifying God. Amen!"

They waved at the crowd and they erupted in cheers. Olivia was just thankful. After the ceremony was over, she went back to the church to eat and hang out. She looked forward to attending college with Jacoby and Victoria. They were talking and laughing while making plans for their last summer before they were college students when a gentleman walked up to her. He had a shy smile, gray eyes, and walnut skin. It was like looking in the mirror, except her skin was fairer than his. They stood there in stone silence, but he spoke after a few minutes.

"I'm Obadiah Morris, your father," he said.

She knew who he was, but he had lost the title of father when he walked out on her. She did not hold any ill will or hard feelings. She did not know what to say. She had never seen him. How was she supposed to respond? She recalled he had surfaced once after she was kidnapped, but he had never returned when she was found. It seemed weird for him to resurface now. Maybe it was the newspaper article about the transformation in Victory Hills. She did not know. She had forgotten Obadiah Morris. She had not given him much thought, and now he stood before her as if he wanted something. Her delayed response got the attention of her friends and family. Capt. Hoover and Miguel were upon the scene before she could utter a response.

"Are you okay, Livvy?" Miguel asked.

"I am. This is Obadiah Morris," she said turning to him. She knew her dad knew who he was.

"I just wanted to see her. I didn't mean to cause no problems," he said looking at Tim and Miguel.

"Obadiah, maybe you ought to sit down over here so you and Olivia can talk together," Tim said looking at his daughter.

They sat down and looked at one another. She felt so distant to him, even though they were inches apart. "Um, so what is it you want?" she asked.

"I want to apologize to you. I am sorry for leaving the family. I thought you were going to be born addicted to drugs. I just could not stand that. Your mother loved her drugs, and I could not take it anymore," he said.

She nodded. "So, you left my brother and me because you could not deal with Nene's drug addiction, but you thought that two children could?" she asked.

He dropped his head.

"Sir, we suffered because of your selfish decision. She blamed me, beat me, and hurt me because you left. I dealt with that. I took it. But when Deek got murdered, I had no one and nothing; where were you then?" she asked calmly.

His eyes met her eyes; now they were filled with tears. "I didn't know. I thought if I left, she'd get her act together. I went back to my family. One month turned into one year; after that, I convinced myself y'all did not need me. So, I married and lived my life. It was not the life I wanted because I was haunted by leaving you. My wife divorced me and moved on. I just did not know how to come back. Then two years ago, when you were taken by those gangsters, I came to see if I could help. But it looked like you had a new family and didn't need me. One year ago, I got diagnosed with an incurable stage three cancer. Before I die, I want peace. I want to do right by you. I visited your mother and brother's graves," he said choking up.

She reached over and placed her hand on his. "It's okay; I forgave you a long time ago. There is no reason for you to be so upset, but you should enjoy the time you have left on this earth. I am so sorry you are ill, but don't waste another day feeling guilty. I am not angry. I have a good family, friends, and church. Maybe the greatest thing you ever did for me was leave. You are welcomed in my life and home," she said feeling horrible about her silent thoughts and harsh response to him. How could she have any anger toward a dying man? It would do no good to bash him. She felt her heart melt as he confessed, he was dying. She would not add to his agony, only to his joy.

"Thank you. I don't deserve your forgiveness, but I thank you for giving it to me. I won't be bothering you anymore," he said.

"Yes, you do. Everyone deserves to be forgiven, because God forgave us. You aren't a bother. You stay here and enjoy yourself," she said.

"Obadiah, you are more than welcome to come by the house anytime," Tim said placing his hand on her shoulder.

He smiled the same kind of smile Deek use to have. She reached over and embraced him. No matter what he had done, he was still part of the reason she was created. At least he apologized, which her mother had never done.

"Well, I probably won't live long enough to see you start your first day of college. But I want to make sure you are financially secured. All that I have own in this world I have given to you. I wrote up a will, and you are my only heir. The house in South Carolina, though it is modest, is yours. It is paid for; all the money I've saved, and my other investments are all yours. I owe you more than that, but it's all I have. I love you. I know you probably think I am saying that because I am dying, but it isn't so. You are everything I prayed to God you would be. When you go to college, I want you to learn for all of us. I and your mother were not as smart and clever as you and Derrick, but I want you to do well in college and never look back on my mistakes or your mother's as a reason to give up. You should always strive for excellence. You are a gift. Don't you ever second guess or think you are less because of adversity; you are a blessing. I just took too long to tell you that. I want to give you these. I bought you a card for every birthday and for Deek's birthdays too. I am forever sorry," he said.

His kindness and fatherly wisdom penetrated her heart so deeply that she could not help but cry. She did have birthday cards. "Thank you. Maybe you should stay with us. We can make sure you are comfortable. Mrs. Castillo is a hospice nurse," she said.

"We can do that. Vivian and I would love to extend our home to you and help with your care," Tim offered.

"Thank you; I don't want to be an inconvenience to you. You have already been taking care of my child. You have done more for her than I ever did. I don't need anything. Really," he said.

"Nonsense. If Livvy wants you to stay, then stay. You won't be an inconvenience to us," he said holding Livvy's hand.

He nodded in agreement. Olivia kissed his forehead and hugged him once more. He smiled.

When the family returned home with their new guest, Olivia found a letter addressed to her. Her heart thumped anxiously as she opened it. There was no return address, but she had a feeling it was from Angelo. She opened it and began to read:

Dear Livvy,

I have had two years to think, to grow, and to understand my wrongs. I am eternally grateful for you. I was wrong; I was wrong for it all. I thought I would die when I discovered you had been taken; it was like someone had ripped out my heart. I guess that is how your adoptive family felt when I took you, and how Deuce felt when I yearned to have you. I took your advice; I confess my sins, and I accepted

Christ. I have done some horrible things that were all in the name of worldly pleasure, so I turned myself in. I have to pay for my actions. Thank you for forgiving me and showing me that I am of value. I hated myself for so long, but not anymore. Prison life is tough; but I awake every morning praising God, and I go to bed every night praying to God. I would not have a personal relationship with Jesus Christ if not for you. I am so very sorry. Please forgive me for every time I hit you, lied to you, hurt you, and mistreated you. In some ways I am glad you were not pregnant. I never want to be an absentee dad. Please continue to pray for me, and I will continue to pray for you. Take care of yourself and continue being that sweet girl you are. I will love you forever...until God calls me home. You saw me; you saw what I thought had died with my mother. Though I was horrible to you, you were loyal to me. You are so right; Deek was the best friend, soldier, and brother that I know. He was brave enough to love God and tell me of his faith. Even knowing the risk, he had the courage to not be phony and stay in a gang. He is the man I hope to one day become. Tell your family that I am so sorry for what I did two years ago. That night when we lost Deek, he whispered to me who killed him and asked that I not let the streets take you. I told him I would take care of you; instead you took care of me. I am forever sorry for the hate and anger I offered you. I was in a pain so deep that I could not give or receive love. I am so proud of you for loving God at a time when I questioned him and went against his commands. You saved me, you saved the hood, and you saved Deek too. You who thought you had nothing to offer used your adversity as a ministry to help menaces to society. May God be in you always; never stop doing what you are doing. You are an amazing woman, and that is what Deek wanted. Congratulations on doing God's work in Hollow Hill, as well as for your graduation. I hear things even though I am still confined in prison. Be all that Deek knew you would be, and I wish I could be. In Him, Angelo G.

She folded up the letter and let two teardrops fall. All she ever wanted for him was to know that God loved him and that Deek was not an enemy. He understood. She was thankful. She walked over to her family and handed the letter to Mr. Hoover; he read it in silence and then handed it to Vivian. She smiled. They prayed.

It was finally over, and now she was all right; that night it rained. It rained like it never had in Georgia. She'd like to think it was her brother crying tears of joy that the people he loved the most had found God. His death saved their souls.

EPILOGUE

The Last Days

O livia had the loveliest summer getting to know Obadiah Morris. He reminded her so much of Deek that she instantly loved him. They laughed alike and made the same facial expressions. It was like having Deek all over again. She loved that. She learned that she had two uncles. His mother and father had long passed away. He told the best stories. The last night they spent together, she had read Psalm 23 at his request and they gazed at the stars and the bright moon. She recalled how that verse had comforted her after her brutal beating. Obadiah said he felt a little tired. She pulled the covers up close to him to warm him. Somehow, she knew it would be his last night. She prayed over him and asked God to let him see Deek. She hummed a little lullaby and watched his chest rise up and go down until movement stopped. She did not cry because she was too busy praising God. Finally, he had rest. It was not violent but peaceful, and he knew it was coming. He was okay with meeting God because he had found God. He had confessed his sins and accepted the Father. That knowledge sent peace through her body. "I love you, daddy," she whispered and kissed him one last time.

The funeral was small and modest. He was laid to rest right beside Deek. Now father and son would be together for eternity. She blew a kiss at each of them and turned to leave.

**

Days later she was packing up what she needed for school. Livvy and Tori were going to be roommates. Olivia was glad; she looked up at the sky and saw a cloud shaped like a smile. She smiled back. Her brother and father were having a family reunion. She hoped that Deek was enjoying him as much as she had, and that Lilly and her family were celebrating as well. Her heart filled with gladness at the thought. She finally was meeting Derrick. She laughed as she recalled telling her he looked like Shemar Moore. That brother of hers sure was handsome. He was a goodhearted man that loved his family.

Standing silently at the door, Timothy watched as Livvy stared out the window and then began to pack her things. A million thoughts ran through his mind, but the one that made him smile was how far Olivia had come and what she had overcome. It made his heart so glad, that God allowed him the opportunity to share in her life. "You need any help?" Tim asked.

"No, dad. I am almost done. I was thinking about something though. Since I am the sole heir, maybe I should offer the Davis family the house in South Carolina. Paul and Mary-Elisabeth can start over and not have to worry about house payments or rent. They wouldn't have to be haunted by their past," she said. She had never forgotten about the family, especially Monty. She personally went to see them regularly so that Paul knew she held no anger toward him. He had been shunned by the community, and she felt that was wrong. Everyone was a victim to something; no one had the right to judge him but only to love him. If she could forgive him, why didn't they? It seemed so two-faced to react to another person in that way. She knew about misjudging; people did it to her and Deek all the time. She did it to Miguel. It was wrong...so very wrong to think that anyone had the right to act as God and make final judgments on people. No one was perfect; all had fallen short, and that was why Jesus died on the cross.

Her kindness humbled his heart. She sincerely cared about everyone. "I think that is generous," he said sitting down in amazement.

"I mean; I guess it is somewhat selfish of me too. But I don't want the house to fall apart. I have at least four years of college, so someone should fill the house with love," she said. She felt like an empty house was a dead house. Houses lived with people; a house needed love too.

"You should share that when they come to the party. I can't believe my girls are going to college. It seemed like you just arrived. I am so proud of you, Livvy. You have taught me so much," he said getting up and holding me closely.

"I have had some really good teachers," she said.

He smiled at her.

"Dad, where are you? I need your help on the grill," Vincent yelled through the house.

"You better go, dad. I'm almost done," she said.

He kissed her forehead and left. She sat down on her bed and looked out the window and she thought about everything. She reflected on how God had brought her through every kind of hardship. People on the outside may feel sorrowful, but not her. She was blessed. She understood the true meaning of love. She had placed human beings above God. But, after being taken away and unable to depend on anyone but God, she knew who was in control. No matter what happened, or what hardships or adversity she faced, she had God. He would always deliver her from any danger or temptation. He said in Revelation 2:17: "He who has an ear, let him hear what the Spirit says to the churches. To him who overcomes, I will give some of the hidden manna to eat. And I will give him a white stone, and on the stone a new name written which no one known except him who receives it." Olivia wrote in her Bible; *I am not who I was; I am what He says I am; much more than what I ever thought. I am royalty and my Father, is the King of Kings, Amen!*

The End!

Y. Deonna's Book List & Contact Info

Duology (Christian Fiction-BWWM)
Battle Scarred Love 1
Battle Scarred Love-Finale

Standalone Novels (Urban Christian Fiction)
Deception Has A Name
Her Mistake, His Masterpiece
Healing A Bitter Heart

Trilogy (Christian/Family Fiction)
Stolen Virtue
A Virtuous Theory
The Theory of All

Connect:
Email: authorydeonna@gmail.com
Join the new Facebook group to be in the know:
Reader Group
IG: bluetygrezz
Twitter:@CrownedRuby
Facebook page: Author Y. Deonna
Would you like to be a beta reader? I just created a new group just for you.
Join here

www.ingramcontent.com/pod-product-compliance
Lightning Source LLC
Chambersburg PA
CBHW032003170626
46807CB00006B/2622